# About the Author

Claire Boston is a contemporary romance author who enjoys exploring real life issues on her way to the happily-ever-after. She writes heart-warming stories, with resilient heroines and heroes you'll love. In 2014 she was nominated for an Australian Romance Readers Award for Favourite New Romance Author.

When Claire's not writing she can be found creating her own handmade journals, swinging on a sidecar, or in the garden attempting to grow something other than weeds.

Claire lives in Western Australia with her husband, who loves even her most annoying quirks, and her grubby, but adorable Australian bulldog.

You can connect with Claire through Facebook (https://www.facebook.com/clairebostonauthor) and Twitter (https://www.twitter.com/clairebauthor), or join her reader group (http://www.claireboston.com/reader-group/).

# Also by Claire Boston

<u>The Texan Quartet</u>
What Goes on Tour
All that Sparkles
Under the Covers
Into the Fire

<u>The Flanagan Sisters</u>
Break the Rules
Change of Heart
Blaze a Trail
Place to Belong

<u>The Blackbridge Series</u>
Nothing to Fear – coming November 2017

<u>The Beginner Writer's Toolkit</u>
Self-Editing

# Under the Covers

## The Texan Quartet #3

## Claire Boston

BANTILLY
PUBLISHING

First published by Momentum in 2015
This edition published by Bantilly Publishing in 2017

Copyright © Claire Boston 2015
The moral right of the author has been asserted.

All rights reserved. This publication (or any part of it) may not be reproduced or transmitted, copied, stored, distributed or otherwise made available by any person or entity (including Google, Amazon or similar organizations), in any form (electronic, digital, optical, mechanical) or by any means (photocopying, recording, scanning or otherwise) without prior written permission from the publisher.

This is a work of fiction. Names, characters, businesses, places, events and incidents are either the products of the author's imagination or used in a fictitious manner. Any resemblance to actual persons, living or dead, or actual events is purely coincidental.

Under the Covers: The Texan Quartet 3

EPUB format: 978-1-925696-03-5
Mobi format: 978-1-925696-04-2
Print: 978-1-925696-05-9

Cover design by XOU Creative
Edited by Kate O'Donnell
Proofread by Melissa Kemble

# DEDICATION

This book is dedicated to the wonderful and supportive Western Australian romance writers' community: Nikki, Rachael, Jennie, Jenny, Michelle, Shona, Peta, Amanda, Lily, Renee, Elizabeth, Nicola, Leah, Carolyn; and of course my critique group, Anna, Juanita, Lorraine, Susy and Teena. Thank you for sharing your knowledge and for supporting me. Our monthly brunches are always a highlight and leave me rejuvenated.

# Chapter 1

This was crazy. How Elle had ever thought she could possibly pull it off, she had no idea.

She had no more than a high school diploma – not so much as a semester of college – and no experience with business, unless you counted the years of bussing tables while at school.

A few online business courses did not an entrepreneur make.

Her lack of experience was really showing now. It was opening day of her bookshop café, Eat, Drink, Read, and she'd lost count of all the things that had gone wrong. The only thing she'd got right was having a 'quiet' opening rather than making a fuss of it – fewer people around to watch her fail.

But still there were enough … and that was part of the problem. Only one of the two waitresses she'd hired had turned up. The other had called in sick, but from the giggling in the background, Elle was sure it was a lie. The other problem was that people were more interested in the bookstore part of her café than she'd anticipated. There hadn't been a bricks-and-mortar bookstore in this part of Houston for years and it was now packed with people browsing. Elle didn't have the time to go over to check if anyone needed any help, or to make sure half her stock wasn't walking out of the door without being paid for.

She placed two coffees in front of a couple who had been

waiting quite a while. "I'm sorry for the wait."

"Man could have died of thirst," the gray-haired gentleman complained.

Elle kept the smile on her face. "Can I offer you a complimentary cookie, to make sure you don't die of hunger?"

The man raised his eyebrows. "Those chocolate-chip ones look good."

"I'll bring one straight out."

Elle left the table and went straight to her cookie jar. She knew today was all about making sure her customers were happy and had a good experience, so they would spread the word and come back. If she had to give away a truckload of cookies, it would be worth it.

After delivering the cookie to the now appeased man, she took orders at three other tables and then went behind the counter to prepare them.

"This is crazy," Nora, her waitress, commented. Nora was a single mother like Elle and had jumped at the chance to work at the café. She had family to take care of her little girl, who was Toby's age – and, thank heavens – they'd agreed to look after Toby today as well.

"We'd be managing if Drew had shown up."

"I'd fire her if I were you," Nora said. "She's obviously had a big night out and is hungover."

Drew was in college and only a few years younger than Elle. She had admittedly seemed a little flighty in the interview, but she had a huge smile and a friendly attitude that would please the customers.

If she ever turned up.

Elle murmured non-committedly and handed Nora the coffee list while she prepared the food order.

"Helloooo, check out the hotties who just walked in," Nora said.

Elle wasn't interested in good-looking men, but she glanced up just the same and groaned inwardly. One of the hotties was Chris Barker, the lawyer who'd been so kind to her and helped her set up her business plan and review her lease. She didn't want him to see her failing on her first day.

She raised a hand in greeting while he and three friends took their seats. Imogen was with him. She had helped Elle find something decent to wear when Elle had run into them at a thrift shop a couple of months earlier. Then Imogen had paid to get Elle's hair styled at a very classy salon. Elle had been horrified when she realized the price but the stylist, Joseph, had told her Imogen could afford it. Elle had called Imogen to thank her again and they'd kept in touch afterward, though Elle had never been able to afford to go out with her. With them were a blond woman and the other guy who'd piqued Nora's interest. He turned when Chris waved back and Elle's heart did a little dance.

Nora was right. He was a hottie.

Broad shouldered, he wore his dark hair short and neat – business-like – and he was tall, a good couple of inches taller than Chris. But it was his face that captured Elle's attention. His expression was open; he was smiling and sexy as hell.

Quickly she looked down before he caught her staring at him. She didn't want or need a man in her life now and she didn't have the time to ogle.

"You know them?" Nora asked.

"The shorter guy is Chris, the lawyer who helped me with my business documents."

"If I had known lawyers were that sexy, I'd have found a reason to visit one long ago."

Elle smiled but her mind was on getting the food prepared so she could take Chris's order before he realized how chaotic this place was.

She checked the details and then hurried on to the floor to deliver the cookies and muffins.

"Your coffee will be right out," she said to the people at the table and then took her order pad out of her apron and turned to Chris's table.

"Hi, Chris. Hi, Imogen. Thanks for coming."

He smiled at her. "Looks like your first day is a success."

Elle nodded. "It's busy, all right. Can I take your order?"

"This place is lovely, Elle," Imogen commented. She reminded Elle of a pixie, small with dark hair and an always smiling face.

"Elle, you know Imogen, and these are my friends, George

and Piper." Chris gestured at the pair.

Elle smiled at them, avoiding looking at George. "Pleased to meet you."

"I can't wait to browse the books," Piper said. "But I'll leave it until we've eaten. Can you give us a few more minutes to decide? Everything looks great."

"Sure." Though she was pleased they liked the menu, she was sure the few minutes would stretch to ten or twenty at the rate she was going. She turned and went to make the rest of her orders.

***

Elle walked away and George admired the way her black skirt shaped her butt as she walked. "When you said you wanted to support one of your clients, you didn't tell me she was a honey," he commented to Chris.

"I didn't notice," Chris said, squeezing Imogen's hand.

George rolled his eyes. He was pleased his friend had found someone he loved, and Imogen was a great woman, but it didn't mean they had to stop admiring other people from afar.

"Are there only two staff?" Piper asked. "It's a lot of work for two people."

"Maybe someone will start soon for the lunch shift," Chris said.

George scanned the room. There was a bookshop area set up at the back, with a couple of comfortable high-backed chairs and coffee tables where people could sit and browse. The bookshelves ran along one wall and provided a colorful contrast to the cream walls. There were a dozen or more tables of different sizes, all a rich dark wood polished to perfection, and in one corner was a play area for children. Imogen was right: the place was lovely – cozy and welcoming. He'd have to tell his mom and sisters about it.

"Are the others coming?" he asked Chris.

"Yeah. Adrian and Libby are picking Kate up from her cousin's place at eleven and will be here for lunch."

George knew both Kate and Libby would love the café. He might even browse through the books before he left. He hadn't had time to read anything lately but that didn't mean he couldn't buy something. He scanned the shelves for the thrillers and noticed a guy take a book from the shelf, look over at the line waiting to pay at the register and then tuck it under his jacket.

He walked toward the door and George frowned. "I'll be right back." He stood and went to intercept the would-be thief. He reached the exit as the man put his hand on the door handle. George stopped him with a hand on his arm.

"You going to pay for that book?"

The man, college age, with scruffy greasy brown hair, scowled at him. "What book?"

"The book you put under your jacket." George nodded at the man's arm, which was pressed tightly against his body.

"Don't know what you're talking about."

Irritation stirred in George. Here was a woman starting her own business and making something better of her life and this schmuck was stealing from her. "I could call the cops if you like, and get them involved."

The guy swore, defiance on his face. "Have you seen the line? I don't have time for that."

Five people were still waiting to pay at the register and Elle and her waitress were serving drinks and making coffees.

"You'll make time," George said, "or you'll leave without it."

The guy dropped the book and wrenched open the café door. "I'm out of here."

George let him go and then picked up the book. It was a thriller and the blurb on the back sounded interesting. He'd buy it himself.

George walked back to his table.

"What was that about?" Piper asked.

"He tried to steal the book," he said, putting it on the table and taking his seat. "Said he didn't have time to wait."

"Jerk," Imogen said.

George glanced around the room and noted how many tables were waiting for food or needed to be cleared.

"Your friend needs a bit of help," he said to Chris.

Chris nodded. "I don't know her well enough to offer. I don't want her to take offense."

"Let me," Piper said. "I spent about a hundred years waitressing. I'll go have a chat with her."

Piper went over to Elle, but George couldn't hear what she said.

***

Elle answered the ringing phone as Piper got up from the table and walked over. She hoped Piper wasn't going to complain about the long wait for service. This day couldn't get any worse.

"Elle, it's Wayne."

It took her a minute to place the name – he was the guitarist she'd hired to play some music that afternoon, to add a little ambience and celebration to the day.

"Hi, what's up?"

"I can't make it today. I've just had a call from my mother and my dad's in hospital. It's serious."

Her stomach fell like lead.

"I'm sorry."

Elle swallowed. "It's fine. Of course you have to go. I hope your father is all right." She hung up, swallowed past the lump in her throat. Nothing was going right today.

She turned and saw Piper standing there. She braced herself. "I'm sorry about the wait. I'll be over in a second."

"No, it's fine. I wanted to check if you needed a hand. You seem a little short staffed."

Elle couldn't ask a stranger to help out. She had no idea who she was. "One of my waitresses called in sick."

"Then let me help. I waited tables all through college. I can clear tables and take orders easily enough and you've got people waiting to pay."

Elle glanced towards the cash register at the line of people. Her eyes welled up. She couldn't possibly keep up with her customers. Perhaps this was the only way. She had nothing to lose. "That would be great. The guitarist I hired just called to say he can't make it and I never dreamed I'd have this much interest." She handed Piper a spare apron and an order pad.

"What was the guitarist going to do?"

"I thought it would be nice to have some music after lunch on Saturday and Sunday. Nothing too loud, but something for ambience, to draw the afternoon crowd."

"Great idea." Piper smiled. "I might know someone who

6

can help out. I'll give him a call if you like."

"I can't pay much," Elle said, worried now.

"I don't think he'll charge. Leave it to me." Piper swept into the café and started taking orders.

Elle didn't have time to worry further. She went over to the cash register and started taking payments, apologizing for the delay and handing out the discount cards she'd made for her regulars' award program.

By the time she had finished, the tables had been cleared and there was a long line of coffee and food orders to deal with. It had tipped over to lunchtime so there was also a list of simple meals to make. She hurried into the tiny kitchen, noted the pile of dirty dishes that needed washing and put a load in her industrial dishwasher.

She'd grossly under-estimated how many staff she needed. She required at a minimum another person to deal with the dirty dishes and one for some of the food orders – at least on the weekends. She doubted she'd be this busy during the week.

Really, if she'd been sensible, she would have opened on a Monday, allowed herself the time to get used to everything while the majority of people were at work and then she'd have had all the bugs sorted out by the weekend rush.

Too late to go back now.

A tap at the door had her whirling around. Chris stood there. Elle forced a smile.

"Piper told me about your no-shows. You could do with a busboy. Can I help?"

Elle was pragmatic enough to know she couldn't let pride stand in her way. The most important thing was her business and its success. Her shoulders slumped and she said, "Yes, please."

"All right. Show me how this thing works."

Elle gave him quick directions on the dishwasher and showed him where the dish towels were. Then she hurried out to assess how the rest of her café was faring. She stopped short: Imogen was making coffees.

Imogen smiled at her. "I'm useless at serving, but I make a mean coffee. Nora's doing the food."

Elle didn't protest. "Thank you." She glanced out at the

café. The tables were all cleared and full of people, Piper was taking orders with a smile, and over in the books area, George was chatting to people, recommending novels. The table where they'd all been sitting was now filled with other patrons.

Elle wasn't sure how or what she was going to pay them, but right now it didn't matter.

"Orders up," Nora said, nodding to the plates of food on the counter.

Elle blinked and picked them up.

She would thank her lucky stars later.

Right now she had a café to run.

***

An hour later, the café suddenly fell silent. Alarmed, Elle looked up from the cash register. Everyone was staring at the person who'd just walked through the door.

Elle's mouth dropped open.

Kent Downer – rock star. And he was carrying a guitar case.

Elle watched, along with the whole café, as he raised a hand to George and walked over to the area she had cleared for the guitarist.

This couldn't really be happening.

The most famous rock star in the world was not in her little café.

Piper had said she was going to call a guitarist.

Elle whipped her gaze to Piper, who was picking up some coffees to take out. "Did you organize this?"

She grinned. "I hope you don't mind."

Elle had no words. Of course she didn't mind. She was frozen to the spot, watching him.

"You should tell him what you want him to do," Piper said.

Was she kidding? He could do whatever the hell he wanted as far as Elle was concerned. If she got a photo of Kent Downer in Eat, Drink, Read, it would do wonders for her promotion.

She hurried over to where Kent was unpacking his guitar and then hesitated, not sure what to say, or do.

"Kent, this is the owner, Elle," George said.

Elle had forgotten about George entirely. She blinked,

8

smiled at him briefly and then turned her attention back to the rock star.

"Howdy, ma'am. Pleasure to meet you." He held out a hand and gave her a wicked smile.

Elle forgot to breathe.

She generally wasn't one to have celebrity crushes, but Kent's music had seen her through the toughest time of her life and she'd viewed him as her lifeline. Now he was standing right there in front of her and wanted to shake her hand.

Quickly she thrust out a hand. "I had no idea … I mean, thank you for coming … nice to meet you." She was babbling, but Kent just smiled, relaxed as could be.

"You want me to set up here?"

Right. She had to focus on why he was here. "Please." She grabbed the stool she'd tucked out of sight and brought it out. "Is this all right?"

"Perfect. What do you want me to play?"

Elle stopped. She'd not thought about that. His music was generally loud and rock. It would be too much for her little café.

But how could she possibly say it? "I, ah, well …"

"How about a light acoustic set?" Kent saved her. "Maybe try out one or two of my new songs."

Relief washed over her. "That sounds wonderful. Can I get you something to eat or drink?"

"A glass of water would be mighty fine."

"Of course." She hurried away to get it. Conversations had started up again around the room, but everyone was sneaking glances at Kent and lots of the customers had their phones out to take pictures and videos.

At the sink, Nora bumped into her. "How the hell did that happen?" she asked.

Elle shook her head. "Wayne cancelled and Piper said she had a friend who could help …"

Some friend.

"Well, girl, our lunchtime rush isn't going to end." She nodded to where people were at the window of the café, peering in.

Elle couldn't think about that now. She took the glass back to where Kent had started his first song. The noise level was perfect, not so loud as to prevent conversation, but not so soft that people couldn't hear. She placed the water on the table next to him and he nodded his thanks.

Elle stepped back, right into George. He grunted and his hands came up to steady her.

"Oh, sorry." She turned and was standing only inches away from him, staring up into his deep sapphire blue eyes. They were the most unusual color she'd seen, such a deep blue, and he was looking rather bemused.

She blinked and moved away, and would have crashed into a coffee table if George hadn't reached out and grabbed her arm. His fingers were warm but his grip was hard, hard enough to break the spell his eyes had cast. Hard enough to remind her of reality and the dangers of not looking beyond a pretty face until it was too late.

Elle shook her arm free. "Thanks."

She headed back to the safety of the counter and her orders.

***

George wandered over to ask if a customer needed help with the books, but his mind was firmly on Elle. There had been a moment – she'd looked into his eyes and he'd felt a connection, but then she'd stepped back, and when he'd grabbed her to stop her falling, her expression had turned to fear.

What had happened to her? Why was she afraid of someone trying to help her? He knew she'd gone to Chris's pro bono office, so clearly she didn't have a lot of money, but perhaps there was more to it. He would have to ask his friend.

Adrian, or Kent as he was known to most people, was playing an acoustic version of one of his rock songs and it sounded great. They'd have to discuss putting out an acoustic album at a later date.

After sending the customer toward the cash register with her new books, George pulled out his phone. He took a picture of Adrian and then tweeted, *Guess at which hot new Houston bookstore café Kent is currently doing an acoustic set?*

It would drive a lot of interest and he'd tweet the answer a little later. He didn't want the café to be mobbed, but it would be good promotion for both Kent and Elle, and as Kent's manager he had to consider the business side of this favor.

Adrian's niece, Kate and his wife, Libby wandered over.

"This place is awesome," Kate said.

"Sure is, Shorty. I might pick up a book or two myself."

His attention was taken by Elle, who was serving the table closest to them. A woman waited until Elle had finished and then asked, "Do you have the last Jessop Chronicles?"

"Of course. It's this way."

George glanced at Libby, who was the author of those books. She grinned.

"You should sign it, Libby," Kate said, loudly.

The customer, who was still close by, turned and said, "Are you Libby Myles?"

Libby nodded and George noted Elle's reaction. Her mouth opened ever so slightly and speculation crossed her face before she gave a little shake of her head.

George knew what she was thinking. Any decent business person would think it. If she got author-signed copies of the Jessop Chronicles it would be another draw card to her bookshop café.

"Could you sign my book?" the customer asked.

"Sure."

They moved over to one of the wing-backed chairs and Libby sat so she could sign the book. Another couple of customers hurriedly grabbed copies of the book and brought them over.

George smiled. He doubted Libby would get out of the chair until all the books had been sold but he knew she'd be fine with that.

The café was filling with people who were standing around watching Kent play. They were crowding the space between the tables and not buying anything. It would become a safety issue if it continued. When Kent finished his song, George stepped up in front of him.

"Listen up, folks. If you're not buying anything you need to move out of the way. Take-out coffee is available at the counter so line up if you want it. There are people who want to enjoy their meals and be able to get out of their seats when they're ready to leave."

People quickly shuffled into a line, many happy to stand at the back.

George chuckled. That would get Elle a few more sales. He stepped away so Kent could continue, and monitored the crowd. It took him back to the early days with Kent, when he'd been both manager and bouncer for his friend.

Then they'd been in clubs and bars which could only be considered seedy. Dark, smoky and smelling of alcohol, with décor that had seen its fair share of hard knocks.

Elle's café was a far cozier option.

A few patrons were lingering after receiving their take-out coffees. He wandered over and when they noticed him they began to browse the books.

Not all Kent's fans would be so well behaved, but these weren't the hardcore ones. They were the ones who'd been in the right place at the right time.

Elle walked by and George stopped her. "You should ask Libby to do a book signing here when her book comes out next month. I'm sure she'll be happy to."

Elle seemed surprised and a little cautious that he was talking to her. George didn't like that at all.

"Thanks for the suggestion," she said. "I'll think about it." She continued to the kitchen with the tray of dirty dishes.

There was something about her that got under George's skin.

And he wasn't the type of man to ignore an itch.

He just needed to figure out how to scratch it.

# Chapter 2

Elle had never been so tired. She'd been on her feet all day and had eaten her lunch on the run. But she wasn't complaining. The opening had been far more successful than she'd ever hoped, though she knew that was largely due to Chris and his friends.

Kent had finished playing at about three but people had kept coming all afternoon. It was now almost closing time and there were only a few stragglers finishing their coffees. Nora was in the kitchen cleaning up the last of the dishes, and Chris and his friends were sitting at one of the tables having a well-deserved drink.

When the last of her official customers left, Elle turned the sign on the door to *Closed* and locked it. She cleared the table, set it ready for tomorrow and then told Nora she could go home.

"I'll take Toby to my place," Nora said. "That way you can pick him up from there and don't have to go all the way out to my mother's."

Elle sighed. A guardian angel must have been helping her today for everyone to be so accommodating. "*Thank you.* That would be great. I'll pick him up by six."

She let Nora out, locked the door behind her and then turned to face Chris and his friends. She had worked out how much she could afford to pay them for their time and she hoped they wouldn't ask for more.

Scrunching her apron up in her fist, she walked up to the table.

George pulled out a seat for her. "You look wiped."

Elle brushed a loose strand of hair away from her forehead. She couldn't imagine what she looked like, but right now she didn't care. She didn't sit; instead she put her hands on the back of the chair. "Thank you for your help today." She reached into her apron pocket and pulled out the pay envelopes for them all. "You all deserve more than this, but I'm afraid it's all I can afford." She handed one to Chris, who frowned.

"What's this?"

"Your pay."

He shook his head and handed it back. "We don't need to be paid." The others shook their head in agreement. "We did it to help you out."

"You've worked all day for me. It wouldn't be right not to pay you." Elle was horrified they thought she would get them to work and not pay them. She might be starting out, but she wasn't going to take them for granted.

"None of us need to be paid," Chris said. "We've got enough money."

So she was a charity case. It stung but she understood how it looked from their point of view. She couldn't afford to be too proud. She knew how much that cost.

"I, for one, enjoyed myself," Imogen said. "I've never worked in a café and it's far harder than I would have expected. It was a good experience."

"I wanted to ask you if I could do a book signing here when my new book is released," Libby said. "You have such a lovely place."

Elle placed a hand on her chest. She'd wanted to ask Libby to do a book signing but she couldn't figure out how to when she had already spent time helping out in the book shop. "I'm sure we can arrange something." She smiled.

"Are you planning on having regular acoustic sets?" George asked.

His eyes distracted her for a moment, blue like the sky just before nightfall. There was depth there.

He was waiting for an answer. She swallowed. "Yes. Just on the weekends though."

"I've got some artists who might be interested in booking a session. I'll see what I can arrange."

It was so very generous. Piper had told her earlier that George was Kent's manager. "I can't pay a lot." She hated to harp on about money, but it was the truth and she didn't want to get her hopes up, only to have them shattered.

"Sometimes they want a small place to try a new idea. This would be perfect." He turned to Adrian. "Today went so well that I've already suggested to Adrian that we do an acoustic album."

Elle knew from the gossip magazines that Kent Downer's real name was Adrian but meeting him in the flesh, now he'd removed all the makeup, she realized he really was a completely different person from his rock-star identity.

"Thank you."

"We're all going to head out and grab some dinner. Do you want to join us?" Chris asked.

The temptation was strong. They seemed like such nice people and she would love to spend some time with them, but she was exhausted and she had to pick up Toby. "Thank you, but no. I've got some things to arrange for tomorrow." Including calling Drew and finding out if she was going to turn up.

They all stood and Elle unlocked the front door. "Thank you again for all of your help."

"Any time," Imogen said.

As they left, George turned and said, "I'll be in touch."

Was he talking about the musicians? It appeared like more by the way his eyes lingered on hers, and her skin tingled in response. She nodded politely, but tried to seem uninterested, and breathed a sigh of relief when she turned the lock on the door again. She did not have time for an attractive man right now.

She checked the café to make sure all the tables were set and all the books were neatly arranged and then began to count the drawer, adding back the pay she'd extracted. When she was finished she sat back and huffed out a breath. Her first day had been a definite success.

Waves of relief washed over her.

She'd had so many anxious dreams of sitting at one of the tables, waiting for the first customer to walk in and no one coming.

But she couldn't relax. She had to string a whole lot of successful days together to make this work. Thirty percent of small businesses only lasted two years. She was going to do better. She had to.

She counted out the change for the following day and put the rest in her safe. Then she picked up the phone and called her no-show waitress, Drew.

The girl sounded bright and chirpy when she answered.

"How are you feeling, Drew?"

When Drew realized it was Elle calling, her voice got decidedly quieter. "I'm all right."

"Will you be in tomorrow?"

"Yes, I should be. I'm sorry I didn't make opening day." The regret in her voice was contrived.

"You missed a great day today. We had Kent Downer play an acoustic set."

"Kent Downer!" Drew shrieked so loudly that Elle had to hold the phone away from her ear. "You didn't tell me Kent Downer was going to play. I would have been there for sure."

Elle frowned. She couldn't fire Drew, as much as she wanted to. She needed the help for the next few days at least. "You weren't well. It was better you didn't give the customers your illness." Had she ever been so carefree? At Drew's age she'd had a two-year-old boy to care for and a whole lot of other issues.

"Yeah, right." Drew sounded despondent.

"I'll see you at seven." Elle hung up. Part of her felt immense satisfaction that Drew had missed out on meeting Kent Downer, though she also knew if Drew had actually turned up, it might never have happened.

Going through and checking the rest of the shop, she grabbed her keys and her jacket and turned out all but the security lights. Then she locked up and went to pick up her son.

***

Toby was one very tired boy. He was just over five years old, but a whole day spent playing with people he hardly knew was too much for him. He'd never been without his mom for that long. When Elle arrived at Nora's, he came running toward her, flung his arms around her and wouldn't let go.

She swung him up into her arms as the guilt hit her.

He was so young to be left with virtual strangers the whole day, but Elle didn't have many options. She couldn't keep him at the café with her, because he'd be constantly under foot and bored in no time, but she also didn't have any family nearby and none anywhere who would actually want him.

She ignored the stab of hurt. She'd accepted her family's rejection long ago.

"Hi, my little man. Did you have a good day playing with Miranda?"

He nodded.

Elle looked over his head to Nora. "Was he well behaved?"

"Mom said she had no problems with them. She took them to the park in the morning and they had a nap after lunch for an hour. Then they played with toys most of the afternoon. There were only a few tears."

Elle cuddled Toby. A few tears were to be expected. "Thank you so much. I'll call your mom and thank her as well."

"There's nothing to thank. You've given me a job and a way to take care of Miranda as well. Harry is having them both tomorrow, isn't he?"

Elle nodded. She and Nora had hired a babysitter to look after both of their kids during the work day, but he'd not been able to start until Sunday. It worked out well because they were able to split the cost and Harry was an older man, a friend of Nora's family, who'd recently retired and wanted something to occupy his time.

She'd been a little hesitant in trusting him until she'd observed him with both of the children and realized he was caring and lonely.

"I'll see you tomorrow." She gathered up Toby's things. She was lucky to have met Nora when she'd first moved in. They were neighbors in the little apartment building they'd nicknamed Single Mother's Condo due to the prevalence of sole-parent families living there. The rent was cheap and the nearest school was within walking distance.

"It was a hell of a day today," Nora said, standing at the doorway with Miranda in her arms.

"Sure was."

"That lawyer of yours sure knows people."

"It was all luck," Elle said. "But I'm so happy about it."

"You should be. We're going to be swamped tomorrow. Are your friends going to help out?"

"Drew is going to be there and I'll have to put up an ad for more staff. I wasn't expecting quite so many people."

"Some of the women around here would be interested in a few hours of work."

"Good idea. I'll chat with them when I get a chance." After her experience with Drew she wanted to find responsible people she could rely on. If she created a roster of the women in the apartment building, they could maybe even work out a babysitting schedule so they didn't have to worry about childcare.

It was one thing Elle had never considered when she'd fallen pregnant. She'd been so happy and sure things would work out between her and Dean that it hadn't occurred to her that she might need to find someone to take care of her baby.

Now money and childcare were constantly on her mind.

She said good night to Nora and went down the hall to her apartment. All she wanted to do was crawl into bed and go to sleep but she had to get Toby dinner.

Putting him back on the floor, she opened the door and let them both into the apartment.

"Why don't you play with your toys while I make dinner?" she said to him.

"No thanks, Mom." He sat at the small kitchen table and watched her with very tired eyes. Quickly Elle dug around in the fridge to find leftovers from yesterday's veggie burgers. She popped them into the microwave and threw a salad together.

When the microwave dinged, she took the food out and checked the temperature before giving it to Toby to eat. She dished up her own portion and sat down next to him, a sigh escaping as she did so. It was good to be off her feet.

"Can you cut it for me, Mom?" Toby asked, stabbing at the patty.

Normally he liked to cut up his own things and she had bought him a plastic knife so he could do it safely. He was obviously too tired today. She pulled over his plate, cut up the burger patty and gave it back to him.

Toby ate slowly, as he always did. It gave Elle time to finish her own meal and clean up the dishes from breakfast before he was done.

"Pass me your plate and go get ready for the shower," Elle said.

He slowly got out of his chair and brought his plate over. "Thanks, Mom. I love you." His smile made her melt. He'd inherited her blue eyes and brown hair and the only echo of his father was a stubborn tilt to his chin when he wasn't happy. Elle was thankful. She didn't want to be constantly reminded of that man, but the tilt reminded her of the dangers of giving in and spoiling her son.

"I love you too." She washed his plate and put it on the drying rack. "What's wrong?" she said when he still stood there.

He held up his arms, his eyes appealing and tired, so she carried him through to the small bathroom. Deciding it would be quicker and easier, she ran the shower and undressed them both. As much as she wanted a long soak, she wanted her bed more and the quicker she got Toby to sleep the better.

After their shower, she dressed him in his favorite pajamas and tucked him into bed. "Which story would you like tonight?" she asked.

He pointed to the picture book on the bedside table: the same book she'd read him the previous three nights about cowboys and their horses.

Elle was tired of reading the story but she smiled and picked it up. Before she'd got halfway through it, he was fast asleep.

Smiling, she kissed him good night, made sure the covers wouldn't fall off and turned off the light.

For all of the trouble she'd had with Toby's father, she

wouldn't have it any other way. Her little boy was the joy of her life – more than she'd ever imagined before she became a parent. He was the reason she was taking the risk to start her own business; he was the reason she would do everything she could to provide a safe and secure home; and he was the reason she couldn't go home.

But she wouldn't change a thing.

Although it was still early, she tucked herself into bed and went to sleep.

***

Sunday was normally George's day of relaxation. He put aside all work and did whatever he wanted to do. Sometimes it meant working in the garden of his newly renovated house, other times it meant sitting on the sofa watching a game – basketball, football, baseball – it didn't matter which sport.

Today nothing captured his attention. It was mid-morning and he'd started half a dozen things and stopped them all. He was honest enough to admit it was Elle's fault. He couldn't stop thinking about her, worrying whether she'd be as overworked today as she had been yesterday. But hopefully she'd have made sure she'd have enough staff by now.

He shouldn't care.

Maybe it was her vulnerability that had drawn him in, making him want to learn more about her.

His phone rang, breaking through his thoughts.

"Georgie boy, we're going for lunch. Do you want to come?"

George grinned at his sister Isla's voice. "Who're 'we'?"

"Mom, Dad, Rose, Janice and me. Adrian can't make it."

"Sure. Where are we going?"

"Not sure yet."

"There's a new bookshop café," George said, before he thought better.

"Oh, tell me more."

His sister loved all things books and food so it was a perfect combination. He told her about Elle's café and before he'd finished she said, "We'll meet you there at twelve."

George hung up, satisfied. With a new sense of purpose, he

got ready.

***

Elle had been right about Drew. The customers loved her. She'd turned up on time and was busy serving coffees to the morning crowd; the cyclists, dog walkers and fitness fanatics who were out early on a Sunday to get their exercise in before starting their day.

Toby was playing quietly in the little area Elle had set up for children who came to the café. It was small but it contained building blocks, a chalkboard and a few toys and books for children to play with while their parents had coffee in peace. Harry would be along later to pick both Toby and Miranda up for the day. Meanwhile Elle was preparing food for lunch. The momentary peace was lovely. Her legs still ached from being on her feet all day yesterday, but it was a satisfying ache. The aches had been earned. She was making something of herself.

At eight o'clock, Sarah, one of the single mothers in Elle's apartment complex, walked in with her two children. Nora had told her about the waitressing job, so Elle made them both coffee, and hot chocolate for the children, and they sat down to chat.

By the end of the conversation, Sarah had agreed to work the lunchtime shift, ten until two, during the week. It didn't help Elle for the moment but was a relief none-the-less.

When Sarah left, Drew called her over.

"Are you looking for more staff?" she asked.

Elle nodded.

"I have a couple of friends who want weekend work."

Elle hesitated. She couldn't afford for them not to turn up. "I'm not sure. I need people who are going to be reliable."

Drew had the grace to blush. "It won't happen again. I am sorry, Elle. I can vouch they're more responsible than I am."

Elle checked the time. "Do you want to call them in? If they interview all right they can do a trial lunch shift."

"Sure."

Elle glanced over to check on Toby. After living with his father, he was used to playing quietly by himself. He'd had to when he was inside and she hadn't been strong enough to stand up for him.

She pushed aside her shame, reminding herself she'd escaped eventually.

Toby was reading through a picture book she'd bought for him, but there was evidence he'd been playing with his cars and with the cowboy doll he had. "How are you going, my little man?"

Toby glanced up and smiled. "I corralled the horses." He gestured to where his horse was surrounded by books.

He sounded so grown up. He'd spent hours mimicking his uncles, who, unlike his father, liked having him around and had occasionally taken him out on the ranch with them when Dean had needed quiet.

"That's great. Can you tidy up now and take your toys to the store room? Harry and Miranda are going to be here soon."

"Can't I stay with you?" The simple question yanked on her heartstrings.

"Not today, my darling. You and Miranda are going to have fantastic adventures with Harry. I'm sure you don't want to miss out."

His bottom lip jutted out, but he nodded.

Elle hugged him.

"Elle, I need a bit of help," Drew called.

She kissed the top of his head and got to her feet. "Love you."

There was a line of people waiting. She was pleased her café was so popular in its first weekend, but having to leave Toby to play by himself was so difficult.

She told herself it was only for a few more months. He'd start kindergarten soon and then he'd be with lots of children his age and enjoy learning new things.

Still, the guilt was ever present.

***

By lunchtime things were in full swing. Nora had arrived at ten, with Harry close behind her. He had taken the children out for their adventure to the park. Drew's friend Mary-Beth had turned out to be a lovely girl with experience waiting tables. Elle had hired her to do the lunch shift and she was working out well.

With the four of them, they were managing the crowd.

Thankfully.

She didn't have Chris and his friends to help and, while she'd been grateful to them, she was glad she had things under control. Besides, there had been something about George that made her nervous. She'd caught him looking at her a few times during the day, assessing her. She didn't know whether it was because of the way she was running her business or if it was the more personal attraction she thought might be mutual.

She didn't want to know.

As if conjured by her thoughts, George walked in the door. He glanced around, smiled and grabbed a table from people who were leaving. Had he and Chris arranged to come by again, thinking she couldn't manage on her own? The idea rankled and she ignored him, keeping herself busy taking payment from the group who had vacated the table.

By the time she'd finished, others had joined George at his table. There were two women about his age, late twenties/early thirties, and an older couple. The man had the same brown hair and broad shoulders as George.

His family?

Why would he bring his family here?

George caught her watching him. He raised a hand in greeting and smiled. The very appearance of his smile made her heartbeat increase.

Caught, she had to acknowledge him and smile back. Now she couldn't avoid going over and saying hello. Not when he'd helped out in the bookshop the day before.

With a sigh, she gathered up an order pad and walked over.

***

Elle didn't appear so happy to see him. It was the first thing he'd noticed when he spotted her watching him. The smile she gave him was perfunctory; it didn't reach her eyes. It was a different experience for him. Usually the women he dated were more than enthusiastic – though of course he wasn't dating Elle. Yet.

She reached his table. "Hi, George, what can I get for you?"

Straight to the point, no chit-chat.

"Elle, these are my parents, Hank and Marla, and my sisters,

23

Isla and Janice." He turned to his family. "Elle owns this place."

"It's a lovely café," his mother said. "Such a great idea having a bookshop with a café."

"Thank you. There were quite a few in LA and I thought it would do well in Houston."

"Is that where you're from?" Janice asked.

Elle nodded.

"I'm going to have to bring my book club here," Marla continued. "Maybe we can use it as our meeting place instead of going to each other's houses. We usually meet every third Thursday of the month."

Elle smiled then, a proper smile which lit up her face. "You're more than welcome. If you tell me how many people, I can set up the tables for you. I was considering starting a book club myself after I settled in."

"Let me know when you do," Isla said. "I'd love to join."

"Sure. Now what can I get for you?"

They gave her their orders with Isla ordering for their sister, Rose, who was always late. George wanted to say something more to Elle, but she was gone before he could comment on how well the café was running.

She had two college-aged women working. One was taking orders while the other prepared them and took them out.

"Hey, Georgie-boy, stop checking out our host and pay attention to me." Isla had a laugh in her voice.

He hadn't heard a word any of them had said. He grinned at his sister. "If you want my attention you shouldn't be so boring," he joked.

She rolled her eyes at him.

"Now children, behave," his mother said, in the same tone she'd used for over thirty years.

They all laughed.

Rose, the baby of the family, came up to the table. "Sorry I'm late, y'all." She slid into her chair.

"I ordered for you," Isla told her.

"Thanks."

It was so typical of Rose to be late she didn't even ask what had been ordered. She knew it would be something she liked.

"So where's Jake today?" George asked Janice.

"He's working."

Janice's fiancé was a nurse and often worked weekends and evenings. George liked him – he was glad his sister had found someone she loved and who loved her for herself.

"Your mother and I have news," Hank said, reaching across the table to take Marla's hand.

George smiled at the love on both of their faces, the shared memories and lifetime of knowing one another.

"We're going to Europe for our fortieth wedding anniversary," Marla said.

Amid the excited noises of his sisters, George sat back. Forty years and his parents still looked at each other like they were newly in love. His heart tugged. That's what he wanted. Someone who he still wanted to be with after forty years of marriage.

"That's great," he said. "Do you want me to organize your flights?" He'd spent years helping to arrange Adrian's tours, so he knew where to go and what to do.

"Everything's arranged," Marla said.

"They don't need you to pay for them, Galahad," Rose said.

George grimaced at the nickname. As children, his sisters had taken to calling him Galahad because he'd been obsessed with knights and the tales of King Arthur. He'd tried to make them play the damsel in distress, but more often than not, they'd twisted it so they were rescuing him.

As they grew older he'd kept an eye on them, as brothers were supposed to do, occasionally rescuing them from an unwanted admirer, and the nickname had been given new meaning.

The thing was he liked helping people, especially his family. He earned so much money, and he enjoyed treating his family to vacations, or helping them out when they needed it.

He hated the idea of his parents spending their hard-earned money on a trip he could have easily paid for. "Let me know how much and I'll transfer some money over."

His parents simultaneously gave him the same look. The look brooked no argument.

"Your mom and I have more than enough money to pay for this trip and we want to. It's our treat to ourselves."

"We appreciate your offer, George, but others could do with the help more," his mother added.

"Yeah, like me. I could do with a vacation," Rose joked.

George knew when to back down. "OK, but we should organize a family vacation. It's almost summer and we could go somewhere nice for a few days."

"Make sure it's a date Adrian and Libby can come too," Janice said.

Aside from being Adrian's manager, George was also his foster brother. Adrian hadn't been able to make the lunch because he'd arranged to take his niece Kate to the movies.

"I'll organize it," George said.

Elle brought their order over to their table and conversation halted while she served them. George examined her. She was tired around the eyes but her smile was fresh and bright.

She drew him in with that hint of vulnerability. She was lovely, and she was clearly ambitious, but ultimately he was always a sucker for a damsel in distress.

"You've got everything under control today," he commented.

She frowned at him, but tempered it quickly. "Drew's back to full health and one of her friends was after work," she said.

He didn't mean to imply a criticism. "That's great," he said, hoping he sounded encouraging rather than patronizing.

She turned her attention to the rest of the table and finished serving them. When she walked away, Isla laughed.

"She's not going to fall for your charms, Georgie-boy."

George ignored her.

He wasn't going to give up so easily.

# Chapter 3

George had some nerve. Elle deposited the dirty dishes she'd collected into the sink and let out a long breath to control her annoyance. He seemed surprised she had everything under control.

Sure she'd made mistakes yesterday – a whole heap of them – but she learned fast and fixed what she could. Today was running much more smoothly than she had hoped.

She loaded the dishwasher and set it running.

Drew was making up for her absence yesterday, charming all the customers as Elle had hoped she would. And Mary-Beth, aside from being an efficient waitress, was also well read, and stopped by to recommend titles to customers who were browsing. More often than not, it ended with a sale.

So George could take his smugness and his surprise, and shove them where the sun didn't shine.

Elle laughed and some of the tension left her.

She wasn't sure why she was letting him get to her. It wasn't as if he was anyone who mattered. He was just a guy who'd happened to help her out the day before. Now he could tell she could take care of herself, he'd leave her alone and she wouldn't have to see him again.

She was fine with that.

Clearing a few more plates, she unloaded the dishwasher

before setting it going again. Calmer than she had been, she went out into her café to keep serving.

***

An hour later, George approached the counter to pay. Elle spotted him rising from his chair and made herself scarce by going to clear some more tables. While she was on the floor, George's mother stopped her.

"Do you have a card?" she asked. "I'll check with my book club and if everyone's in agreement, we'll come here for our meeting next week."

"Sure." The idea of attracting book clubs to her café was exciting. Though they might monopolize the tables for a couple of hours, she was sure they would buy enough coffee and cake to make it worthwhile. Maybe even books too.

Elle went behind the counter and grabbed her business card. "Be sure to call me with numbers."

"Absolutely," Marla said. "I'm pretty sure everyone will agree. It's become a chore to host the club because everyone's always trying to outdo each other with the catering." She laughed.

"I'm happy to cater for you all," Elle told her and handed her the card.

Before she could escape, George came over. Elle stifled her groan.

"Ready to go, Mom?" he asked.

Marla nodded.

He turned to Elle. "Can I grab a business card too? I'll be in touch this week about the artists."

Elle closed her eyes briefly. She'd forgotten he'd offered to find her musicians to do the weekend sets. She really didn't want to have to deal with him again, but she couldn't refuse this opportunity. She handed him a card. "Great."

He opened his mouth to say more, but his mother took his arm. "Come on, George. Elle has work to do and your father is waiting for us."

Relieved, Elle said goodbye and headed to the kitchen to regain her equilibrium. As she unloaded the dishwasher she acknowledged the tightness of her skin and the giddiness of her heart: George was an attractive man but she wasn't eighteen any more. She wasn't going to fall for the first man who showed her any attention like she had with Dean. No, she was twenty-five, and a mother. She didn't have time for that kind of nonsense.

Perhaps she should mention Toby to George the next time she saw him. It was sure to send him running. From what Nora said, no man was interested once he found out there was a child in the picture.

And she was more than happy with that.

The only male she wanted in her life was Toby.

***

The rest of the afternoon ran smoothly. Harry brought Toby and Miranda back at three o'clock. Nora finished her shift and took her little girl home, and Toby went in to the play area, where a couple of other children had congregated.

Elle hated the fact she didn't have time to spend with Toby at the moment. She really hoped once she'd fallen into a rhythm, she'd be able to leave Drew to close up so she could steal a few extra hours with her son. But it would be some time away. Drew had to prove she was responsible.

By the time the last customer had left, Mary-Beth had restocked the bookshop and Drew had cleared and set the tables. Elle tallied up the tip jar and split it between the girls based on the hours they worked, and put Nora's aside to give to her later.

Then she locked the café door behind them as they left and went to tally the register. Toby was playing happily where she could keep an eye on him.

"I'm hungry, Mom," he said as she brought the till tray to one of the tables.

"I know. I'll get dinner for us soon. I need to count the money first."

"I'll help." He got to his feet and hurried over. He was tall for his age and, after learning to ride on the ranch, had great coordination.

Toby would insist, so she took out the pennies and put them on the table in front of him. "Awesome. Put them into piles of ten for me." She showed him what she meant, helped him to count out the first ten and then concentrated on the bills in front of her.

By the time she'd counted out the bills, made up her change for the morning and started on the coins, Toby had finished with his pennies.

"How many piles have you got?" Elle asked him.

He stuck out his tongue and counted the piles aloud. "Six and not a full pile."

Elle smiled. "How many are in the not full pile?"

While he counted she surreptitiously checked his stacks to make sure they were correct.

"Five."

She added the total to her list and got him to count out the nickels. When they'd both finished he said, "I was a real help, wasn't I, Mom?"

"You sure were," she said, giving him a hug. "You've been such a good boy all day that I think there should be ice cream for dessert. What do you think?" She turned and put the money away.

He nodded in all seriousness. "Yes, I deserve it." Then he added, "Even if Dad doesn't think I do."

The laugh Elle was biting back died.

It had been six months since she'd left Dean, and Toby hadn't mentioned his father in all that time. He'd asked about his uncles and his Memah and Pepah, and Elle had explained they needed to have a break from them, but he'd never asked about Dean.

Elle wasn't at all surprised. Dean had barely tolerated Toby's presence, particularly if he'd been working on a screenplay. Then he'd needed total silence and even Toby's quiet murmurings when he was flicking through a picture book had induced acts of rage.

Toby's Memah, Dean's mother, had often taken him out on the ranch to watch the horses and cattle while Elle was required to stay in Dean's study and act as his muse. She'd been too eager to please, too scared of his rages, to disagree.

At the end of the day, Toby's Pepah would take him for a ride, first sharing the saddle with him, and then with Toby sitting up by himself. The first time Elle had found Toby on the back of a horse she'd freaked out. He'd only been two and she was sure he would fall off, but Dean's father had calmed her and explained all his boys had been riding since that age. She hadn't wanted to cause a fuss, and Dean had been unconcerned, so she'd allowed it. By the time she'd fled the ranch, Toby had been as comfortable on the back of a horse as he was on the ground. It was one thing she regretted about cutting all ties with Dean's family. She'd really had no problem with them, only their son, but she knew if they knew where she was, so would Dean. She couldn't risk Toby in that way.

"It doesn't matter what your dad thinks," she said. "We've got each other and *we* know you're the best." She tickled his sides and it brought a smile to his face. "Let's go home."

She took his hand and kept up a light banter all the way to the car. But on the inside she was cursing herself for not having the courage to leave Dean sooner.

***

The next week flew by. The café had its quiet moments mid-morning, before the lunch rush, and late afternoon, for which Elle was grateful. It gave her a chance to tidy up, catch her breath, and ensure Nora got her coffee and lunch breaks.

Aside from Sarah's shifts, Elle had set up a roster for another two women who wanted a few hours' work during the week. So far it was working well.

Marla had convinced her book club to hold the meeting at the café on Thursday afternoon, and that session consisted of a riotous two hours of women laughing, arguing and eating cake.

Elle envied their camaraderie, and hoped when she formed a book club it would be as lovely as theirs. There was real friendship in it and she'd never had that. Nora was the closest Elle had to a friend, but even they weren't close. They helped each other out, but that was more because they were neighbors and because Toby and Miranda were the same age than from any deeper bond. Nora had no idea about what had happened with Dean, and Elle wasn't going to tell her. She was the biggest gossip in the apartment building.

Toby was getting used to his new routine. Harry picked up him and Miranda at ten o'clock and brought them back around three. The rest of the day he was with Miranda either in the converted store room/playroom or out in the café play area. There were the inevitable fights or tears but they were generally well behaved. However, by the end of the week, it was obvious both children were tired.

Harry had dropped them off while Elle was at the bank, and when she returned to the café she found both children screaming, Nora completely flustered and Drew trying to appease the customers.

As she rushed forward to herd the children back into the playroom she registered a man seated in one of the high-backed chairs in the book area. She glanced at him, registered with dismay it was George, and then continued to Toby. Sweeping him up into her arms, she left Miranda to Nora and took him out the back.

"Shush, Toby-boy. What's the matter?" she said as she lowered him to the ground again.

"Miranda took my horse."

"It's my horse," Miranda said as Nora carried her in.

"Is *not*!" Toby shrieked and Elle winced.

She dug a tissue out of her pocket and wiped Toby's eyes, making soothing, shushing noises, and he began to settle.

She glanced around the room and noted the horse that was obviously at the root of the problem clutched in Miranda's hand. She met Nora's eyes and saw the same exhaustion in them as she was sure was in her own.

"The horse is yours, but it would be nice if you let Miranda play with it," Elle said.

"But it's mine!"

"Toby, we've talked about sharing before. You'll have a chance to play with the horse after Miranda goes home." Toby scrunched up his face but before he reverted to tears again Elle added, "I bet Miranda's never seen a real horse before." Hoping she was right, she turned to the little girl. "Have you?"

Miranda shook her head.

"Toby used to ride the horses at his grandparents' ranch."

Miranda's eyes opened wide and Toby wriggled out from under his mother's arm.

"I did. I rode them by myself."

"Why don't you tell Miranda all about it?" Elle suggested.

Toby walked over and took Miranda's hand. "You can play with my horse," he said and led her to the mat to tell her all about his grandparents' ranch.

Elle stood and exchanged a relieved look with Nora, who was still shaken.

"I'm sorry, Elle. I couldn't get them to stop."

"It's not your fault. It's inevitable. Why don't you take a minute and I'll go and help Drew?"

Nora nodded and Elle went out to check the damage.

There were only a few people left in the café. Elle walked over to Drew, who was cleaning the coffee machine. "Any complaints?"

"One couple, but they complained about everything: the temperature of the coffee, the selection of pastries and the types of books available. I wouldn't worry, people are used to kids having tantrums."

Drew was right but Elle worried about the image it portrayed to her customers. She wanted people to come back.

She surveyed her place and found George watching her, his expression thoughtful. She jolted. Damn, she'd forgotten about him.

Forcing a smile on to her face, she wandered over. "Hi, can I help you with anything?"

George was silent for a moment, before he said, "I was in the neighborhood and thought I'd drop by to discuss your music needs."

There was something about the way he said "needs" that sent a shiver through Elle. She ignored it. Now wasn't the best time to discuss music, but she was afraid if she postponed it he'd suggest after hours, and that wouldn't work *at all*.

"Sure, what do you want to know?" She perched herself on the edge of the chair across from him.

"Why do you want music?"

It wasn't the question she was expecting and she took a minute to consider her answer. "For the ambience and to draw people in."

He nodded. "Any preference for the type of music?"

"It needs to please the family crowd, and it can't be too

loud. Acoustic only so those who want to chat aren't drowned out."

He was silent for a long time.

"It was only an idea, something I thought I'd try." She hated that she was so defensive, so ready to back down from an idea both Nora and Drew thought was fantastic. She shut her mouth firmly and waited for a response.

"Could the singers sell their merchandise?"

"Of course." She figured if they were willing to do a gig at the price she could afford to pay them, they should be able to earn more from CD sales.

"Do you want a commission?" he asked, watching her.

She hadn't considered it. She supposed they might take sales away from her books, but she doubted it would be much.

"It won't be necessary."

"Will you advertise?"

"On my website and a flyer in the front window." She couldn't afford any more than that; as it was every change to her website cost her. "Will you?"

"Of course." He appeared to be enjoying their negotiating and Elle had to admit she was too. It had been far too long since she'd been treated as an equal by a man.

"I've got some artists for you to consider." He handed her a CD. "Have a listen and get back to me."

Elle took the CD. She only had a player in her car, so she'd have to listen to it on her way home from work.

"Mom." Toby's voice and his hand on her arm had her turning, but she caught the surprise on George's face.

"Yes, sweetheart?"

"Can Miranda go riding at Memah's?"

Elle's heart sank. This wasn't a conversation she wanted to have now. "We'll have a chat about it later," she said. "Would you like to meet –?" She paused, not knowing what George's surname was. Face flushed she said, "I'm sorry, I don't know your last name."

"Jones."

"Toby, this is Mr. Jones." She turned to George. "This is my son, Toby." Did he hear the defiance in her tone?

"Nice to meet you, Toby," George said, holding out his

hand. "Call me George."

Toby hung back, examining George's hand, and then turned to his mother for confirmation. She nodded.

He stepped forward and shook George's hand. "Pleased to meet you."

"Pleasure's all mine." George sounded sincere. "How old are you, Toby? Aren't you too young to be riding motorbikes?"

Toby frowned. "I'm five and I don't ride motorbikes."

"Oh, I thought you said you wanted to take your friend Miranda riding."

Toby laughed, the same way as he used to laugh when his uncles teased him, so loud and carefree. It tugged at Elle's heart.

"*Horses*, not motorbikes."

"It sounds mighty scary to me. Aren't you afraid?"

"Nah. My Pepah says if you treat them right, there's nothing to be afraid of. I give them carrots and apples."

Toby hadn't been that animated with an adult since they'd left the ranch. She debated whether she should interrupt them, because she didn't want George knowing their history.

"Toby, can I go?" Miranda shouted from across the café.

Elle turned in time to catch Nora's wince. "Why don't you go play with Miranda and we'll talk about it tonight?"

Toby nodded. "Bye, George," he said and headed back to the playroom.

Elle waited for George's comment but when it didn't come, she asked, "Where were we?"

"I was about to ask you whether there's a Mr. Carter I need to be aware of," George said, his gaze focused on her.

Elle gaped at him as heat flooded her body. They hadn't been talking about anything of the sort. What had they been talking about? She cast her panicked mind back and her gaze rested on the CD she held. She was going to listen to it.

"No," she said and stood. "I'll listen to the CD. Do you want to leave a card with Drew? I need to ... do something out the back."

She fled.

***

George was surprised by the panic in her eyes. Surely she'd had men ask her out before? She was an incredibly attractive woman.

She was also young to have a five-year-old boy.

Toby brought a whole other set of values into the equation. Not only would Elle have less flexibility to go out to dinner, but also – where was Toby's father? Had he left her, died, had she left him?

He needed to tread carefully because he did want to get to know Elle better. She fascinated him.

Here she was setting up her own business with a young child to care for. Did she have a lot of family to support her? Toby had mentioned his grandparents, so perhaps she did.

She had a quick mind too. Watching the thoughts race over her face while they discussed music was fascinating.

He was glad he'd dropped by. Elle had been on his mind all week; he couldn't shake her from his thoughts. It didn't matter to him that she had a son. He liked kids – he had always spent a lot of time with Kate, who was effectively his niece.

Standing, he went to the counter to leave his business card. He needed to figure out how he could spend more time with Elle, find out what he needed to do to get her out of his system.

He handed his business card over to Drew, who smiled and batted her eyelashes at him. She probably wasn't much younger than Elle, but she held no interest for him at all. "Tell Elle I'll call her at the end of next week if I haven't heard from her," he said. That would give Elle something to mull over. He wasn't going to go away if she ignored him.

As he moved toward the door, Toby and Miranda came prancing out of one of the back rooms, neighing and pretending to be horses. He caught annoyed glances from a couple sitting having coffee and Nora was right behind them.

"Whoa there, horses," he called as they went to pass him. Both children stopped and looked up at him.

He wasn't sure what the right thing to say was. He'd guessed by the way Elle had picked up Toby and hustled him into a back room that they weren't supposed to be on the shop floor. He felt sorry for the kids, but also knew it would be difficult being a single mother who needed to earn a living.

"You've broken out of the corral."

Toby shot him a wicked grin and George immediately knew

Toby was going to make a break for it. Before he did, George grabbed both of their hands. "Gotcha. Let's go quietly and you might get a carrot."

Luckily that satisfied the children and they trotted alongside him, neighing.

Nora took Miranda's other hand. "I told you both you needed to stay in the playroom," she said.

"We broke out," Toby said proudly.

"Well good children don't break out." Nora's tone was full of frustration.

George couldn't imagine what it was like to work so hard *and* have kids to care for.

"But we're horses, not children," Miranda told her mother.

"Good horses wouldn't break out either," George said. "If you're treated well, like your Pepah said, you'd want to stay."

Toby was silent for a moment, then he nodded. "That's why Mom and me broke out."

# Chapter 4

Toby turned to Miranda and grabbed her hand. "Come on, we can pretend the mat is grass." George watched as both kids disappeared out the back.

Did Toby mean his grandpa hadn't treated them very well, or was it someone else?

If it had been her ex, it would explain why Elle was so skittish.

Nora was watching him closely.

George forced a smile. "I'll see you around," he said and left the café.

He had a lot of thinking to do.

***

Nora came into the kitchen where Elle was hiding out, doing the dishes and waiting for George to leave. She'd been so stupid to get flustered. It might make him think she was interested.

Which she wasn't.

She should have made it clear. Or better yet, lied and said yes, there was a Mr. Carter. That would have kept him away.

She groaned.

"He's good with kids," Nora said, placing dirty dishes on the sink.

"I don't want to know," Elle told her. "It doesn't matter. I'm not interested."

Nora scoffed. "Which is why you ran scared and are hiding out here, while that sexy man calmed down the kids and got them to return to the playroom."

Elle looked up then. "What happened?"

"They decided to play horses out in the café. Your George told them good horses didn't break out of the corral, especially if they were well cared for, and they went back."

"He's not my George."

Nora ignored the comment and said, "Toby said something you should know about."

The tone of her voice made Elle stop her frenetic cleaning and pay attention. "What?"

"He said that's why you both broke out."

Elle's stomach sank. "What did George say?"

"Nothing. But he got a very thoughtful expression on his face."

"Maybe it will be enough to scare him away. I'm too busy for men right now."

"Honey, I wouldn't be so quick to dismiss him. If he's still interested after meeting Toby, there's a chance he's a keeper."

Frustration rose in Elle. Nora didn't know what she'd been through with Dean. Nora's ex had left when she'd fallen pregnant, which was bad enough, but at least she hadn't suffered years of abuse. "I don't want or need a man." She said it slowly, trying not to let the anger show, but some of it must have.

"I know it hasn't been long since you left your ex, but you need to remember some men are worth it." Nora ran a hand down Elle's arm and left the kitchen.

Elle let out a breath and bowed her head over the sink.

She shouldn't be getting this worked up over a man. What she would do was listen to the CD, tell him she didn't like any of his singers and that would be the end of it.

Easy.

***

Elle dumped the fast-food bags and mail on the kitchen table and sank into a chair, sighing. She'd been too tired and stressed to worry about cooking and figured the occasional treat wouldn't hurt.

Toby sat next to her and reached for the bag.

"Hold on a second." Elle pulled it out of his reach and then handed him his fries, burger and juice.

He attacked the fries with gusto and there was a short period of silence.

Elle would have killed for a mint iced tea, but she didn't have the ingredients. Instead she had to settle for the over-sweetened soda that had come with her meal. Still, at least she hadn't had to cook.

As she ate her fries, she sifted through the mail, mostly flyers and other junk, but an envelope caught her eye, and then the logo on the front made her heart race.

Slowly she picked up the envelope and examined it.

It was from the women's shelter she'd run to when she'd first left Dean. The only reason they would be sending her something was if it had come from Dean or his family.

After she'd left the shelter, she'd written to Dean's mother, Lindsay, and told her if she wanted to contact them, she should send it to the shelter. Only the women there knew where she was now.

Tearing open the envelope, she let two letters fall out. The first had the address handwritten and Elle recognized Lindsay's handwriting. It was postmarked Monday.

The second was worse.

*Simpson, Cook and Partners.*

Lawyers.

Elle's heart thumped as she debated which she should open first.

She wouldn't be a coward.

She pried open the lawyer's letter and flattened it out on the table. Taking a deep breath, she read it. Then she read it for a second time, not quite believing what it said.

"Can I leave the table?"

"Mom?" Toby tapped her on the arm.

Elle looked over. "Sure. Why don't you get your pajamas out and find a story book to read?"

Toby raced out of the room.

Elle closed her eyes.

Dean wanted custody of Toby.

She'd never heard anything more ridiculous. He hadn't spent any time with his child. No, a relationship with Toby was definitely not his real motive. He just wanted to keep control of *her*.

She would fight it. There was no way she was going to allow that asshole to have Toby. She didn't even want him to have joint custody. There was no reason for him to want it. He hadn't paid any attention to his son since he was born, had often said Toby was a nuisance and had even suggested she have an abortion when she first told him she was pregnant.

No, she would fight this with all she had.

Which wasn't a lot.

Dean had his family's money behind him. He could afford to hire lawyers whereas Elle would have to go back to the pro bono place.

Thinking of his family, she reached for the letter from Lindsay.

*Dear Elle and Toby,*

*I hope you are well and safe. You have both been missed at the ranch and we hope you will be back soon.*

*Elle, I don't know why you left, but I do know that since you've been gone Dean has been beside himself. He is going to get in touch and I think you should consider counseling, for Toby's sake if not your own. A boy deserves to be with his father.*

*Martin and I miss our little man as well. Tell Toby we have a couple of new foals. I know he would love to visit them.*

*Love,*

*Lindsay (Memah)*

Elle put the letter aside, her heart twisting. Despite living in such close quarters, Lindsay and Martin never witnessed the abuse. She and Dean had lived in a little cottage not far from the main house, but far enough for them not to know what happened in her day-to-day life.

Dean didn't beat her often, just when the rage overwhelmed him, or when she made him mad. And he learned to hit where the bruises could be covered up.

Anyway, the worst punishment had been the feeling of being trapped. She'd been in a cage with the door left open, daring her to take a step out and face the punishment, and that was almost worse. She'd had no money and there was no one she could run to.

It had taken her five years to build the courage to leave, and then it was only because Dean had hit Toby. She might have had no money, no transport and no prospects, but she had to protect her son.

There was no way she was going back to Dean, and no way she would let him have care of their son.

Her one ray of light was she'd never married the creep. He hadn't believed in the institution of marriage and so she didn't need a divorce. Of course there were still de facto and parenting legalities she had to deal with, but she'd not had time to think about them until now.

At least she had her diaries and photos to back up her allegations of abuse.

She'd kept a diary since she was in high school and Dean hadn't had an issue with it early in the relationship. Then when Toby was born and things became rocky she'd kept a fake journal, full of her love for Dean and her sorrow at making him mad; the real one, well hidden, detailed his rages and violence, his tight control of her movements and her concerns for her child.

Elle rose, gathered both letters and went to the closet of her room, all thoughts of her dinner forgotten. She took the box out of the bottom and opened it, to check the diaries were still there. She really should get a safe deposit box for them, in case Dean found out where they lived.

She'd check with her bank in the morning.

Right now she wanted to spend some time with the one male in her life she would do anything for. The one who relied on her to take care of him.

And she *would* take care of him.

No matter what Dean threw at her.

***

Why the hell had George agreed to take this diva on? Sure, she had an amazing voice, but damn, she could caterwaul if she wasn't getting her own way. She was nowhere near successful enough to be throwing these theatrics at him. He sat at his desk as she stalked around his office.

"Can you *believe*, George, they only offered water, tea or percolated coffee as refreshments? What kind of radio station is that? I won't go back to them." She took a breath and before George could change the subject she continued, "*And* they made me do some stupid name-the-song game without any warning. I mean who knows songs from the nineties?"

Anyone who was born before then or who had an interest in music.

George let it lie. Instead he said, "A lot of radio stations don't have the money to cater as well as they would like to, Ophelia."

"Well they should."

This wasn't getting them anywhere. He needed to change the topic. "How's the latest song going?"

Ophelia sighed, deep and heartfelt, and George wished he hadn't asked.

"Jay wants to add rapping and the thought gives me the heebie-jeebies."

Jay had sent him a sample the day before, along with a whole heap of complaints about the girl. The rapping gave the song an edge and a different sound from Ophelia's other songs. It worked.

"Why?"

"Rapping is so passé. Everyone's doing it."

George clenched his teeth together. The girl had no clue. She was eighteen, blond haired and blue eyed and had never had a difficult day in her life. When he'd met her, she'd spun him a sob story of poverty and struggle and he'd fallen for it.

The damn Galahad syndrome again.

He was too proud to admit he'd made a mistake about her, and damn it, she was such a fantastic singer – there was a tone to her voice that gave him chills. He just needed to show her that hard work and networking meant a damn sight more than voice in their industry, and that being a diva would get her nowhere she wanted to go.

Somehow.

"Rapping is an incredibly difficult art form," he said to her. "It gives the song extra depth."

If there was one thing Ophelia wanted it was depth and meaning to her music. She didn't want to be a Katy or Taylor – her words not his.

She pursed her lips. "Maybe I should listen to it again."

George clicked open the file on his computer. "I've got it here."

They listened to the song twice, the second time with Ophelia singing along. Her voice was perfect. When they got to the recording studio it would be a piece of cake – as long as she'd lost the attitude before then.

"Jay's got the mix right," he said.

Ophelia tilted her head. "Do you really think so?"

There was the tiniest hint of vulnerability there, but George refused to be pulled in to it. He'd learned his lesson.

The problem with Ophelia was she'd never been through the battle to find gigs, never had to sing in dives to make a few dollars and a few fans. No, Ophelia had graduated high school and come knocking at his door. She hadn't even been the songwriter she'd said she was.

Perhaps that was the solution. He should book her into a few small places to do a short set and check what she was like in front of an audience. She could do a couple of covers as well as the song they'd released.

Elle's place would be perfect for her.

But Ophelia might be too much for it.

He could start somewhere else. Mind made up, he said, "I'm going to book a couple of gigs. We'll try a couple of the new songs and check the audience reaction."

Ophelia was truly panicked. "But I don't have a full set."

"We'll add in a couple of covers. You don't want to give them a free concert."

"Free? I'm not going to work unpaid." Her tone was incredulous.

"You'll be paid but the patrons won't need to pay. I'll find a couple of bars and set something up."

"Bars? What about concert venues?"

George laughed then. He couldn't help himself. "No one knows who you are, Ophelia. You need to start off small. The concert venues will come, if you master the smaller ones and attract fans."

Ophelia flopped down into one of the chairs. "Do I have to?" She was like a whiny child.

"Yes. Why don't you go and work on your next song? You've got another session with Jay tomorrow, don't you?"

She nodded, pouting a little, but George ignored it. When she realized she wasn't going to get any further reaction from him, she stood and walked out the door.

George waited until it closed behind her and then let out a deep sigh. His other artists were nothing like her. Which was just as well.

Grabbing a pen he jotted down the names of a few bars and clubs that might suit Ophelia's music. Then he picked up the phone and started calling.

***

An hour later he had a schedule he was happy with. He'd left Elle's place at the bottom with a question mark next to it. It was too early in the week to call her. He'd promised himself and her that he wouldn't until Friday. But that didn't mean he wasn't thinking about her.

After Toby's bombshell about escaping, George had asked Chris about her. Chris had worked for her at a pro bono session, but he didn't know much about her circumstances.

It was obvious from her skittish behavior that she hadn't had an easy time. George knew he needed to take things slowly, but she was on his mind constantly.

His cell rang and he picked it up, then smiled. "Hello, Elle."

There was a sharp intake of breath and some stuttering before she said, "Hello, George."

His smile widened. He liked that he flustered her. It meant she wasn't indifferent to him. "What can I do for you?"

"I've listened to the CD you gave me."

"Great, what did you think?"

A long pause, then a big sigh. "They were all good." She didn't sound happy.

George grinned. He'd made sure the song list he'd put together was perfect for her small venue and full of artists who would enjoy the gig. There were some on his books who would gig anywhere because they loved to play, loved to sing. Some of them were breaking into the big time now, but they wouldn't mind doing a one-off secret session. It would be great for interest and social media. Elle was too professional to let the chance go.

"Do you want me to come around later and we'll work out a schedule?"

"Can we discuss it now?"

That didn't fit his plan. "I've got a meeting in five. I'll check the artists' schedules and come around Friday about four. Does that work for you?"

"That's fine."

"How's Toby?" George asked.

"He's well." She seemed surprised by the question, but pleased.

"Did Miranda get to go riding?"

"No." Her tone shifted, screaming 'back off', and so he did.

"All right. See you Friday." He hung up.

Placing his cell on the table, he leaned back. Was he being too pushy? Was he inviting more issues than he should, by trying to get Elle to open up? What was she hiding? On a whim, he typed her name into the search engine on his computer. He scanned through the results. There was nothing that matched her.

Who didn't have an online presence these days? Her name didn't even come up in conjunction with her bookshop café.

Was she hiding from someone?

He closed his eyes, pictured her standing in her bookshop, vulnerable but determined, and the protectiveness in him kicked into gear. Someone, somewhere had treated her badly, of that he was sure.

He wanted to show her not everyone was like that.

He wanted her to trust him.

***

Elle flitted around the shop, brushing non-existent dust off her books and wiping already-clean tables again. She checked the clock for the tenth time – five to four – and cursed the fact that for the first time all week, the café was quiet, with only a few customers.

The tables were set, the books were restocked, and the sugar containers were full. Any other day she'd send Nora home now, but George was due to arrive any minute.

He was the reason she was in such a state.

Calling George hadn't gone the way she'd hoped. Initially she'd intended telling him all his artists were unsuitable, but damned if he hadn't chosen wonderful voices that would be lovely in her shop. She wanted her business to succeed too much to refuse them because she didn't want to deal with George again. But then she was sure they could have arranged it over the phone.

No such luck.

To give herself a boost of confidence, she'd changed out of her uniform and dressed in the one business suit she owned. She wanted to portray the image of a successful business owner. Checking her reflection again in the display cabinet, she huffed out a breath. She was being ridiculous.

Annoyed with herself, she turned to head out the back to check the kitchen – and the chime on the door sounded.

He was dressed in a gray suit with a white shirt. The tie he wore took the look from completely professional, adding a bit of fun with its bright, colorful cartoon knight.

Elle's heartbeat increased and she swallowed. While he searched for her, she started forward, determined to be polite, professional and to the point.

"Elle, nice to see you again." He held out his hand as she approached and she had no choice but to take it.

"George." His hand was warm, strong but gentle as she shook it. She ignored the zing that shot up her arm, or tried to. "Can I get you a coffee?"

"A latte would be great."

Glad for the excuse to distance herself, she said, "Why don't you take a seat over there and I'll bring it right out?" She pointed to the table she'd set up ready for their meeting and hurried away.

Nora walked over as Elle put the required amount of coffee in the scoop. "What do you need?"

"Two lattes," Elle told her and put the cups under the nozzles.

"Let me finish them. You go and start your meeting with George." She nudged Elle away from the coffee machine. "If you're nervous, pretend he's naked."

Elle's eyes shot towards George and heat filled her face. She was relieved he wasn't close enough to hear, or see her reaction. That image was the last thing she needed. She rolled her eyes at Nora, who was grinning at her. "Thanks a lot."

Elle stepped away from the machine, took a moment to make sure the flush was fading, and then she sat down across from George. "Nora will bring the coffees shortly."

"How's business going?" George asked.

Elle ignored the instinctive defensiveness rising up in her. He was making polite conversation, not challenging how she was doing. "Very well so far," she said and forced herself to smile. "Your mother's book club had a lovely meeting here and must have spread the word because I've had a number of other clubs contact me to ask if they can hold their meetings here. I've had to work out a calendar roster as most of them meet monthly."

"That's great." He seemed genuinely pleased for her.

"I've put up an expressions of interest form to start my own book club as well," she added and then immediately wished she hadn't when he said, "I might put my name down for it."

That was the last thing she needed. "It will be during the day," she told him.

"A benefit of working for yourself," George told her. "You can choose your own hours." He grinned and Elle couldn't help smiling in response. It was infectious.

Nora served the drinks.

"Thanks, Nora," George said. "How's Miranda?"

Nora beamed at him. "She's doing swell, though a little obsessed by horses at the moment. I'm going to have to find somewhere to take her."

"My niece Kate went through a horse phase," George said. "It didn't stick."

"Well I hope this doesn't stick. I can't afford to feed a horse." Nora laughed and went to serve another customer.

Elle sipped her coffee. "The red-haired girl who came in on opening day? I thought she was Adrian's niece? Are you brothers?" Piper had said George was his manager.

"Foster brothers," George answered. "Kate's father, who was Adrian's brother – and my foster brother – died in a car crash eighteen months ago." He was silent a moment. "Kate's mother died too, and Kate lives with Libby and Adrian now. She's always been like a niece to me."

How awful, but Elle was intrigued. She wanted to know more about how they came to be foster brothers, because she'd met George's sisters the other day – there were already four Jones kids. What would make his parents take on another two children?

She couldn't ask though. She could hardly pry when she wasn't willing to tell him anything about herself. "I'm sorry to hear about Kate's parents."

He acknowledged her sympathy with a small nod. "She's been amazing. What about you? Any siblings?"

This was veering into territory she needed to avoid. "An older brother." Her heart squeezed when she thought about James, who'd always been her protector and her hero when she was younger. Until Dean came into her life.

She doubted she'd ever be able to fix their relationship, and James had never even tried.

"What fees will you charge for these artists?" she asked, pushing the CD toward George.

George raised his brows at the abrupt change of topic, but answered smoothly with an amount. "That's for a two-hour acoustic set on the weekend. Do you want the same artist on Saturday and Sunday?"

"I'll go with just Saturday," Elle told him. "On Sundays I might do poetry readings, or author talks or something similar."

"Great idea."

Pride surged up in her. She'd thought it was a good idea as well. She wasn't sure if it would work, but she'd try it.

George took out a computer tablet and tapped on it. "I've got a few availabilities."

They discussed dates and times until they locked in what suited them both.

"I'll send you an email with all the details," George said as he switched off the tablet.

"Thanks." Elle had her scribbled notes but she wanted to check and confirm everything before she signed.

It was close to closing time and she was far too comfortable sitting across from George. He was surprisingly laidback and easy to be with. He wasn't scornful of her ideas, and if he disagreed, he did so politely, but let her make her own decision.

"Now the business is done," George said, giving her a wicked grin that made her skin prickle, "what do I have to do to convince you to go out to dinner with me?"

Elle sat back, shocked. She'd been comfortable, relaxed and he had to throw this curve ball at her.

"Ah –"

"You're so pretty when you get flustered."

Heat rushed to Elle's cheeks. She didn't know what to say, but she had to get out of there.

The bell over the door rang as a customer came in.

Saved.

She half stood, looked over and froze.

It couldn't be.

What the heck was she doing in Houston?

# Chapter 5

Elle wanted to hide, but Lindsay had already seen her. Dean's mother stopped, stared.

"Elle?" The older woman moved toward her.

Elle's legs went weak but she braced them firmly. She wanted to run out the back and wait until Lindsay went away but it was too late.

"Hello, Lindsay."

Lindsay reached her and threw her arms around her. "Thank the Lord: you're all right. We've all been so worried about you, you up and disappearing like that. We all thought something terrible must have happened."

"I wrote you a letter."

"Which could have been coerced! Dean's been beside himself since you've been gone. He'll be so relieved to know where you are."

Elle's blood ran cold. "No. You mustn't tell him."

Lindsay showed her surprise. "Of course I must. He's been depressed for months."

Elle couldn't have this conversation now, not with George sitting right there. "Are you in Houston by yourself?"

"Martin's with me. He's got an appointment with his accountant down the road so I popped in here for a coffee."

If she'd known their accountant was on the same street, she

never would have leased this place.

"How about we meet for dinner about six-thirty? There's a restaurant a few doors down," Elle suggested. "We can talk then."

"You'll bring the Toby monster, won't you?"

He shouldn't be there for the conversation she needed to have. "He's having a sleep-over tonight at a friend's house." She hoped Nora could babysit him.

"Oh." Lindsay was disappointed and then she noticed George. "Who's this?"

Elle hesitated. She didn't want Lindsay to discover she owned the café. "This is George, he's a ... friend." She hoped he wouldn't dispute it.

Lindsay's face changed instantly, her expression one of disbelief, not unlike the expression Dean used to get when she disobeyed him.

"Friend? Is he the reason you left Dean? Have you been shacking up with this man while my poor son has been beside himself with despair?" Her voice rose as she spoke and one of the customers glanced over in interest.

Before Elle could answer, Lindsay continued.

"You harlot!" she hissed. "You leave my son, take Toby away from his family and we were thinking the worst had happened. How long were you having an affair before you left?"

Elle couldn't believe Lindsay was suggesting such a thing. She'd barely ever left the ranch and never unaccompanied. There was no way she'd had the opportunity to have an affair.

George stood. "I'm afraid you've made a mistake, ma'am," he said and gave her a friendly smile. "Elle and I are recent acquaintances. She's a friend of a friend and was kind enough to meet me for coffee so I could discuss some business matters with her." He held out his hand. "I didn't catch your name."

Some of the indignation left Lindsay. "It's Lindsay. I'm Elle's mother-in-law."

Elle didn't dare correct her. It wasn't worth the scene it would cause.

George didn't react to that piece of news at all. "Mighty pleased to meet you," he said. There was something in his tone and Lindsay blushed.

He sure had an effect on women.

Elle needed to get them both out of there before anything else happened.

"Memah!"

Too late.

All Elle's hope fled. How the hell was she going to explain Toby's appearance without giving away she was working there?

"Toby!" Lindsay held out her arms and Toby leaped in to them, giving her a big hug.

Elle's heart squeezed. She hated the fact Toby couldn't visit his grandparents; she'd had nothing against them, it was just she couldn't figure out how to keep him safe from his father.

"What are you doing here?" Lindsay asked.

Before Toby could give away any secrets, Elle blurted, "I brought him. His friend's mother works here and she's going to take him home for the sleep-over."

"It's wonderful to see you. Did your mother tell you the foals have been born?"

Toby shook his head. "Really? Can I come and play with them?"

"Any time."

Things were rapidly getting out of control. Elle had no idea how to get them back on track again.

"I think the café is about to close," George said, coming to the rescue. "How about I walk you back to the accountant's, Lindsay?"

Elle could have kissed him.

"I'll wait for Elle."

"Oh, I have a few things I need to discuss with my friend." Elle pointed to Nora. "I'll meet you and Martin at the restaurant at six-thirty." She held a hand out for Toby and he took it reluctantly.

George offered his arm to Lindsay and she grasped it, letting him lead her toward the door.

At the door she turned. "You will be there?" she asked.

Elle nodded.

"Bye, Memah!" Toby called. "I'll see you soon."

"I hope so."

George held the door open for Lindsay and as she went

through he looked back.

Elle mouthed, "Thank you."

He nodded and left.

He would want an explanation, Elle was sure. She would figure out how much to tell him when the time came. Right at that moment she had to deal with her café and with Toby.

"Mom, which restaurant are we going to?" Toby asked.

"Go and play with Miranda and we'll talk in a minute. I need to finish up here."

He pouted, but she nudged him toward the playroom and he went. Elle sighed and walked over to Nora, who was cleaning the coffee machine.

"What was that all about?" Nora asked.

Nora knew little of Elle's story. "Lindsay is Dean's mother. She doesn't know the reason I left him."

"And so Dean has been acting like the depressed son?"

"It won't be an act." Elle was sure. "He never thought he was doing anything wrong. Plus if it will get him more sympathy, he'll milk it for all it's worth." She ran a hand over her hair. "Can you take Toby for a couple of hours tonight? I don't want him coming to the restaurant. I need to explain things to Martin and Lindsay and he shouldn't hear them."

"Shoot. I can't tonight. We've got tickets to the Wiggles." Nora was really apologetic.

"Of course. Never mind. I'll work something out."

Though she had no idea what. Sarah, her lunchtime waitress, had left early because she was going away for the weekend with her kids, and Elle wasn't comfortable asking her other neighbors.

Which left her with no one.

"Why don't you head off now? There's nothing to do here, and it will give you time to get ready," Elle said. She needed space to plan.

"Are you sure?"

Elle nodded.

"That would be great." Nora untied her apron and called for Miranda. They were out of the door in minutes.

The final customers in the café took the hint and paid their bill, leaving right behind Nora.

Elle followed them to the door to lock it and turn the sign.

George was there.

She'd hoped he would give her some time to get herself together, decide what to tell him, but she held the door open so he could come in.

"I'm sorry about Lindsay's accusations," she said.

George waved them off. "I'm not concerned about them. I'm concerned about you." He stepped closer and Elle stepped back.

He sighed. "When Lindsay mentioned your husband, you were scared."

"Not my husband." Elle wanted to be clear. "We never married. Dean didn't believe in marriage."

"What are you scared about?" His voice was gentle.

Elle closed her eyes. What did she say? She walked over to the table that had been vacated, and cleared it. She knew George would follow, so carried the dishes to the kitchen to give herself a bit of time. When she'd loaded the dishes into the dishwasher and switched it on, she faced George.

"Dean was abusive. I left when he turned the abuse on Toby. Lindsay and Martin didn't know it was happening."

There was anger in George's eyes but it wasn't directed at her. "They didn't know where you moved?"

"No. I went to a women's shelter at first. When I moved into my apartment, I sent them a letter to tell them we were fine and to direct any correspondence to the shelter."

"You'll tell them the truth tonight?"

"Yes." She sighed. "I didn't want to take Toby with me, but Nora has plans."

"I can babysit if you want." He was serious.

Elle hesitated. She barely knew George.

But she didn't want Toby to hear what needed to be said at the restaurant. Lindsay wouldn't take it well and Elle wanted Toby to have a good opinion of his grandparents.

"Ask Adrian or Chris for references. I've looked after Kate before."

She could call. But it wasn't just that. Toby was going to be furious about being left behind. He'd missed his Memah and Pepah. She didn't have a lot of choice. She wasn't sure how much he would understand but he'd been there and he understood enough. Plus he'd be a distraction, wanting to talk to his grandparents, and she might not get the chance to explain why she left.

Elle huffed out a breath. "I don't know why you're being so nice to me. Why won't you run in the opposite direction?"

"I'm a nice guy," George said and grinned, but then sobered. "There's something about you that fascinates me and I want to learn more."

Oh, hell no. Dean had had a similar intensity when they'd first started dating. Then she'd been thrilled to have someone's undivided attention; now, she was a lot more wary.

"I'm not interested," she said flatly.

"I know." There was something self-deprecating in his stance.

Closing her eyes briefly, she made her decision. "Do you have Chris's number?"

He tipped his head in surprise, as if he'd expected her to let him take care of Toby without checking first. "Sure." He rattled it off and Elle dialed. George walked out of the kitchen to give her privacy.

A woman answered.

"Imogen?" Elle asked.

"Yes."

"It's Elle Carter here."

"Hi, Elle. How are you?" Imogen sounded pleased to hear from her, even though they'd only spoken a few times. These days Elle was wary of things that seemed too easy.

"I wanted to ask you about George."

There was a murmur of surprise.

"He's offered to babysit Toby for me tonight and I wanted to check his references."

"Oh, sure! George is great with kids," Imogen said. "Kate adores him, as do her cousins. I wouldn't hesitate to leave children with him."

"Toby's only five."

"Mmm. I still think he'd be fine. Hang on, let me check with Chris." There was a murmur of conversation. "Chris said he was great even when Kate was a baby."

Elle hesitated.

"It must be hard to leave your child with someone you don't know so well. I could come over and help if you like. That way there'd be two of us."

Having both of them there *would* make her feel better as she knew Imogen a little better than George, but could she take Imogen up on yet another offer? "Are you sure you don't mind?"

"I'd be delighted to. What's your address?"

Elle gave it to her and then said, "Can you be there by six?"

"Sure. See you then."

Elle hung up and went out to find George playing with Toby in the playroom.

"What's the verdict?" he asked.

"It would be great if you could look after Toby. Imogen's going to come around as well."

He looked a little surprised again but nodded. "Why don't you finish up here and I'll follow you back to your place?"

Elle checked the time. She would be cutting it fine if she wanted to finish shutting the shop and get home and back in time to meet Lindsay and Martin.

"All right."

George kept Toby busy while Elle counted the till and finished up. Then he walked them to Elle's car. He was parked nearby and followed them back to the apartment building.

Imogen was waiting when they arrived and Elle was grateful. She didn't want to be in her tiny apartment alone with George.

She let them in, showed them around and got out some vegetables for dinner. Nerves zinged over her skin.

Toby dragged Imogen into his bedroom to show her his toys, which left Elle alone in the kitchen with George.

"I've got the makings for a stir-fry. I'll cook it up for you and then Toby can eat." She started to chop up the vegetables.

George moved closer. "I can cook," he said, putting a warm hand on her arm. "Why don't you take a few minutes for yourself? Figure out what you want to say to them." His voice was gentle.

Elle squeezed back tears. She hadn't asked for comfort but there he was offering it, and she desperately wanted to take it.

"It's going to be all right," he said.

She shook her head. "You can't know." She put down the knife and fled to the bathroom before she could break down.

She only had a few minutes, but she jumped in the shower, hoping the water would soothe her. Pushing aside her confusion about George, she focused on what to say to Dean's parents. Standing under the steamy spray she ran options through her head. The best thing would be to take the photos. People always said a picture painted a thousand words. She'd had a Polaroid camera – an old one Lindsay had given to her to take pictures of Toby. Dean had never been interested enough to keep track of how many slides she used or what she took with them. She'd used it to her advantage.

She sighed.

Damn, she really didn't want to do this now. She didn't have the strength to confront them. But if she didn't turn up, they would probably turn up at the café asking Nora where she lived. She had to do it. This was a necessary step toward her freedom. Admitting what had happened to her, what she'd allowed to happen to her, was part of putting it behind her and Toby.

She turned off the water and dried herself, quickly dressing in the clothing she'd brought in from her bedroom. She checked the mirror, put the lightest touch of makeup on and then checked the time.

Time to go.

Happy play noises were coming from Toby's bedroom and Elle poked her head in. Imogen sat cross-legged on the floor playing with the horses. She smiled.

"Toby, I have to go out for a little while. Imogen and George are going to take care of you until I get back."

"Ok, Mom. Bye." He didn't look up.

Relieved he'd forgotten about his grandparents, Elle collected the copies of the photos and then hurried into the kitchen. George was finishing the stir-fry. He'd taken off his jacket, rolled up his sleeves and loosened his tie. He looked competent and sexy as hell.

He looked right at home.

His gaze met hers and then traveled down her body and back up again. Something warmed in her belly.

"I'm off," she said, trying to keep her voice steady.

"Take care," he said. "You've got my number in your phone?"

She nodded.

"Call me if you need me."

Elle had no intention of calling him, but she appreciated the gesture. "I won't be late."

"We'll take good care of Toby."

She believed him.

Elle was at the door when Toby called, "Mom, wait!"

He ran into the room, pulling on a jacket. "You're going to meet Memah. I want to come."

Elle groaned inwardly. "Not this time, Toby."

"But I wanna see Memah!" The loud whine was so like Dean's that Elle froze for a moment.

"No. I need to talk to them about some things."

He screwed up his face, getting ready for the full theatrics.

George entered the room. "Hey Toby, dinner's ready."

Toby ignored him. He opened his mouth and screamed, "I want Memah!"

George winced and Imogen hurried out.

Elle couldn't leave while he was like this. Her heart ached at denying him but she stood firm. "No. You're going to have a nice night playing with Imogen and George. You can visit Memah another time."

"No, now." The sobs started, big tears and chest shaking sobs. "I miss Memah."

Elle was the meanest mother in the world, but she couldn't possibly take him. She couldn't even promise Toby when he'd see his grandparents next. She wasn't willing to guarantee anything until she discovered how Lindsay and Martin reacted to what she had to say. Crouching down, she held out her arms and brought him close. "I know you miss them. They miss you too, but tonight I need to talk to them about your dad."

The sobs lessened a bit. He peered up at her, fear in his eyes. "We don't have to go back to him, do we?"

She cursed herself for staying so long with Dean. "No, but I need to tell them why."

He didn't quite understand but the sobs had lessened into

tears. The thought of Dean was sobering for them both.

"I need to go now. You'll be a good boy for George and Imogen, won't you?"

He nodded, tears still running down his face. Elle squeezed him tightly and kissed both cheeks. Her heart was aching as she stood up.

Imogen approached and put a hand on Toby's shoulder, giving Elle a look full of sympathy and understanding. "Come on, Toby, we need to eat George's dinner before it gets cold."

"Will he get mad if it goes cold?" Toby whispered, glancing up at Elle, frightened again.

Elle's heart clenched. It was her fault her baby was so fearful. "George won't get mad," she told him. "Now go and eat. I'll be home shortly."

George laughed. "Of course I won't be mad – it just won't be as nice if we wait." He stayed where he was, over by the kitchen, seeming to understand he shouldn't approach, that it might scare Toby.

Toby slowly reached out and took hold of Imogen's hand and walked toward George. When he got to the man, he hesitated and then held out a hand for him to take.

A hundred expressions crossed George's face as he took Toby's hand and walked into the kitchen.

Elle blinked back tears. She would do everything in her power to make up for the sorrow she'd put her baby through.

Including deal with Dean's parents.

***

Elle was ten minutes late by the time she arrived at the restaurant. Martin and Lindsay were already there, and Martin was checking his watch. Elle hurried over.

"I'm sorry I'm late."

Lindsay smiled coolly and stood, giving her a hug. Martin nodded to her.

Elle slid into the seat across from them.

"You're looking well." Martin was a man of few words, but Elle always felt he took everything in. She liked him.

The waitress came over and took their orders. Elle ordered the first thing on the menu: a burger. She wasn't hungry.

When the woman left, Elle clasped her hands together, not sure where to start.

"It was so lovely to see Toby today. I can't believe he's grown so much in six months. It will be great to have him out on the ranch to see the foals." Lindsay seemed as enthusiastic and as oblivious as ever. Seeing as the older woman had only just been calling her names, Elle wondered for the first time how much of her southern courtesy was an act.

Martin put a hand over his wife's. "We need to ask Elle why she left." He said it quietly, no threat under the words.

Elle closed her eyes, took a deep breath and opened them again. "I left because Dean hit me."

There was silence at their table, and the noise around the restaurant swelled to fill it. Martin's face was stony, but Lindsay's fine skin flushed immediately with indignation.

"Well, I never heard anything more ridiculous in my life," she exclaimed. "You shouldn't be telling these lies."

Martin patted Lindsay's hand. "Would you like to explain?"

Elle had expected Lindsay to react that way. She'd always doted on Dean, her youngest boy. Elle was glad Martin was here. He'd listen before he'd make his judgment.

"When we first moved to the ranch, it was a little easier because I could take Toby out in the yard if he was crying and give Dean the quiet he needed. Then when Toby stopped sleeping through the night, Dean would get angry and he would yell."

Lindsay tutted. "That's normal. He would have been tired."

Elle nodded. "I used that excuse as well. There were a few times when I couldn't keep Toby quiet, and Dean would lash out and hit me."

This time Lindsay slapped her hand down on the table. "Nonsense." The noise in the restaurant hushed at her exclamation and several people looked over. She lowered her voice. "We would have noticed the bruises."

Martin stayed silent so Elle continued.

"Most of the time I could cover them with long shirts or makeup." She took a breath. "There were other times, when I'd made him unhappy, that he would make me stay in the house when he went out. If he found I had disobeyed him, he would hit me. He wanted to have total control over me."

"The only time you didn't go out with Dean was when you were sick," Lindsay stated.

Elle nodded. "He often said I had the flu, despite having no one to catch it from. Apparently I had bad period pains, or chickenpox or any number of other diseases." Elle smiled tightly. "Funny how I've not been sick once since I left him. If I'd had everything he said I had, I should have been at the doctor once a month. I'm not sure whether you ever offered to come and check on me, or to help with Toby, but I'm sure if you did, he came up with some excuse."

Lindsay's mouth shut.

Elle got the photos out of her purse and handed them over. "I took pictures."

Lindsay gasped and covered her mouth. Martin's expression was unreadable but he slowly flicked through all the Polaroids. Finally he looked up. "Why did you stay? Why didn't you tell us?"

"I had no money, no car, nowhere to go. When I went into Brenham, Dean only ever gave me enough cash to buy what we needed, and my parents didn't want me after I left California."

"So what changed?"

Elle looked Martin in the eye. "He hit Toby. The broken wrist wasn't because he fell down the steps: it was because Dean backhanded my baby on to the coffee table. I had to protect him."

Lindsay shook her head, trying to deny it, but Elle held Martin's gaze. His eyes acknowledged her words.

"You won't be coming back," he said.

"No."

"Wait a damn minute," Lindsay said, putting up a hand. "You can't mean to say you believe her, Martin."

"I suspected you weren't happy," he said. "I should have asked if you needed help. I'm sorry."

The relief he actually believed her was a balm to Elle.

"No. I *won't* believe it. Dean *loves* her. When I told him I'd run into her, that we were having dinner, he jumped straight in his car to come here."

Goosebumps leaped to Elle's skin and her breath caught in

her throat. She jumped to her feet, sweeping the photos up and thrusting them in to her bag. "You told him?" The ranch was an hour's drive from the outskirts of Houston and, depending on the time Lindsay called, he could be there any second. She wasn't hanging around.

"I told you not to call him," Martin said.

"He had a right to know," Lindsay shot back.

Elle was already moving toward the door.

"Elle, wait a minute. At least let us get your number," Martin called, following her.

Elle reached the door of the restaurant and flung it open.

Only to be face to face with the one person she didn't want to see.

Terror gripped her heart at the sight of the long, lank hair, those dark eyes and the small hands, which didn't look as if they could hurt a fly.

Dean.

# Chapter 6

Elle backed away instinctively, crashing in to Martin, who was right behind her.

"Elle, thank God: you're all right," Dean said, striding forward, arms outstretched as if to hug her.

She flinched and pushed past Martin, moving further into the restaurant and away from the door. Her breath came in gasps. She had to get away from him. She wouldn't be trapped.

Dean's mouth dropped open and hurt crossed his face. "Darling, what's wrong?"

That caressing, caring tone had once been so soothing to Elle, had once made her think everything would be all right, had once made her believe in happily ever after.

Now it made her ill.

"I'm not your darling," she said.

A waitress strode over and asked them to be seated or leave. Elle desperately wanted to leave, but if she did, Dean would follow her. She was certain.

Choosing the lesser of two evils, she led the way back to their booth and let Martin slide in first. Then she followed him, not allowing room for Dean to sit beside her.

He slid in next to his mother, frowning at her.

Nerves were dancing such a ferocious jig on her skin that she was shaking. She clenched her hands together. She needed to deal with this and leave. She needed to make him understand, needed to be rid of him. "Dean, it's over. I made it clear in the letter I sent you. I want nothing to do with you and you won't get to see Toby. Not after you broke his wrist."

He frowned, more hurt filling his eyes. "I didn't mean to hurt my boy. It was an accident. I didn't know he was behind me."

Elle gaped at him. It had been no accident. Her anger gave her courage. "Your parents have seen photos of what you did. The bruises on my arms, those on my stomach and the black eye, from before you got careful. They know all about how you used to hit me and keep me locked in the house."

Dean turned to his parents. "You know it's not true. I don't know anything about these photos, but we lived with you. Elle was often out on the ranch, never hidden."

Lindsay nodded.

"Those photos were taken at the house," Martin said. "How did she get the bruises then?"

Dean was a little uncertain when faced with his father, but he wasn't backing down. "I don't know. Maybe she fell off a horse. They've probably been photoshopped."

Elle had had enough. She wasn't going to let herself be drawn into an argument about who was telling the truth. She had to get out of there, away from him. She stood. "I will fight your custody claim," she said to Dean.

Turning to Lindsay she said, "I wish Toby could come to visit you at the ranch, but I do not trust Dean with him and therefore if you wish to visit him, you will have to contact me." As much as she wanted to cut all ties with them, she couldn't do it to Toby. She knew how much it hurt to be cut off from family. She took a breath and directed the next sentence at Martin. "I will give you my phone number, so you can arrange visits, but only if you don't give it to Lindsay or Dean." There was no way Lindsay wouldn't give it to Dean, but Martin was stronger.

"Agreed."

Elle turned to Dean. "Don't come near me or Toby. If you do, I'll get a restraining order."

"You can't do that. He's my son. I love him."

"You don't. You never did." It had taken her so long to realize. "You called him a nuisance, you wanted me to abort him, you kicked him out of the house for disrupting 'your muse'. I won't let you harm either of us any more."

She walked over to the waitress and asked for some paper. She wrote down her cell number and gave it to Martin.

Dean was on his feet. "You can't walk away from me. I need you. You give purpose to my life – you're my muse."

It was always about him. "Goodbye, Dean." She turned to walk away.

Dean grabbed her arm so hard she gasped, his fingers pressing in to her skin. "You can't go." He pulled her back, gripping both of her arms now, and tears sprang to her eyes at the pain.

"Let go of me." She'd intended to say it loudly but it came out as a whisper. The pain took her right back to the house, when she'd been alone and defenseless with a baby to think of.

"You're mine. We love each other."

"Let go of her, son." Martin had a hand on his son's arm. "You're hurting her."

Dean blinked and let go. "I'm sorry."

She'd heard those words more times than she could remember. She backed away from him until she got to the door. Then when she was outside and away from the windows, Elle broke into a sprint, the fear finally releasing and pushing her into action. She raced to her car, only checking briefly over her shoulder to ensure Dean wasn't following her.

He wasn't.

Still Elle wasn't taking any chances. Taking a couple of breaths to control the shaking, she started her car and drove straight to the nearest police station. She walked in the door and up to the counter and said, "I'd like to file for a restraining order."

***

Half an hour later, Elle returned to her car. The officer at the station had been very kind to her. He'd taken down her details and explained she had to go to the courthouse for the order itself, but had promised to send some officers to the restaurant to get a statement from the waitress who had witnessed the altercation.

Elle suspected it was because she'd burst into tears after announcing what she wanted, and had taken five minutes to calm down enough to explain why.

But at least now she knew what she had to do.

She started her engine and drove home, keeping a close eye on her rearview mirror in case she was being followed. Her common sense told her Martin would have kept Dean with them but she wasn't willing to risk it. A couple of times the car behind her took the same turns as she did, so she doubled-back to make sure it didn't follow. When she finally pulled into her apartment building parking lot, there weren't any cars behind her.

Grabbing her bag, she hurried inside.

The first sound she heard was laughter from Toby's bedroom – his childish shriek, followed by a deep belly laugh that had to be coming from George.

Some of her stress evaporated.

Taking a couple of deep breaths, she calmed herself. She couldn't let Toby see her in this state. In the kitchen, she splashed water on her face and dried it.

Hoping she looked halfway normal, she followed the voices through to Toby's bedroom just as Imogen said, "It's time for bed."

"Ain't no filly gonna tell us when to go to bed," came George's voice.

"Yeehaw," Toby yelled.

Elle walked into the room and stopped in surprise, her head tipping to the side.

Toby was sitting on top of George, who was on all fours, pretending to be a horse. They were facing away from the door, George's gray pants stretched over his butt and Toby pretending to whip him. Imogen was perched on Toby's bed, holding a book and tapping her foot.

Imogen was the only one who noticed her. She grinned at Elle's expression. "Oh I think Elle mentioned seven was bedtime and it's way past."

"Don't be a spoilsport, Imogen. We're having fun."

The whole scene chased away the residual chill she'd felt from the meeting with Dean and his parents. She couldn't resist seeing George's reaction when he realized she was there.

"It's not as much fun in the morning when someone's a cranky pants because he hasn't had enough sleep," she said.

Toby twisted towards the door. "Hi Mom!"

George turned around more slowly so Toby didn't fall and lifted his head, a sheepish grin on his face. If Elle wasn't mistaken, there was also a slight flush on his cheeks, but whether it was from the exertion or embarrassment she wasn't sure.

"Uh oh, we've been caught red handed," George said.

"Quick, run." Toby dug his heels into George's side and George winced.

Elle moved forward and lifted her boy from George's back before he could do more damage. "No you don't, Cowboy," she said. He struggled in her arms and she put him down on the floor. He turned to jump back on George but George had already raised himself up to his knees.

"Aaw."

Elle hated to break up the fun, but it would take another half an hour to calm Toby down enough for him to sleep. "Have you brushed your teeth?"

"No." He pouted and then frowned. "What happened to your arm?"

Elle glanced down at the bruises in the pattern of fingerprints on both of her forearms. She crossed them to cover the marks. "Nothing to worry about, Toby boy."

George was on his feet in an instant, his expression concerned.

Imogen stood, sensing the tension. "Come on, Toby. Show me how well you can brush your teeth." She took his hand and they left the room.

***

George put a tight rein on his anger. Unless he was very much mistaken, there were fingerprint bruises on Elle's arms. Someone had touched her; someone had hurt her. He waited until Imogen and Toby were gone before he asked, "What happened?"

Elle glanced over her shoulder and then gestured for him to follow her into the living area. "My ex turned up at the restaurant. He didn't want me to leave."

George clenched his fists. He couldn't fathom how anyone could want to hurt Elle, or any woman. Before he could respond, Toby came running out.

"Teeth are clean," he announced.

"Then put on your pajamas and choose a book to read," Elle told him.

"George, would you read me a story?" Toby asked, his voice hopeful.

The kid sent a cupid's arrow straight through his heart. There was no way he'd refuse. "Sure thing."

The grin Toby gave him was like the Cheshire Cat's. He raced back toward his room.

"I might head off now," Imogen said, gathering up her bag.

"Thank you so much for babysitting Toby," Elle said.

"Any time. He was an angel. Besides, he was more interested in George than me. I was good enough for lassoing and that's about it."

Elle grimaced. "Sorry."

"I had fun." Imogen walked to the door. "Listen, I'm arranging a girls' night next weekend. Piper, Libby and me. You should come. I'll send you the details."

"I'm not sure. I'll have to find a babysitter."

"I'll do it," George said. Elle could do with some down time and if he couldn't convince her to spend time with him, then at least he could help her have fun with Imogen and the girls. They'd take care of her and let her know she wasn't alone.

Elle hesitated and Imogen smiled. "I'll give you a call." She opened the door.

"Hang on. I'll walk you down." George crossed over. It was dark and not the best neighborhood. "I'll be back in a minute," he said to Elle and walked Imogen out.

As they moved away from the apartment Imogen said, "You're going to have to take it slow with her."

"I know." It was going to be hard, but it mattered because, somehow, she mattered.

"Find out who put those bruises on her and tell me. I want to know how I can help."

It was one thing George loved about Imogen. She cared for everyone and she did whatever she could to help them.

"I will. Tell Chris I'll call him later. Elle's going to need a good family lawyer and I want to know who's the best."

"She won't be able to afford the best," Imogen said.

"She will if she believes they're working pro bono."

Imogen turned to him. "I'll help pay."

George knew she could afford it: her father owned a fashion empire and she had an inheritance of her own.

They reached Imogen's car and George gave her a hug. "Drive safely."

"Will do. Take care of them both."

Imogen backed out of the parking lot and drove off.

George turned and jogged back to the apartment. He didn't want Toby to think he'd left without saying goodbye.

The kid was absolutely amazing. When Elle had left it was clear Toby was a little scared of George. That in itself told him a lot about the household Toby had grown up in. It killed him that a child could be treated that way. He'd kept his distance physically while keeping up a light conversation with Imogen and Toby and by the time they'd finished eating, Toby had lost his fear and was giving George the rundown about Pepah's ranch and everything he knew about horses.

Which was surprisingly a lot.

George had learned much and made a note to check how much was actually correct.

That of course had led to playing cowboys and Imogen, being the good sport she was, had let them pretend to lasso her.

He'd been having an absolute ball and couldn't wait to read a story to him.

Tapping on the door he waited for Elle to let him in. She looked a little uncertain so he kept it simple. "Did Toby find a book?"

"Yes, he's waiting in his room for you."

George grinned at her and walked through to find Toby sitting up in bed, trying his hardest to keep his eyes open. George doubted he'd be awake for the end of the story.

"All right, kiddo. Snuggle down. What story have you got for me?"

Toby passed him the book. Cowboys. George grinned and settled on the bed next to him, opening up the book. He started to read.

Five pages in, Toby was fast asleep.

Carefully, George closed the book and stood up. Toby stirred but didn't wake. George pulled the sheets over the child and turned out the light. Then he went to find Elle.

She was sitting on the couch in the living room, a cup of tea next to her. "That was quick."

"He's out for the count."

Elle smiled. "I thought he'd fight it some more."

George settled on the couch next to her, but far enough away that she didn't feel crowded. "He's such a great kid."

"He is. You shouldn't have let him ride you. He's going to want you to do it every time he sees you."

He liked that. He liked that Elle was thinking they would see him again. "It's no problem." He'd often been accused of being the biggest kid anyway.

"Do you want a drink?" Elle asked.

"No, thanks." Though he hated to break this casual, comfortable setting, he needed to know what had happened. "Do you want to tell me about tonight?"

Elle searched his eyes for something. Perhaps she found what she was looking for because she said, "I met Lindsay and Martin at the restaurant. We were living on their ranch until recently."

"They didn't know about the abuse?" How could anyone be so clueless?

She shook her head. "Dean was good at covering it up." She rubbed her arms. "Anyway, Lindsay thought we should get back together and didn't want to believe the photos I showed them."

"You have photos?"

"I took them every time Dean got physical – it wasn't often but it was enough. I wanted to get away, but I wasn't sure how I was going to do it."

George felt a surge of pride. Even if it took her a while to escape, she was sensible enough to make plans, to record the evidence. "Can I have a look?"

Elle watched him for a moment, considering his request, and then reached for her bag. She must have made up her mind to tell him everything. It gave him a ray of hope.

She pulled out the photos. "I made copies and put the originals in a safety deposit box."

He reached for the photos and she held on to them for a moment longer before letting go. It was difficult for her, he could tell. Slowly he reviewed them.

The first photo showed her with the mother of all black eyes. It was swollen shut and dark purple in color. The date was four years ago.

The next one was bruises on her stomach, the third on her arms and legs.

There was a range of different photos, including one with a broken wrist.

Queasiness swirled around George's stomach as he flipped through. Finally when he could talk through the nausea he asked, "How could they not know?"

"Dean is very charming, very convincing. He never showed his violence to others. He would pout or whine but he is an artist and none of his brothers would have even considered he had enough muscle to do something like that. They were always busy on the ranch and with their own families so we didn't see them much." Elle paused. "Lindsay doted on Dean. He never did any wrong in her eyes and so I'm sure it never occurred to her to question him."

"What about Martin?"

"He was busy as well. I didn't see him a lot and though we got along well, he thought I was sickly and as weak as his son. Dean used to tell them I was unwell when I had bruises from the beatings. He'd lock me in the house and take Toby over to Memah's to play."

"How long did you live like this?"

"Four years."

George counted the photos. A few beatings a year.

He reached out, wanting to touch her, to comfort her in some way.

She leaned away and he dropped his hand.

"I think Martin believed me tonight, because he hushed Lindsay, which he never does normally. He adores her. Perhaps he suspected something was wrong after all. He said he knew I wasn't happy there. Then Lindsay got upset and mentioned how she'd called Dean and he was on his way." She shuddered.

George swore.

Elle nodded. "I was going to leave but I was too late. Dean arrived, caused a scene about wanting me back and grabbed my arms to stop me leaving. Martin told him to let me go, which he did, and I left." She spoke with little emotion as if reciting something she'd read.

"Does he know where you live?" Could she be in danger?

"No. I went to the police station, and I made sure I wasn't followed home from there."

She was right to be careful. "What did the police say?"

She gave a wry grin. "They told me I need to get a restraining order from the courthouse but they'd take statements from the restaurant waitress who witnessed the whole thing. I was a bit upset when I arrived."

"You could have called me."

She shook her head. "If you'd come to the restaurant it would have made things worse."

"I'll call Chris tonight and get a name of a good lawyer for you, and you might be able to get an order this weekend." The sooner she was protected the better.

Elle touched his arm lightly. "Thank you. I'll call Chris myself. I was planning to anyway."

George didn't comment and didn't move. She'd reached out to him for the first time. Her hand was soft and warm. It was delicate – but it was strong. He covered her hand with his own, caressed it. He wanted her to know he was there for her, that he wasn't a threat, that he would never treat her the way Dean had treated her.

Her lips parted, but she didn't pull away.

He took her hand in his, rubbed her palm with his thumb. "You're a strong woman."

"I don't feel like it." Her voice was a little breathless and she was watching him warily, uncertain.

"You've raised a great kid in such difficult circumstances. I'd say that's strong." He let go of her hand and shuffled a little closer. She didn't back away. "If you need help, I'm here for you."

Elle stood then, scowling. She stalked away and then turned back to him. "Why? I don't understand why you would possibly want to help me. I'm a mess. What's in it for you?" She put her hands on her hips.

George raised his eyebrows, but stayed seated and replied, "I want to get to know you better. You're a beautiful, intriguing woman."

Elle screwed up her nose. "But I've told you I'm not interested. I don't want a relationship; I don't want a fling."

"And yet I just can't keep away." He realized how ridiculous it must sound to her. "How about we agree to be friends?"

"Friends?"

"Yes, friends. You know, people who hang out together, go to the movies, call each other to chat about their day? Friends."

She frowned. "So you'd stop telling me I'm beautiful?"

"Honey, I tell my female friends they're beautiful all the time."

It seemed to surprise her. She was quiet for a moment and then nodded. "All right. Friends."

George felt liked he'd made a touchdown. He wanted to jump in the air and chest bump someone but instead he stood up. He needed to go slow. "I should get going."

"Of course. Thank you for looking after Toby for me."

"Did I pass the test?" he teased.

"With flying colors," she said.

"Fantastic." He walked to the door and she followed him.

"Adrian's having a barbeque tomorrow night," he said, turning to face her. "Do you and Toby want to come?"

Elle hesitated. He hoped there would come a time when she wouldn't hesitate, when she'd trust and say yes.

"What time?"

"I could pick you both up at seven."

"Toby needs his car seat."

He grinned. "Fine. You can pick me up at seven." He got a business card out of his wallet and wrote his address on it. "I'll see you then." Before she could disagree, he was out the door.

As he walked out to his car, he started whistling.

***

Elle cursed agreeing to go to the barbeque with George. Though in her defense, she never actually said she'd go, but somehow there she was, driving to pick up George after a long day at work and having to apply for a restraining order. As she'd predicted, Toby had been tired and when Harry had dropped him off in the afternoon the man looked exhausted. Elle had bundled Toby into the playroom with a pillow and told him he had to have a nap or they weren't going to the barbeque.

Amazingly the threat worked and he had slept for two hours.

Which meant he'd be a bundle of energy tonight.

She hoped she could contain him a little.

"Are we there yet?"

Elle checked her rearview mirror and Toby wriggled in his seat with excitement. She smiled. "Almost."

Turning into a street, a pang of envy went through her. This neighborhood was lovely. The street was tree-lined, all the lawns were mown and the houses were in a good repair. She glanced at the business card George had given her to check the number and then pulled into the drive of a brick-and-tile house.

There was a big tree in the front yard, which begged to have a swing attached to it and the garden was well tended, with flowers in bloom. Did he have time for gardening or did he pay someone to do it for him?

Before she got out of the car, George came out of the front door and waved his greeting.

"There's George!" Toby called.

"Sure is."

He was dressed casually: red board shorts and a black T-shirt with some band's logo printed on the front of it. He carried a beach towel.

It was another thing Elle wasn't sure of. George had called to tell her to bring swimsuits and she didn't have any. There was nowhere to swim on the ranch and she hadn't needed any since. Besides, Toby didn't know how to swim.

Not wanting her boy to miss out, she'd bought them both

something to swim in on the way back from the courthouse –
but she still wasn't keen on the idea.

George opened the passenger door and climbed in.
"Howdy."

Immediately the space in her small car felt smaller.

"Howdy, pardner," Toby called. "We have the same shorts!"

George glanced into the back seat. "Hey, kiddo. So we have.
You have impeccable taste."

"What's impeccable?"

"Perfect."

Toby beamed.

"Where to?" Elle asked.

George gave directions and Elle concentrated on driving
while George and Toby kept up a conversation about the day's
events.

She had to admit, George was good with kids. Dean had
never spent that much time talking to his son.

Not that she was thinking of George as a father figure.

Before long she pulled up in front of Adrian's house. It
wasn't what she was expecting for a rock star's place. For starters
it was single story, with a high-pitched roof. The bright blue
door contrasted with the red brick, giving it a bit of interest and
flair.

There were already a couple of cars in the drive.

"Who did you say was coming?" she asked George, nerves
suddenly appearing. She hoped he'd told Adrian he was bringing
them; otherwise there might not be enough food to go around.

"Imogen and Chris will be there, as well as Piper."

At least she'd have someone to talk to. "And you told them
we were coming?"

George unbuckled his seatbelt. "Sure did. Don't worry." He
smiled and winked at her, then glanced in the back seat. "You
coming, kiddo?"

Toby had already unstrapped himself and was sitting,
waiting for the command. "Yes!" He thrust open the car door
and that spurred Elle into action.

Together they walked up the path, but rather than knocking
on the door and waiting, George knocked and went straight in.

Elle hesitated, not sure of her reception.

Then she took a deep breath and followed him.

# Chapter 7

Elle hovered in the hallway, not sure about walking in to someone's house uninvited.

"Come on, they're out the back by the pool," George said.

There were voices and laughter coming from somewhere in the house. Elle shut the door behind them and followed George through. Toby grabbed on to her hand, suddenly not so brave. Elle knew the feeling.

They walked through the kitchen and out the back door to where the others were gathered.

Elle scanned the faces. There were Imogen and Chris, who waved, and sitting next to them was Piper, who'd been such a great waitress on opening day, and then there was Adrian and his wife Libby.

Libby stood, gave George a hug and then turned to Elle. "I'm so glad you could come," she said and hugged her. She turned to Toby. "You must be Toby. My name's Libby." She held out a hand.

Toby glanced up at her and then shook it.

"Would you like to meet the others?" Libby asked him.

He held on to Elle's hand tightly, but nodded, glancing over to the pool where Kate was splashing about.

Libby made the introductions and then said to Elle, "He's welcome to get in the pool with Kate."

Elle shook her head. "He can't swim, so I'll need to go in with him." What she really wanted to do was sit down with a nice cool drink. The day had been crazy busy at work and she was tired.

"I'll take him." George was suddenly right next to her. "I'm dying for a swim."

"You always are." Libby laughed.

"If you sit right here, you can keep an eye on us," George said, waiting for her answer.

Bless him for understanding it wasn't him she was worried about, but the idea of her baby in the water.

Elle crouched down to Toby's level. "Do you want to go for a swim with George?"

He nodded, a little uncertain himself.

"All right, but you need to do what George says, agreed?"

"Yes, Mom."

George held out his hand. "Come on, kiddo, we might even find ourselves a couple of seahorses to wrangle."

Elle watched them go.

"He's great with kids," Libby said.

"I know." She sighed and sat down in the chair George had indicated. It had been a hot day but the humidity had dropped – it was pleasant enough for swimming or sitting outside. Libby handed Elle a drink as Toby slowly descended the steps of the pool, holding George's hand. When the water got up to his chest he stopped and didn't want to go further. George stripped off his T-shirt, threw it on the paving, out of splash reach and sat on the step next to him, talking to him.

Elle had to admit he kept himself in good shape.

Kate swam up and then hurried out of the pool, going over to a chest on the side and pulling out a kickboard. She showed Toby how to use it and then gave it to him.

Elle could tell he really wanted to try it, but he was scared.

Should she go over and encourage him?

As she was deciding, George stood up and waded into the pool, a couple of feet in front of Toby. "Come on, kiddo, I'm right here."

Kate stood next to George, encouraging Toby, and Toby's face set in determination. He launched himself off the step, kickboard pinned under his chest, and splashed furiously toward George. When he reached him, George picked Toby up in his arms and gave him a high five.

The others at the table all cheered. Elle hadn't been aware they'd been watching.

Toby turned and fist punched the air. "Let me do it again, George."

George carried him back to the steps and placed him down. "Go for it."

Her heart swelled in pride and tears pricked her eyes.

Dean had never given Toby even that much of his time.

Annoyed at herself, she dabbed her eyes and took a deep breath. Toby would be fine in the pool with George and she should be paying attention to her hosts.

"George is a good teacher," Adrian said. "He taught me and my brother how to swim."

Elle was intrigued, but didn't want to pry. She knew from magazine articles Adrian was a private person.

"He's certainly good with Toby," she said.

"He'll have a whole posse of children when he finds the right woman."

Elle didn't like the direction of the conversation. What George wanted was nothing to do with her. "That's nice."

"How's the café?" Libby asked as she placed a bowl of chips and salsa on the table.

"Really great." Happy with the change of subject, she chatted to Libby about the bookshop café and organized a date for a Jessop Chronicles book signing.

Adrian and Chris had left the table to stand around the grill to cook the meat, and it wasn't long before Libby was calling the kids and George out of the pool.

Elle grabbed Toby's towel and went over to him.

"Did you see me, Mom?" he asked. "I can swim the whole length of the pool with the kickboard."

"I saw." She wrapped the towel around his small body, which was starting to shake.

"After dinner I'm going to try two lengths."

Elle smiled at his enthusiasm. "After dinner it will be too dark for swimming," she said.

"Aaw."

"It's OK, Toby. We can play inside. Have you ever played Go Fish?" Kate said.

Toby slid on his T-shirt at Elle's urging and turned to the girl. "No."

"Everyone needs to know how to play Go Fish." Kate took his hand. "Come on, we'll get some food and then I'll teach you."

Without a glance or word to Elle, Toby followed Kate, his eyes wide and his mouth slightly open. The conversation tomorrow would be all about Kate did this and Kate did that. Elle smiled.

Kate had to be about six years older than Toby, but she didn't mind playing with him.

"Kate's good with kids," George said.

Elle turned to find George toweling himself dry. He was standing close, too close really, and some of the water from his hair flicked on to her. It was suddenly difficult to breathe. George was a formidable presence with his clothes on, but without them he was magnetic. His chest was muscled and she itched to run her hands over it. She backed up a step.

"Sorry," he said and grinned.

"I should help Toby with his dinner," she said.

"Kate's got him taken care of," George said.

She had. Toby and Kate had found seats together at the table and Toby had some ribs on his plate. Kate handed him the potato salad and they both seemed perfectly happy.

Elle acknowledged the pinch of loss – her little boy was growing up and didn't need her any more – but part of her was pleased. She didn't want him to be clingy, didn't want him to be scared of the world.

George handed her a plate. "Help yourself."

He'd yet to put on his T-shirt and the temptation to help herself to something else was strong.

She shook her head, surprised at herself. She hadn't been interested in sex for years; she'd hated the way Dean had made her feel so vulnerable, had her begging him for release. The last thing she should be feeling now was attraction for someone she was determined not to get involved with, as anything other than a friend.

Without benefits.

To distract herself, she dished up her plate, not really paying any attention to what she was putting on there.

When she sat down again, George sat next to her.

"Thank you for taking Toby swimming."

"Any time. Swimming lessons will be starting soon. Maybe you can get him enrolled in a class."

Elle would love to and she was sure Toby would love it as well, but she wasn't sure if she could afford it. Right now all the money she had went back into the business. She only took what she needed to pay her meager bills and for food. "I'll look into it."

Piper, who was sitting across from Elle, said, "I've heard the Sea Monkeys is good."

"Thanks." She took a mouthful of food.

"So Elle, where are you from originally?" Piper asked. "That's no Texan accent you've got."

She didn't want to be talking about herself. "California." When Piper continued to wait she added, "LA. I moved out here when I met my ex."

"You must like it here to stay."

She nodded. There hadn't been much choice. She'd had no money for a long bus trip and by the time she'd got back on her feet she'd decided it was as good a place as any.

"Do you have any siblings?" Imogen asked.

Elle's heart hurt. "An older brother, James." They'd been so close until she started dating Dean.

She'd let Dean ruin all of her relationships.

She needed to get this conversation away from her. "What about you?"

Imogen smiled. "I'm an only child but I've got a bunch of cousins who I've recently met and they're amazing."

The conversation thankfully turned to other topics and Elle was happy to listen while the others talked about football, fashion and politics.

"May Toby and I leave the table?" Kate asked, looking at Elle for an answer. "I'm going to teach him how to play Go Fish in the living room."

Kate had shown she was good with Toby and Elle needed to trust at some stage. "Sure. Toby, you need to behave yourself and do what Kate says."

"Yes, Mom," he said as he scrambled out of his chair and followed Kate inside.

"They'll be fine," George murmured to her.

His breath on her ear was warm and sent a shiver down her spine. "I know. But I can't help worrying."

"You're a good mother and Toby's a fantastic kid. You should be proud."

He was getting under her skin, telling her things she wanted to hear. She desperately hoped she was doing the right thing by Toby. She wanted to believe George, but she'd learned to doubt what was said. Dean had taught her that.

Adrian started clearing the table and Elle grasped the opportunity to leave. She grabbed some plates, flashed George a quick smile and then carried the dishes inside.

***

George watched Elle go. She was relaxing, appeared happy to sit and listen. The tension he normally saw in her wasn't there tonight. She'd trusted him to take Toby into the pool and that meant so much to him.

He knew she'd been treated cruelly by her ex, and that it would take a lot to get her to completely trust again, but he'd obviously proven himself in some small way. He'd had so much fun teaching Toby to swim. The enthusiasm of the kid and the level of determination and trust he showed were incredible considering the atmosphere he'd grown up in. Elle had obviously been a supportive, protective influence.

He remembered what Adrian had been like when he first joined their family. Adrian had been physically and mentally abused by his father and had jumped at every shouted word or potential conflict. It had taken months for him to stop running every time he was scared and longer still to stop flinching and expecting the worst.

There were elements of Adrian in Toby but perhaps it was because the child was younger, or because most of the abuse had been directed at Elle, that Toby was less cautious.

George was glad.

The kid was great and didn't deserve such an asshole as a father.

Chris sat down next to him. "I got you the list of family lawyers you asked for." He handed George a piece of paper.

There were three names on it.

"Do any of them do pro bono?"

"Victoria does and she's the best, but people know her reputation and there's usually a long wait."

George was sure he could arrange to pay Victoria's fees without Elle knowing, if needed. "I'll give this to Elle."

"Give what to me?" Elle asked as she sat back down.

George handed her the list. "These are the family lawyers Chris recommends. Victoria's the best."

Elle's face clouded and her shoulders hunched. He wished he'd left it until later. "Thanks." She tucked the list into her bag. "I'll call her on Monday."

"If you want someone to go with you, let me know." He hated the thought of her dealing with this all on her own.

"I'll manage. I'd better go check on Toby." Elle hurried back inside.

She'd shut right down. Turned away from him and his offer for help.

"Don't let it get to you," Chris said, patting his back. "Your charm will win her over in the end, I have no doubt."

George appreciated his friend's confidence but he wasn't so sure.

When Elle came back out, she was deep in conversation with Imogen. She sat down the other end of the table, but she was obviously enjoying herself because she'd relaxed and was laughing at something Imogen said.

While he missed her company he was glad. He didn't know how many friends Elle had, but there couldn't be many if she'd asked him to babysit Toby. If she wasn't comfortable enough to call him, he hoped she'd be able to call Imogen or Libby.

The situation with her ex really worried him. The man didn't sound particularly rational and Elle's apartment complex wasn't the most secure.

He would keep an eye on her whether she wanted him to or

not.

***

It was after ten when people began to leave. After playing Go Fish, Kate had read Toby a story and he'd fallen asleep on the couch. George had talked shop with Adrian and watched while Libby, Imogen and Piper brought Elle out of her shell and into their world. He wasn't even worried when they'd all burst into laughter and glanced at him.

Whatever made Elle happy, made him happy.

George couldn't quite understand why. After so many years of casual but fun relationships, he suddenly felt this overwhelming sense of protection toward Elle. Perhaps it was because she was the first woman he'd known to go through such an abusive relationship, but then again, he'd been attracted to her before he knew about that.

He wasn't in the mood to analyze it. He was happy to go with the flow and discover where it led.

Elle stretched and stood. "We should get going. I've got an early start tomorrow."

"What time do you get to the café?" Piper asked.

"Six. There's a bit of prep work to do before the doors open at seven, and on Sunday, the coffee crowd starts early."

"Do you get a day off?" Chris asked.

Elle shook her head. "Not yet. I want to work toward taking a half or full day off, but at the moment I'm still setting up the routine."

"If you get into a bind and need a waitress on the weekend, give me a call," Piper said with a smile. She gave Elle her number.

"Thank you."

George got to his feet and said his goodbyes. "Thanks for dinner, Libby."

Libby laughed. "It was Adrian who did most of the work, but I'll take your thanks."

He followed Elle in to the living room where Toby was sleeping on the sofa, one arm draped over the edge. "Do you want me to carry him?"

Elle turned, surprise on her face. "Yes, please."

George bent over, carefully slid his arms under the little boy and lifted him up. Toby murmured but didn't wake.

Elle opened the front door and then the car door so George could put Toby straight into the car seat. George examined all the straps in the dark and backed out. "The technical stuff is up to you," he said.

Elle flashed him a grin, so quick and full of fun, before she leaned into the car to do up the restraints. George stepped back, his heart doing a funny beat. It was a glimpse of her lighter side, the Elle she'd probably been before getting mixed up with her ex, and he wanted to see more of it. Much more.

He waved goodbye to Libby and Adrian, who were saying goodbye to Piper, and got into the front seat. Elle gave Libby and Imogen a hug and then joined him in the car.

They were silent for the first part of the drive. George was content to let Elle speak first; he had no need to make unnecessary conversation and he liked how relaxed she was.

"Thank you for inviting me tonight. You have such lovely friends." Her voice was quiet, perhaps because she didn't want to wake Toby.

"They're your friends too. Aren't you planning a girls' night next weekend?"

Elle nodded. "I'll have to check if Nora can babysit Toby."

It irritated him a little that she wouldn't ask him for help but he understood. He simply said, "If she can't, my offer still stands."

"Thank you. I do appreciate it." She glanced quickly at him and then back to the road.

There was sincerity in her voice.

She pulled into his driveway and the casual atmosphere changed. He felt the subtle shift from her, a tensing of her spine, and reminded himself to keep it light. They were just friends.

"Thanks for the ride."

Elle turned to face him. "No problem."

The light from the headlights showed her wary expression.

He wanted to kiss her. Wanted so badly to cup her cheek in his hand, lean forward and touch his lips to hers.

But he'd given her his word.

Instead he opened the car door and said, "I'll call you later."

He hoped the soft sigh she gave as he closed the car door behind him was disappointment.

***

Elle was too busy to be giving any thought to George. At least that's what she kept telling herself, but her mind had other ideas.

During the early-morning prep work she'd caught herself staring off into space thinking about him, remembering specifically the goodbye moment in the car. She'd wanted him to kiss her – she had been so sure he was going to – but he'd simply said goodbye and left.

And she'd been disappointed.

She was a hypocrite. She'd told him to back off, to stay away, and now she was cross he hadn't kissed her. She should be pleased he respected her boundaries instead of being frustrated. She'd barely slept the night before, replaying the moment over and over in her head.

One thing was certain.

He'd got under her skin.

Now every time the bell above the door chimed, she looked up, hoping it was going to be him. She had to get a grip.

She didn't have time for men in her life.

Indulging in fantasies about Dean was what had got her into this situation in the first place.

She needed to focus on her business.

During the week she'd hired two more waitresses for the weekend so Nora didn't have to work every day and to ensure she had enough staff should someone fall sick. They were students and happy with the casual hours, but Elle needed to keep an eye on them until they understood the routine.

Which meant she had to focus.

Next week was the first meeting of her book club and she needed to call around and confirm numbers. There were half a dozen people who had put their name down on the expressions of interest list, along with the days and times that would suit them. Elle had considered holding it after hours, but with Toby, it was too difficult. So instead they were meeting on Tuesday at two o'clock. It worked out well because it was after the lunch-hour rush.

Leaving her staff to run the shop, she went into the kitchen to make the phone calls. By the time she had only one more call to make, it was noon. Telling herself she wasn't a coward for leaving George to last, she went out to help serve the lunch customers.

***

The first of George's musicians arrived on time, just before two, to set up for his music set. Elle greeted Joel and showed him to his area. He was young, maybe twenty, and cute. Drew gave him more than a second glance.

"George said to play my acoustic versions and keep it low; is that right?" Joel asked.

At George's name Elle started and then cursed herself. "That would be great." She would not ask if George was dropping by to watch the session. It would be immature.

He started his set and Elle wandered over to a customer who was browsing the books.

She needed the distraction.

***

An hour later the shop had settled into the quiet rhythm where everyone had been served and were focused on their conversations, and the staff were filling up sugar jars, cleaning up the kitchen, and restocking the bookshelves. Elle was so pleased with how everything was going. In two weeks she already had her regulars and her little café was often full.

She'd never dreamed so big.

Her cell phone rang so she headed to the kitchen to answer it. It wasn't a number she recognized. "Hello?"

"Elle, it's Martin."

The elation Elle had been feeling deflated.

"What can I do for you?" she said, keeping her tone polite but distant.

"We've decided to spend an extra night in Houston and were hoping we could visit Toby if you're free."

"Who are we?"

"Just Lindsay and myself. Dean returned to the ranch."

Elle was glad but could she trust him? She certainly didn't want them coming to the shop or her apartment, but perhaps this would show them she was serious about letting them see their grandson.

"There's a park about ten minutes from the restaurant we met at on Friday. You probably drove past it on your way," she said.

"I know the one."

"We could meet you there at five-thirty. There's a playground Toby can use." And it was a wide open space so no one could sneak up on them. Plus there were always people around.

"Great. I'll see you then." He sounded relieved.

Elle hung up, her stomach awash with nerves. She didn't want to turn up without telling anyone where she was going.

Her first thought was George.

Which was utterly ridiculous. She should be considering Nora or Imogen even.

She sighed. George was strong enough to help her if she needed it.

Following her instinct, she phoned him. She had to talk to him about the book club anyway.

"Hey, Elle," he answered. His tone was warm.

"Hi. I'm calling about the book club. You expressed an interest and we're going to meet on Tuesday at two."

"Let me check my calendar." There was silence before he came back on. "I'll be there."

"Great." She took a deep breath. "There's something else."

"What's wrong?" His tone was immediately concerned.

"It's probably nothing, but I wanted to tell someone about it. I'm meeting Martin and Lindsay this afternoon so they can play with Toby before going home."

"Where and when?"

Elle gave him the details.

"Do you want me to come with you?"

She really did, but she didn't want Lindsay to see him again and think they were an item. It would complicate matters.

"No. I just wanted to make sure I told someone. We'll only stay an hour or so and I'll call you when I get home."

"I haven't been for my jog today. That park has some good trails."

Elle smiled, already lighter. "Far be it for me to stop you from exercising."

"I'll keep an eye on you both and won't come near unless you need me."

"That would be great. I'll wave if I need you." She hoped he could hear how grateful she was.

"I'll call you later."

Elle hung up. Whatever this thing was between her and George, she was glad he was there.

***

The rest of the day flew by as it always did when she wasn't looking forward to something. She managed to lock up the café by twenty past five and get to the park on time, stopping only to buy a T-shirt to replace her uniform shirt. Martin and Lindsay were there, sitting on a park bench waiting.

"Memah! Pepah!" The second Toby saw his grandparents he took off across the grass toward them.

Elle locked up the car and followed more slowly.

Toby flung himself at his grandfather, who picked him up and whirled him around, with Toby's delighted shrieks filling the air.

The guilt that was never far away slunk back.

There had to be some way Elle could make this work. Toby only knew this set of grandparents and it wasn't likely he would ever meet her parents. It wasn't fair to punish either her son or his relatives because she and Dean hadn't been able to make things work – or rather because Dean was such a jerk.

As she crossed a path, a jogger came toward her. It was George. He was wearing loose black jogging shorts and a white T-shirt. His breathing was even as she gave him a brief smile but kept walking. By the time she reached the group, Lindsay had smothered Toby in kisses and he was dragging them toward the swing set.

"You'll push me real high, won't you, Pepah?"

Elle greeted them cautiously. Lindsay's smile was forced, but Martin's was genuine.

"Thanks for meeting us today," he said.

"Toby missed you," Elle said simply.

"Come on, Pepah!" Toby tugged on Martin's hand.

"I'm going to sit down here while you play with your grandparents," she told Toby. She wanted to give them space and the playground was only a dozen yards away.

"OK."

He wasn't the least bit concerned. He'd often spent time with his grandparents.

Elle settled on the bench. It was a beautiful summer evening and there were a few other children playing at the playground. Several families had settled into the picnic area nearby to have dinner and there were a number of people riding or jogging along the path. Across the park George was setting a good pace. It was like having her own personal guardian angel.

She breathed in deeply and her muscles relaxed.

On Monday she would call the lawyers whose names Chris had given her. Why she hadn't organized it sooner she didn't know. She supposed there had been so much else to organize, what with finding a job and somewhere to live and getting away from the women's shelter, which was entirely too depressing. Plus she hoped Dean wouldn't care enough to search for her.

Wishful thinking.

He'd been so obsessed with her in the beginning that it had been overwhelming at first and oh so flattering. Boys had never really been interested in her at high school. She was average looking and had received high grades. She'd been one of the smart kids – pity her intelligence hadn't stretched to members of the opposite sex.

She'd met Dean at the café where she'd been waitressing after she started college. He'd been hunched over his laptop, frowning, and she'd been a little afraid to disturb him. When she'd asked for his order, he glanced up and his brown eyes had been so full of longing that she'd taken a step back. When he'd continued to stare at her, not really seeing her, she'd said, "Can I help you?"

He'd blinked and focused even more intensely on her. "Yes, you're perfect. You're my heroine."

That had freaked her out, and she'd backed away. But he

chuckled and said, "I'm a script writer. I was searching for inspiration for my latest heroine and here you are." His smile had dazzled her. He was several years older and yet *he* thought *she* was perfect.

At the end of her shift they'd gone for coffee and by the end of the week she was spending more time at his place than she was at college.

It had been so thrilling to be wanted so desperately. He'd treated her like a princess, had told her she was his muse and had seduced her so slowly and passionately that she'd fallen in love.

A month later she moved in with him, much to her parents' dismay, and six months later she was pregnant. Of course Dean hadn't wanted the baby but Elle was sure it would only bring them closer together.

She'd been wrong.

After Toby's birth their relationship struggled until one day Dean had said they were moving to Texas to his parents' ranch. There hadn't been any consultation and Elle had still been desperate to make things right between them so she'd packed up, said goodbye to her parents and left.

That was the last time she'd heard from them.

Toby's shrieks brought her back to the park and she smiled as Martin pushed him high on the swing.

She was glad she'd come – glad she was able to give Toby time with his grandparents. Family was important.

Toby got off the swing and Lindsay said something to him, pointing toward the bayou and the bridge that ran over it. There were ducks swimming along and Toby was keen to watch them. It was a little further away than Elle was comfortable with so she scanned the area. She didn't like Toby near the water, even if he'd practiced swimming the evening before.

It was then she spotted the man sitting on a bench on the other side of the bayou. It wasn't so much his appearance that struck her, but the way he sat, hunched over and focused, very much like Dean when an idea struck him.

And his focus was on her.

# Chapter 8

He was sitting under the shade of one of the trees lining the bayou and it was difficult to distinguish his face properly, but Elle was certain it was Dean.

They'd lied to her.

Lindsay and Martin were getting closer to the bridge that led over the river to Dean. Elle leaped up.

"Toby!" she called.

Toby glanced back at her call and she hurried toward him.

"It's time to go."

"But I want to feed the ducks," he said.

Lindsay tugged him forward and out of the corner of Elle's eye she saw the man rise. She didn't want Toby to see his father; she wasn't sure what reaction Toby would get.

"We'll feed the ducks another time," she said as she reached them and grasped Toby's hand.

Toby stepped back into the protection of his grandmother's arms and Lindsay smirked at her.

"Please, Toby, we need to go."

"Let him feed the ducks." It was Dean's voice, loud but cajoling.

Toby's eyes widened in fear and he stepped toward Elle only to be held back by Lindsay.

"Momma!" Toby reached for Elle.

Fear swept across Elle's body like a wild fire. Would Lindsay let any harm come to her grandson?

Martin turned to his son. "You were supposed to be back at the ranch." His voice was angry. Then he turned to his wife. "You called him."

"He has a right to see his son." Her voice was shrill.

"Let go of me." Toby struggled against his grandmother.

Anger rose in Elle as Toby was held against his will, but she turned her attention to Dean, who was now too close. He was the danger, but she needn't have worried. Dean didn't pay the slightest attention to Toby.

His focus was all on her.

That was fine for the moment. She reminded herself that Dean was always on his best behavior around his parents. There was no need for him to get violent now. Still she moved a couple of steps away to lure him from her son.

"What do you want?" she asked.

"You. It's always been you."

Toby shrieked, "Let me go!"

"Shut up, kid," Dean roared and Toby stopped struggling, his eyes wide in fear, and he shrank back again into his grandmother's arms. Dean blinked and his face smoothed into a smile. "Will you take him to the ducks?" he asked his mother, as sweet as could be. "I need to talk to my wife."

Martin shook his head at Lindsay and she stayed where she was, but Dean didn't notice.

Elle breathed a sigh of relief. They weren't going to leave her alone with him. "I am not your wife."

He waved her words away and his tone was soothing. "Honey cakes, don't be like that. We were so good together, we didn't need the certificate." It had been this tone that had convinced her everything was going to be all right, that he wouldn't hit her again and that they had turned a corner to a bright future ahead.

It was this tone that she'd believed time and time again.

It was this tone that lied.

"We've had a couple of rough moments, but we can get through them. We always have before. I haven't been able to write a word since you left."

So that was the reason he'd come. Not because he missed her or loved her, but because his writing was suffering.

"Then perhaps you shouldn't have broken your toys," she said. It was how she'd felt in the last couple of years. Like some kind of toy that he rolled out when he needed inspiration and kicked under the bed when it was not required. There'd been weeks of neglect, when she couldn't get any response from him because inspiration had struck and he'd write from the time he woke up to the time he fell asleep, usually exhausted, at his desk.

In the later years, those periods had been a blessing.

Dean reached out a hand to placate her and she stepped away. "Don't be like that. I'm sorry you left."

Yes, he was sorry she'd left, sorry he'd lost his muse, but not sorry for the way he'd treated her and Toby. Anger began to win out over her fear. "Dean, you're violating your restraining order. You should leave before I call the police and have you arrested."

"There isn't a piece of paper in this world that would keep me from you. Stop being silly. You've had your tantrum. Come home."

"So you can beat me again? So you can lock me in the house, neglect me, keep me by your side with no money and no one to turn to? I don't need you now. I have friends and I have a job."

He was a little uncertain. Perhaps she was getting through to him.

Toby was standing a few yards away, watching; Lindsay had let go of him, distracted by their conversation.

"We are over and you need to move on. I'm sure there's someone else out there who can be your muse." Not that she'd wish Dean on anyone. She took a step toward Toby and held out her hand. He came running over and tucked himself into her side.

Dean didn't so much as glance at him. He was considering her words.

"Hi, Elle, how are things?" George's voice from behind made her want to groan. He couldn't have chosen a worse moment. She'd told him to stay away unless she waved.

"George!" Toby's voice was delighted.

Dean's expression went dark, furious. "Who the hell is this?"

There it was, the switch from calm to dangerous. She'd never seen him do it in front of his parents before. Her skin tight and every sense on high alert, Elle turned to George, keeping her tone light. "Oh, hey! What are you doing here? George, this is my ex, Dean; Dean, George is a friend of a friend."

"Bullshit. He's your new lover, isn't he? He's the reason you left me? You've been having an affair with him all this time, while I've been struggling to provide a living for us."

Elle wanted to wail. She'd been so close to a civil outcome until George had to interfere. She pressed Toby into her hip.

"No. I only met him a couple of weeks ago."

Dean ignored her, turning on George. "Have you been fucking my wife? You're not able to get your own woman so you have to go stealing from another man?"

Lindsay gasped, put a hand over her mouth.

Toby pushed further against Elle. She had to get them away before fists started flying.

George held two hands up in front of him in the surrender motion. "No. I was on a run – I saw Elle here and thought I'd say hello."

Dean wasn't going to listen to a word he said.

"It was nice seeing you, George. Tell Imogen I said hey." Elle kept her voice light but her expression said, Get the hell away.

George hesitated.

"You'd better finish your jog, I don't want you to cool down too much."

"I'm sure you don't," Dean snarled. "You want him hot for you."

Elle turned back to Dean and his parents, who'd approached when Dean had raised his voice.

"Isn't this the man you were talking to in the coffee shop the other day?" Lindsay asked.

Elle wanted to throttle the woman. Instead she said, "Yes. He's familiar with Houston and was giving me some tips."

It sounded lame to her ears but she couldn't tell them the truth.

"You're a whore," Dean hissed. "You sucked me in with

your innocent eyes but it turns out you knew exactly what you're doing. You probably fuck everything that moves. I wonder if the kid is even mine."

She wanted so desperately to say he wasn't. To say she had cheated on Dean and Toby was the result, but it wasn't fair to her child. He had a right to know his lineage, who his grandparents were and where he belonged.

"You believe whatever you want, Dean," she said instead. She had to get out of there, had to trust Dean would behave in front of his parents, had to trust George would have enough sense to leave when she did – in the opposite direction. "Goodbye."

She took Toby's hand and turned.

A hand on her shoulder whirled her back around. Toby stumbled and fell to the ground with a shriek.

"Don't you turn your back on me." Dean was right up in her face, his face screwed up in fury. "You've been a lying, cheating whore. It's no wonder I haven't been able to write. You've been sabotaging my creativity." His fingers pressed hard into her shoulder and she wasn't able to shake him off.

Even now, it was all about him.

"Let go of me." Her voice wasn't as strong as she wanted it to be. The pain was letting her fear seep in, the memories of past hurt all clouding around her.

"Dean!" Martin's voice.

She needed to focus. She needed to overpower her fear.

To the side, George was helping a silent Toby to his feet. He was holding his wrist to his chest and tears ran quietly down his face.

Dean finally noticed his son.

"What the hell are you doing with my boy?" he growled, keeping his hand on Elle's shoulder.

George ignored him, talking to Toby, examining his wrist.

Dean didn't like to be ignored.

He let go of Elle and took a step toward George. "Give me my son."

George finished whispering to Toby, and Toby hurried over to the park bench Elle had been sitting on earlier.

George had gotten him out of danger.

The relief was a balm. Elle was about to tell George to go when he spoke.

"I don't know about your relationship with Elle, but if she were my wife, I wouldn't treat her like you do."

He may as well have waved a red flag at a charging bull.

The punch was fast, vicious, heading straight for George's face.

George must have been expecting it as he ducked and it only glanced the side of his face.

George tripped as he stepped back and went down on one knee, and Lindsay shrieked. Elle rushed between the two men as Dean kicked at George.

The kick landed squarely on Elle's thigh and pain radiated through her body before going numb.

Dean grunted in shock as George leaped to his feet and pushed Elle behind him. Martin grabbed his son's arm and yelled, "Enough!"

The shout got through some part of Dean's brain and he took a couple of steps away, breathing heavily.

Elle massaged some feeling back into her leg and reached for George. "Let's go," she said.

George turned and his eyes were full of anger too, but she wasn't scared. The anger wasn't directed at her.

"Elle, I'm so very sorry about this," Martin said.

"I know." It was obvious Lindsay had set the whole thing up. It was a shame, but she'd been right to give them a chance. She wasn't going to do it again. She couldn't risk Toby or herself.

She turned to Dean, her hands shaking. She needed to be confident. Drawing on her strength reserves, she stood tall. "You've violated your restraining order, you've hurt Toby, George and myself. I will report you to the police." She took a breath. "You need to stop this. I'm not coming back." Then she thought of the one thing that might convince him to leave them be. "You'll end up in jail, and then you'll never get your scripts made."

She hoped some of what she said would sink in, or that Martin would be able to talk some sense into his son.

Elle hurried over to the park bench where Toby was

standing, wide eyed, holding his wrist.

"Momma." He held his arms up to her and she picked him up.

"It's all right, my little man. Show me your wrist; does it hurt?"

He nodded, his eyes filling with tears.

The wrist was a little swollen. Anger rose in her chest but she kept her voice soothing. "We'll get you to a doctor then." She turned to George, who was behind her. "How's your face?"

"Sore," he admitted.

Elle didn't want to leave with George but she could hardly leave him there when he'd taken a hit for her. Though if he'd listened to what she'd told him, he wouldn't have been hurt at all.

"Could you have a concussion?" she asked as they crossed to the parking lot.

"I don't think so."

She opened the car door for Toby and when she tried to do up his seatbelt she found her hands were shaking. "Do you need a ride to your car?"

"I jogged over."

Of course. George's house wasn't far from the park.

She belted Toby up and shut the door, turning to face George. "I can drop you off on the way to the hospital."

"How's your leg?" he asked.

"I've had worse." Now Toby was safe, the fear turned to anger. She was angry at Lindsay, she was angry at Dean and she was angry at George. If he'd stayed at a distance, like he'd promised, none of the violence would have happened. Her rational side knew she should be pleased he'd been there for her as she'd asked, which was why she wanted to get away before she blew up. It wouldn't help the situation.

She opened the driver's side door and slid in. "Do you want a lift?"

"Sure." His tone was easy but he had a wary look in his eye. At least he realized she was mad at him. It made things so much easier.

When he'd climbed in, he said, "I might come to the doctor with you, if that's all right. I'd better get this checked out. Then we can go to the police station together. It will save time."

She couldn't argue with his logic but she didn't have to be happy about it.

*** 

George gave Elle directions to a nearby emergency clinic and fell silent. What he'd just witnessed was hard to understand. Sure, he'd seen the pictures but it was a hell of a lot different from experiencing that level of venom directed at you. She must have been living in hell.

When he'd seen the confrontation he'd wanted to run straight over. It was obvious even from a distance that the man was Elle's ex and that she was scared. And that Toby's grandmother was keeping Toby very close.

It made his blood simmer.

It was one thing to try to get your son back together with his partner, but an entirely other matter to put your grandchild in danger.

Would Lindsay still be making excuses for her son after today?

They arrived at the clinic and he stood back while Elle helped Toby from the car. She was angry but he wasn't certain whether it was with him or the situation.

It was best to give her some space.

The receptionist got an icepack for Toby's wrist and luckily the waiting room wasn't very full.

They sat down and, as Elle did, her pencil skirt rose a little on her thigh, exposing a big bruise that was getting darker.

George ran his hand gently over it. "You're hurt." It was a very nasty bruise.

She slapped his hand away. "It's fine. It will fade in a few days."

That wasn't the point. The point was she'd been hurt trying to protect him because he'd been stupid enough to bait the man.

He abhorred violence, but he'd wanted to hit Dean for all the things he'd said to Elle, let alone what he'd done. But the guy had been much quicker than he'd given him credit for – if it hadn't been for Elle, he'd be a lot worse off than he was.

"I'm sorry." He laid a hand on her arm.

She shrugged him off. She glanced at him with damp eyes but looked quickly away.

His heart squeezed.

Hell, he'd made her cry.

He had to do something to make up for it.

"Toby Carter," the doctor called.

Elle and Toby got to their feet. George hesitated. Maybe he shouldn't go in with them.

"Come on," Elle said, without looking at him.

They went through to the examination room and the doctor examined Toby's wrist. "It's not broken," she said. "Ice it for twenty minutes every hour until he goes to bed and give him Ibuprofen for the pain. It should get better in a day or two."

"Thank you. Could you please check George for concussion?" Elle asked.

The doctor frowned. "What happened to y'all?"

"A run-in with my ex."

The doctor gaped at her. "I hope you're reporting him."

"That's the next stop."

She nodded and stepped over to George.

George answered her questions as she examined him.

"You'll be fine but someone should keep an eye on you tonight. You're not going to be alone, are you?"

"I'll figure something out," he said.

He had friends he could call on.

***

As they left the doctor's clinic, Toby said, "Momma, I'm hungry."

Elle sighed. It was dark now and way past Toby's dinnertime. It was a wonder he hadn't asked for food sooner. They would have to get some takeout on the way to the police station. "We'll grab something now."

She drove through a fast-food place, checking her purse before ordering.

"I'll pay," George said.

"No, it's fine." She didn't want to owe him anything. She was still simmering, despite his apology. She didn't want to soften toward him. Elle ordered Toby some fries and chicken nuggets,

101

the meal George wanted and then some fries for herself. Her purse contents didn't stretch to more.

"You're not eating much," George said.

"I'm not hungry." She wasn't either. Her stomach was still tied up in knots.

They'd finished eating by the time they reached the police station, so they went straight in. It was the same station as Elle had gone to two days before and the same young officer was at the desk.

He fidgeted as she approached. "Everything all right, ma'am?"

"I'd like to report a breach of a restraining order and an assault."

The man seemed relieved she didn't burst into tears this time. She smiled as he got out the paperwork and started writing.

***

Elle was exhausted by the time she arrived home. Toby was asleep in the car and George was still in the passenger seat. Against her better judgment, she'd offered her couch for him to sleep on, since the doctor said he shouldn't be alone.

Unfortunately he'd accepted.

She let George carry Toby inside while she locked the car and unlocked the apartment. Leading him through to Toby's bedroom she said, "Put him in bed." She pulled back the sheets and George laid him down. She wasn't going to wake him up and make him brush his teeth. It had been a rough day and one night wouldn't hurt.

When George gently brushed Toby's bangs out of his eyes, Elle refused to acknowledge the tug on her heart. She kissed her son good night and went into the kitchen to start coffee brewing.

She didn't know what to say to George, didn't know what he thought about the altercation in the park.

Plus she was still angry about him interfering.

Elle busied herself getting out mugs and milk.

"Do you want to talk about it?" George asked, standing at the table, his hands on the back of a chair.

"No." She handed him his coffee, then, annoyed she was being so petty, she said, "Lindsay called him. Martin didn't know he was going to be there."

"He wanted to see Toby?"

She laughed. "No." While it was a relief, she felt the pain of rejection for her son. "He was only interested in me, until you turned up." Elle addressed George then. "Surely a father should have some regard for his child?"

George shook his head. "It's not always the case. Some people weren't meant to be parents."

She should have realized when Dean had been so angry when she'd told him she was pregnant. Still, she hated the fact her child didn't have a father who loved him.

"He's not normal, you know?" George said. "The obsession with you and the flip from calm to anger."

"He would have been fine if you hadn't shown up," Elle retorted. "I had him calmed down and I was about to leave when you came over. Damn it, I told you to stay away unless I called you." Even as she said the words she knew she was being unfair, but she'd been holding in all of the fear from the afternoon for so long, she had to get it out.

George raised his eyebrows. "From where I was, you looked outnumbered. I wasn't going to leave you there by yourself."

"You should have. I don't need you."

He put down his mug and walked around the table to her. She fought the urge to step back. She wasn't afraid of him.

"You need someone you can turn to when things get tough, you need someone who will stand by you and help you out, you don't need to do it alone." His voice was low, sympathetic.

Tears stung her eyes and her throat burned. Why was he being so nice? Why hadn't he walked out the door when she'd started blaming him? She shook her head, wanting to deny what he said but no words would form.

"I said we were friends, didn't I? I wouldn't let any of my friends – Piper, Imogen, Libby, Adrian, Chris – face what you've had to face alone. It's not who I am."

"But I asked you not to."

He nodded. "I know and I'm sorry I made it worse. I couldn't stand by and watch you face that bully by yourself. I care for you." He brushed away the tear that had escaped her eye. "I should have trusted you had everything under control."

Her anger deflated.

She squeezed her eyes shut. She didn't want this, this kindness, this caring, these warm and contented feelings that were being stirred up inside her. She couldn't trust those. She'd felt those with Dean and she'd been oh so wrong about them.

But, damn, she was tempted.

George stepped closer, gathering her into his arms, and she didn't resist. How could she? She wanted to be able to lean on someone, even if only for a minute.

Giving in to the temptation, Elle wrapped her arms around his waist and felt him relax.

He was as uncertain as she was.

That made her smile.

George stroked her back, sending lovely, shimmery warmth everywhere. She gave herself a minute to enjoy it and then stepped back.

His eyes captured her; something in them said he would protect her, that he cared for her.

After five years of having no one she could turn to for help, the invitation was beyond enticing. She wanted someone she could rely on, someone she could talk her worries over with, someone to just be there.

But was she wanting too much?

George watched her, waiting. He was letting her make the choice. He was giving the power to her.

That was what made her decision for her.

She leaned forward and kissed him.

# Chapter 9

Elle's lips met the warmth and softness of George's. She wanted to keep it light and gentle, but the moment they touched, she melted in to him. It was slow and maybe a little cautious as she went deeper, tasting him. There was a lingering coffee flavor and then there was George. There was something about him that drew her in.

No.

Taking a step back she noticed his breathing was a little uneven – like hers.

She wanted more, so much more, that it scared her.

"I …" She didn't know what to say.

"You," George agreed and brought her back against him, kissing her, deepening the contact and causing her to hold on for fear of being washed away.

It was so sweet: long luscious kisses that made her heart sing and her body zing. She sensed the control behind the kisses though, felt it in the slightly tense way he was holding her. He was holding back, being careful for her.

He stepped back, rested his forehead on hers. "Do you want to go make out on the couch?"

Elle laughed, surprised she could after the emotion of the day.

She did, she *really* did but she wasn't sure where it would lead and she couldn't deal with any more today.

"Yes, but I'd better get you a pillow and some sheets for the couch instead."

"I like where your thoughts are going," he said, causing her to laugh again and step back.

"I'm not sure where this is going," she said.

George shrugged. "Neither am I. Do we need to be?"

It made her pause. Could she start something not knowing what the outcome she wanted was? Was it fair to either of them to do so?

But then again, life made no promises.

"I guess not."

George squeezed her hand. "Don't overthink it, Elle. We like being together: it's a good thing."

"There's Toby to consider too."

"I know you two are a package deal. He's an awesome kid."

From conversations with Nora, Elle realized how rare that was. She was lucky.

"All right." She kissed him quickly and stepped away before it could go deeper. "Let me get you those sheets."

After she'd made up George's bed on the couch, she spent a long time lying in her own bed, staring up at the ceiling, thinking of him.

***

George woke to the high-pitched, delighted shriek of a young boy.

"George!"

He opened his eyes to find Toby crouched by the couch, staring straight into his face.

"Morning, kiddo," he said and stretched, groaning at all the kinks in his muscles. He'd not cooled down properly after his jog and a night on the couch hadn't helped matters.

"What are you doing here?"

"The doctor said I had to be watched, so your mom invited me to sleep over."

Toby frowned as he remembered what happened yesterday. "You could have slept in my room. I would have shared."

George smiled. "Thanks for the offer. The couch was fine."

"Or you could have shared with Mom. She's got a bigger bed and sometimes she lets me sleep with her."

The idea held a lot of appeal but he didn't say so. Instead he sat up as Elle padded into the room wearing only a pair of thin summer pajamas, rubbing the sleep out of her eyes.

Other parts of him woke up.

"Morning."

Elle gasped and stopped still, eyes blinking until she recognized him, and then quickly crossed her arms over her chest. "George. I, ah, forgot. Oh I hope Toby didn't wake you … Let me get dressed."

She disappeared back down the hallway.

George grinned and focused on the boy in front of him. "What time is it?"

"The clock in my room had a five first, then a zero and a seven."

George swallowed a groan. Way too early to be up in his book, especially since he'd lain awake for hours after Elle had left, thinking about the kiss, about her and about how to deal with her violent ex.

"What do you normally have for breakfast?" he asked as he stood up and stretched again.

"Cereal."

"Right, let's see what we can find." He took Toby into the kitchen and the boy showed him where everything was. By the time Elle returned they were both sitting at the table chatting and eating their breakfast.

Elle stopped at the kitchen doorway and George studied her. She must have taken the time to have a quick shower because her hair was damp and she was already dressed in her work clothes: the black, hip-hugging skirt and the neat shirt with the shop's logo on it. She was divine.

"Coffee?" George asked, getting to his feet.

She blinked at him. "Yes, please." She rubbed her arms, hesitated and then poured a bowl of cereal and sat next to her son. She was obviously used to doing everything.

Well, he could help now.

He put the coffee in front of Elle and took his seat next to her. Their knees bumped and she flinched.

He hoped it was just because she was unused to the situation and not because she was regretting their kiss. Finishing his breakfast, he cleared his and Toby's bowls and washed them.

"What time do you need to leave?" he asked.

Elle checked her watch. "Damn. About ten minutes." She was only halfway through her cereal, but she stood.

George held out a hand. "Finish your breakfast. Toby and I can get him ready, can't we, kiddo?"

"Yep," Toby said.

Toby ran down the hallway to his room and George found him digging through his drawers.

"I'm going to wear my superhero shorts and top today. Then I can pretend I'm like you, protecting Mom from the bad people."

George's smile froze on his face. He kneeled down. "Toby, kiddo, I admire you for wanting to protect your mom, but you could get hurt. Your dad is a lot bigger than you."

Toby scowled. "He's not nice. I wish he wasn't my dad. Can't you be my dad?"

George swallowed past the lump in his throat. What the hell did he say? Was he being unfair to the kid by spending so much time with him when things between him and Elle might not work out? He'd not considered it from Toby's point of view before.

"It's not that easy," he said instead. "How about we go brush your teeth and then you can get ready?"

"All right."

George followed Toby into the bathroom, the reality of what Elle and Toby as a pair really meant hovering over him.

***

Elle dropped George off at his place just before six. George waved goodbye to the ever enthusiastic and wide-awake Toby and then trudged inside.

He was tired.

The temptation to slip into bed and get another hour's sleep was strong. Instead he went into his kitchen, put on his coffee machine, and headed for the shower to wash the fatigue away.

Standing under the spray, letting the warm water flow over

him, he reviewed his situation.

He was involved with a woman who had a beautiful five-year-old boy and an abusive ex-husband.

Dean didn't scare him. He'd spent the early part of Adrian's career dealing with possessive fans and even now one occasionally popped up.

No, he was more worried about Toby. How would Toby react if he and Elle split up? What would it do to his already fragile state? He needed to be so careful. He didn't want to lose either of them, but he needed to consider Toby more than he had been.

He didn't want to hurt the kid.

***

Elle rearranged the plate of cookies for a third time and stepped back. It was fine. She didn't know why she was so nervous about her first book-club meeting.

She was lying to herself. She knew exactly why she was nervous. George would be there.

He'd called her yesterday to check how she was and they'd talked for an hour. He made her laugh. He was able to do it so easily and she felt as if it had been so long since she'd really laughed.

Dean had always been too controlled, never indulged in moments of whimsy and silliness, though Toby had often made her smile.

But George made her laugh out loud with stories of his day and tales of his childhood. She was unable to follow suit. Talking about her childhood made her so sad. She didn't know how she'd ever repair the bridge which had burned down when she'd left with Dean, was too scared of rejection now to reach out and try.

The bell over the door jangled and one of Elle's regulars walked in. It was such a thrill to say she had regulars, and this woman, Jude, had been the first to put her name down for the book club.

"Hi, Jude; we're over here today."

"Howdy, Elle. You've set this up so nicely."

Elle smiled at the woman. "Thanks. Take a seat. Do you

want the usual?"

"That'd be great."

Happy to keep her mind busy, Elle went to make Jude's drink. She'd decided she would provide a free drink and cookies and when that was gone, people could buy their own.

When she returned to the area, another guest had joined Jude, this one a little younger, possibly in her early thirties. After the introductions were made and Elle had turned to make Bethanie's order, someone else entered the café.

Bethanie looked up and under her breath said, "Hubba, hubba. I hope he's coming to our group."

Elle turned as George walked toward them. She raised a hand in greeting and said to Bethanie, "He is."

"Thank the lord. Is he taken?"

Elle didn't know what to say. Was he taken? Was what they had with each other exclusive? They'd said they'd be friends but that was before. They'd not discussed what the kiss meant to their *friends* status.

George answered the question when he reached her. "Hey, beautiful," he said and kissed her on the mouth, longer than was perhaps proper in this situation.

Bethanie whispered, "Damn it."

Elle stepped back, flustered and George grinned at her. "Hi." She blinked, willing her blush away. "George, this is Jude and Bethanie." She took George's order and let them talk while she escaped to make the drinks.

Nora met her at the coffee machine. "When did that happen?" she asked.

Elle wanted to pretend not to know what Nora was talking about but her friend would keep on at it until she got an answer. "Sunday."

"Girl, you've been keeping secrets. You need to tell me all about it after work."

She wasn't sure she wanted to talk to anyone about what was happening with her and George.

She wasn't sure she understood it herself.

She took the drinks over and busied herself with introductions.

The book club was a mixture of ages and races, with

George the only male. Maria was a Hispanic woman in her eighties, who'd insisted her daughter and granddaughter come along too, Nicole was an African-American woman who'd just retired from her high-powered corporate job and was looking for something to fill her spare time, and Jude and Bethanie, who were both mothers whose children were at school. George's sister Isla hadn't been able to make it. It took George all of five minutes to charm the women there.

There was something about him that was so easy and likable.

They discussed books they'd read over the last few months, made recommendations to each other and argued about what types of books they should cover in their book club. Elle solved the argument by suggesting everyone took a turn at choosing the book and had them choose a number out of a box to decide what order they would go in.

"How much time do you need to order the books?" George asked Elle.

Elle hesitated. "You don't all have to buy from me," she said. She couldn't compete with the prices of online retailers and she wasn't going to force the group to buy from her.

"I read all my books on my e-reader," the Latino grandmother said. "Bigger text."

George was waiting for an answer.

"It would depend on the publisher but maybe two weeks."

"So if the person who chooses next calls Elle two weeks before the meeting, she can order enough books so those who want them can pick them up at the meeting."

The others nodded. Half of them were happy for her to order the books.

As the mothers were packing up to go and pick their children up from after-school care, Toby arrived back with Harry and Miranda in tow.

He saw the group and made a beeline toward it, ignoring his mother completely and going straight over to George.

"Hey, George!"

"Hey, kiddo." George hugged Toby and pulled him on to his lap. "How was your day?"

"Great." Toby launched into his tale but Elle didn't hear it.

She was too caught up in the picture they made together. The sexy, kind man, chatting quite happily with her five-year-old son. She couldn't remember a time when she'd found Toby sitting on Dean's lap, telling him about his day.

"That's a pretty picture," Jude said and winked at Elle.

It was.

Her heart squeezed so tightly in her chest she wasn't sure she'd be able to breathe.

"See you next month," Bethanie said, breaking Elle's focus.

Elle blinked and said goodbye to the women.

Not quite sure what to do about her heart.

***

That evening Elle was sitting on Toby's bed reading him a bedtime story, when Toby asked, "Momma, why doesn't Dad like me?" He fiddled with his sheet, clenching and unclenching it, not looking at her.

Elle stared at the page in front of her. What could she say? "Honey, your dad isn't very well. Most men don't hit women and children. Your dad is an exception and he doesn't really like either of us."

"He only talks to me when he's yelling."

Elle brought her arm around her son and hugged him close. "I know." She could hardly deny it. "You need to remember I love you so much and so do your Memah and Pepah and your uncles."

Toby frowned. "Memah and Pepah are Dad's mom and dad, right?"

"Yes."

"Where are your mom and dad?" He squinted at her. "Do they not love us either?"

Elle hesitated. She didn't know the answer. "They live in California, which is a long way from here. I'll show you on the map when we next get it out."

"Is it too far to drive?"

"No, but it would take a long time – two or three days."

Toby was silent while he thought about it. What was his mind running through?

Finally he asked, "Will George become like Dad?"

"No, honey." The answer was immediate and she stopped for a moment to consider why. George had a kindness Dean had never had. She knew for certain he would never hit either of them.

"Good. I like George."

Elle wasn't sure she liked where the conversation was heading. They'd only known George for two and a half weeks. It wasn't long enough to get to know someone. "Do you want me to finish the story?"

Toby considered it. "Yes, please, Mom." He hugged her tightly. "I love you."

"I love you too."

After she'd finished the story and tucked Toby into bed, she sat on the couch with a cup of tea.

Her little boy was growing up. He was asking the kinds of questions she'd known he'd ask eventually. What child didn't want to know where he came from?

But she really didn't know how to answer him about her family.

When she'd left California she'd written them letters – Dean had said it was more personal than email and he was always using the single laptop they had anyway – but all of them had been unanswered.

She'd been sure her brother would have at least responded, but there'd been nothing from him.

Since she'd left Dean, she had considered contacting them, but a mixture of pride and fear stopped her. She didn't want to go crawling back, showing them they'd been right about Dean and begging for help. She would have received, at best, 'I told you so' and, at worst, full rejection. She hadn't been in a mental state where she could have coped with the rejection.

Now however she was doing better. The café was running fine so far, though it was too early to tell whether it would continue its success. She could call or write and tell them of her changed circumstances, in case they wanted to get in touch.

But still fear entwined itself into her. Her mother had told her she was making a mistake, her father had asked her not to go, but neither had ever checked if she was doing OK. They knew little about Toby.

She sighed.

Part of her reluctance was also anger. She'd been the perfect daughter all through her childhood and the one time she'd done something they disagreed with, they had turned on her. James's betrayal was the worst of all. She'd idolized him and had loved him so much – her big brother had always been there for her – until she'd really needed him.

The phone rang and she answered it before the ringing could wake Toby.

"I had fun at the book club today."

George.

Just the sound of his voice made her smile.

"I'm glad. You certainly charmed all the women there. They all wanted to take you home."

"There's only one woman I want to take me home," he answered.

Elle blushed and said, "If you'd told Maria, she would have ordered her girls to put you in the car."

George chuckled. "You know who I mean."

Elle was silent.

"Is Toby already in bed?"

"Yes. I just turned out his light." She sighed, thinking about the conversation they'd had.

"What's wrong?"

Should she tell him? Should she share her concerns with a man she really didn't know very well but had become part of her life so quickly?

"Is he sick?"

"No." She paused. "He asked me why his dad didn't like him."

"Oh. What did you say?"

"I said he was unwell."

"You're right. From what I've seen of your ex, he's pretty extreme."

It was a relief to hear it coming from someone like George.

"How did Toby take it?"

"I'm not sure. He thought about it, asked some more questions and then seemed all right as long as I love him and so do his Memah and Pepah."

"What about your parents? Do they see him much?"

The question echoed Toby's earlier one and it took Elle by surprise. She'd not mentioned her parents: they could be dead for all he knew. But suddenly she had the urge to tell someone about the situation, to confide in.

"They haven't seen him since he was a baby. When I left with Dean, they weren't happy and we fought. I tried writing to them, but they never responded."

"Writing? As in letters?"

Elle chuckled. "Yes. You remember those old fashioned things? Bits of paper, and a writing implement? Though I used a pen not a quill."

"Who sent them?" George asked slowly.

"Dean." He'd controlled everything, including the mail.

There was a pause and then George's voice was quiet. "Are you sure he sent them?"

The question was like a thunderclap in her ears. At that time of her life she was still in love with Dean. It never occurred to her that he wouldn't have sent her letters to her parents.

But what if he hadn't?

What if they thought she'd left and wanted nothing more to do with them?

What if they'd tried to write and Dean hadn't given her *their* letters? She knew he'd given them the address of the ranch — she'd made sure.

But had he given the right address?

She hadn't known where she was going to check it was correct.

"Are you still there?"

George's concern broke through her what ifs. "Yes. I don't know. I never considered ... I was still in love ..." She couldn't explain.

"Do you want me to come over?"

Yes.

"No." She couldn't follow her pattern of letting a man take over her life. There were some things she had to work out on her own. "I need to think about this. I'll call you later." She hung up before he could argue, and stared into space.

Would Dean have really done that to her?

It was possible.

But then, her parents could have tracked her down. They knew Dean's surname, they knew the ranch was in Texas and the nearest major city was Houston. They hadn't tried to call or visit.

Maybe they didn't want to see her after all.

How she could find out the truth?

Was she brave enough to pick up the phone and call them?

She shook her head. No, not yet. She had to consider it some more, not rush into anything.

She could use the computer she had at the café to look them up. James had been into social media before she'd left and she might even be able to remember her own passwords, if the accounts hadn't been closed due to inactivity.

If she wasn't too busy tomorrow, she'd take an hour and do some research.

She closed her eyes, satisfied she'd worked out the next step.

If Dean had hidden correspondence from her family, she'd take the first step to fix things.

To find Toby more family.

# Chapter 10

George was too busy at work to be worrying about Elle, but that didn't stop him. She'd sounded shocked and confused when he'd suggested Dean had lied to her about her parents, but she hadn't wanted to turn to him for help.

He'd been on his way out the door to go anyway when Isla had called, and after he'd explained the situation she'd told him flat out he couldn't go over.

Unfortunately, her reasoning had been sound, but it didn't mean he liked it, or that he hadn't fretted all night whether Elle was all right.

He'd wanted to go over and give her a hug, support her, show her she wasn't alone.

But Isla had pointed out Elle had said she was fine and if he'd disrespected her wishes, he'd be like her ex, forcing her to suit his needs.

Sometimes being logical sucked.

That morning he had been rushed to death. He was due to fly to California next week with Ophelia and had all those last-minute details to confirm. She was appearing on a talk show, doing an exclusive performance for a radio station and a hundred other general promotional things. Not for the first time, he considered whether he should hire a marketing assistant, but he knew he'd double check everything himself to make sure it was done the way he needed it done anyway, so it would be a waste of time.

At lunch he gave into his urge and Googled *Carter* and *California*. Perhaps he could find something about Elle's family for her. If he could show her they were worried and missing her, she'd definitely call them.

As the search results appeared he sighed. It was too much to hope there would only be a few. Thousands of names in the phone directory and too many on social media to narrow down based on a surname. He had no idea what her parents did for a living or what their names were.

But she had an older brother. She'd mentioned his name at Libby's dinner, but he couldn't remember.

He dialed Imogen's number.

"Hey, Shorty, do you remember what Elle said her brother's name is?" he asked when she answered.

"Give me a second," Imogen said. She paused, then asked, "What are you planning?"

George thought fast. "Nothing. I just don't want to look like I wasn't paying attention."

Imogen laughed. "It was a J name. Something common, not John or Jason …"

"James," George said as he remembered.

"Yes, that's it."

"Thanks, I owe you one."

"Hey, you're babysitting Toby so we can take Elle out on the town. I think that makes up for it."

He grinned. "All right." Elle had asked him during the week to babysit after all.

He hung up and typed *James Carter* into the social media search engine. He scrolled through the names, discarding those who were of the wrong age bracket or ethnicity. There were only three that fit. One was a graphic designer, one was a fire fighter and the last was a teacher.

The graphic designer's profile was clear and George studied the picture. Was he being overly hopeful, or did the designer have the same smile as Elle? The profile didn't mention family, just awards he'd won and what he liked to do in his spare time.

Should he send the guy an email and ask?

The worst that could happen was the guy didn't answer, but it could be Elle's brother and George knew she'd love to be reunited with him. George could scout this guy out, make sure he wasn't harboring any ill feelings for Elle and then organize for him to fly to Houston. Elle would love it, he was sure.

Decision made, he typed the email.

***

The retail gods had been kind to Elle that week and she'd been flat out. What that meant was she didn't remember she wanted to search for her family until she was on her way home. She could hardly drag Toby back to the café to wait while she searched. It wouldn't be fair to him.

And if she was honest with herself, the whole idea made her feel so vulnerable – she wanted privacy in case she failed.

Anyway she didn't have time to dwell on it now. If she was going to be ready in time for her girls' night, she had to shower and get dressed.

She'd managed to get Toby to clear away his toys in the living area and he was so excited about having a boys' night with George that he'd been bouncing around singing since they got home.

"Toby, quieten down or you'll have Nora over here complaining," Elle said as he started on the chorus of his favorite song. Unfortunately they were the only words he knew and it had been like a song stuck on repeat for the last ten minutes. "I'm going to take a shower. You need to get into your pajamas before George arrives."

"OK!" He raced into his bedroom, still singing.

George didn't know what he was in for.

Checking the time, she showered and stood in her bedroom with her towel wrapped around her and examined her wardrobe.

She had no idea what to wear.

Was the girls' night casual – jeans and a nice top? Or was it fancy – a stylish dress and heels?

It didn't really matter either way, because she had neither a nice top nor a stylish dress.

When she'd left Dean, she'd left with the clothes on her back and a couple hundred dollars. The women's refuge had given her some clothes – basics like jeans and T-shirts, and she'd bought a few things as she'd needed them, but she'd had no need for going-out clothes.

And she'd been too busy in the café to buy something during the week.

What was she going to do?

There was a knock on the door.

"I'll get it!" Toby yelled.

Damn. It had to be George. "Check who it is before you open the door," she called after her son, hoping he would listen.

She had to throw something on because George couldn't find her in a towel.

George's voice sounded in the hallway. "Where's your mom?"

"I'll be right out," she yelled, frantically pulling on a clean pair of jeans.

The voices came closer and she adjusted her towel, took a step toward the door to close it – and came face to face with George.

"Oh, sorry," he said as he saw her state of undress. He turned but his eyes lingered on her, absorbing everything, and her body flushed.

"I won't be long," she said, pushing them both out of the door and closing it behind them.

She shook the towel, fanning herself.

Holy hell the man could start a forest fire with that much heat.

Never before had a man caused desire to shoot through her with a single look.

She breathed out, dropped the towel, and dressed quickly. She decided on jeans and the white shirt she'd bought for the loan interview. Slipping her feet into the sensible black heels she'd bought for the same interview, she hurried across the hallway to the bathroom to do her hair and makeup.

George and Toby's voices were coming from Toby's room. Her son was explaining to George how foaling worked on the farm.

"– and then plop, out comes the baby, easy peasy."

Elle grinned at his simplistic explanation. He'd never

actually witnessed the foaling take place, but had heard about it from his Memah. He'd get a real shock if he saw what really happened.

She finished her makeup and checked the time. Five minutes.

"Toby, I need to tell George a few things," she said as she walked into his bedroom.

Toby looked up. "Wow, you look real pretty, Mom."

"She sure does," George agreed.

Elle smiled. "Thank you, Toby-boy. Now follow me."

She led the way into the kitchen and showed George the spaghetti sauce she'd prepared the night before. "The pasta is in the pantry."

"Got it."

"Bed time for Toby can be seven-thirty tonight."

"Yippee!"

Elle laughed at Toby's exuberance. It was only a half hour extra. "You've got my cell phone, so call me if there's any problem. Nora is next door if you need anything."

"We'll be fine, Elle," George said. He was calm and confident.

There was a knock on the door. "That will be Imogen," Elle said and went to answer it.

Imogen stood at the door, absolutely stunning in a pastel blue dress that fit snuggly and fell to just above her knees. She was wearing a pair of black stilettos that rivaled the Eiffel Tower in height and a gorgeous pair of sparkling diamond earrings.

Elle's stomach dropped and her spirits fell. She was completely underdressed. There was no way she could go out dressed as she was. She'd look like the poor cousin next to this gorgeous woman.

She forced back her disappointment. It was her own fault really. She should have bought something to wear during the week.

Or refused the invitation. Nothing she could afford would rival this.

"Hi. You look gorgeous," Imogen said. "I love what you've done with your hair. Are you ready to go?"

Imogen was being kind – Elle knew that. "I ah … Maybe

not." How could she possibly go out as she was? Forcing herself to be casual, she shrugged. "I don't have anything as nice as you to wear and well, they might not let me in wherever we go." Her cheeks burned.

"Nonsense. You're casual chic. You've got nothing to worry about. Libby and Piper are both wearing jeans as well."

The parking lot wasn't visible from Elle's door so she couldn't check, though she was almost sure Imogen wouldn't lie. "Are you sure?" The last thing she wanted was to be self-conscious all night. She'd never enjoy herself.

"Of course. I've been looking forward to this all week." Imogen beamed at her and tugged her hand. "Say goodbye and let's go."

Imogen's enthusiasm was infectious, but Elle wasn't entirely convinced. She sucked in a deep breath. She'd been looking forward to this too and she shouldn't let her lack of fancy clothing stop her. Turning, Elle gave Toby a hug. "Be good for George, all right?"

"Yes, Mom."

She turned to George. "Call me at any time."

"Yes, ma'am. We'll be fine. After dinner we're going to build ourselves a corral and fill it." He winked at her.

Not entirely sure that was a good thing, she waved goodbye and followed Imogen down to the car.

No, not car – to the limousine.

Elle gaped at the sleek, black limo parked in the parking lot of her apartment building. The back window rolled down as they walked toward it and Piper stuck her head out.

"Hi! Hurry up, we've got places to be, food to eat and music to dance to."

Imogen laughed.

Where were they going? Was she going to have to spend a lot of money on this night out? She didn't have a whole lot – nothing saved and she only took enough money out of the business earnings to make it through the next week. She hadn't calculated for an expensive girls' night.

Imogen was the daughter of a fashion mogul, and Libby was a bestselling author and wife to Kent Downer who probably never had to consider price when going out. But Piper was a journalist, and single – she probably just had her salary. Surely they'd make sure it was within her budget. Elle hoped so.

She slid into the car and greeted Piper and Libby, who were both wearing more casual attire. She sighed in relief and settled in.

"Where are we going to?" she asked.

"We're going to the Wooden Spoon," Libby announced, naming the most expensive restaurant in Houston.

Elle's mouth dropped open.

"It's my treat. We're celebrating," Libby said.

"Celebrating what?" Piper asked.

Libby paused, a big grin on her face. "I've been offered another four-book contract – they want more of the Jessop Chronicles. *And* I've sold the movie option for the first book to Hollywood."

Imogen and Piper both squealed in delight.

It sounded like a big deal and Elle was happy for her. "Congratulations!"

"Thanks. I'm so excited. I know movie options rarely actually end up with a movie being made, but the fact someone is considering it is amazing."

"What did Adrian say?" Imogen asked.

"He's stoked. We had our own celebration." Libby blushed.

"This is definitely cause for celebration." Piper uncorked the bottle of champagne that was chilling and poured a flute full, handing it to Libby and then pouring them each a glass.

"To Libby. The best damn author there is," she said, raising her glass high.

"To Libby," Imogen and Elle echoed.

Elle took a sip of the sparkling wine. She'd not drunk a lot of alcohol because Dean said it messed with his creativity. The drink was light, a little bit fruity, and the bubbles danced along her tongue.

She could get used to it.

The limousine pulled up to the restaurant and the driver opened the door. They all poured out and into the restaurant. The maître d' met them at the door and took them straight over to their table, which was in a discreet corner.

The furnishing of the restaurant belied its name. The only

word that came to Elle's mind was sumptuous. Everything was classy: there had to be a lot of money involved to make everything so gorgeous.

The flooring was a plush carpet that cushioned Elle's steps as she walked, the tables were covered in a white so sharp it would have reflected the lighting if it had been any brighter. The walls were painted in a gorgeous light earthy tone and there were a few large pieces of Native American artwork on them. The overall ambience was one of comfort and good taste.

It was still relatively early and there were only a few diners already seated, but Elle noted they were a mixture of people who had dressed up in their finest and those who were as casual as she was. Both types of diners fit perfectly in the restaurant.

The tension that had been hovering since she'd opened the door to Imogen melted away.

She slid into a chair next to Imogen and across from Piper.

The waiter arrived to pour them all water and to explain the specials of the night. Imogen and Piper argued over what to drink and in the end ordered two bottles of wine for them to share.

Elle perused the menu and inhaled sharply when she saw the prices. You only came here if you could afford it.

She couldn't comprehend having so much money.

Still it wasn't right to take advantage of it. She didn't know these women very well and they'd been very kind to invite her out with them. She'd get an appetizer and say she wasn't very hungry.

"I've heard such amazing things about this restaurant," Piper said. "The food critic at the paper has been once and he didn't stop talking about it for days."

"The chef's a bit of a recluse," Imogen said. "He's about our age and he's a genius. Papa tried to get him out front so he could thank him for a meal and he refused."

"George has met him," Libby told her. "We had a meal here a few months ago and he walked into the kitchen to speak to him. He's the brother of one of George's artists. Apparently he's very nice."

Elle hadn't paid much attention to the restaurant when she was researching options for her bookstore café because it hadn't been within the realm of what she wanted to do, but she had read a glowing review of it in the newspaper. The food was a fusion of all things Texas: barbeque, Mexican and Native American. She couldn't wait to try it.

The waiter arrived with the wine and Imogen went through the tasting process. Elle was glad she was with them, because otherwise she'd have no idea what to do. It was a world she hadn't lived in since she was in California, and then she'd been under age and never drunk any wine.

When the waiter was gone, they discussed what they were going to eat.

"The fajitas here are out of this world," Imogen said. "I don't know what he does with them but they make your taste buds party."

"I had the ribs and they melted in my mouth," Libby told them.

There were so many delicious-sounding meals on the menu, but Elle would go with the cheapest thing. She wasn't going to take advantage of Libby's generosity.

When the waiter returned she ordered her appetizer along with the others. When they ordered entrées as well she said, "I don't need anything else, thank you."

Piper looked at her. "You can't just have an appetizer. They're not that big."

"I ate a lot at the café," Elle lied.

Piper examined her, her gaze direct and searching, and Elle itched to look away, but she held the other woman's gaze.

"Libby can afford it," Piper said. "Otherwise I wouldn't be eating either."

Elle blushed. How had Piper known?

"Of course I can," Libby said. "I know what it's like to have next to nothing. When I met Adrian, I was so desperate to pay my rent I worked as his nanny. Now, while I'm not a big spender, I do like to treat myself and my friends from time to time."

Elle was conscious of the waiter still standing there listening. "You barely know me."

"I knew you were one of us from the moment George brought you to the barbeque," Libby said. "It's the first time he's ever invited a woman to our place, and that means you're someone special."

Elle stared at her. She'd had no idea. "But we're just friends." She pushed aside thoughts of their kiss.

"Honey, I've seen you two together. It's more than that," Imogen said.

"What do you like on the menu?" Piper asked.

Elle wavered, but the waiter was waiting and she got the feeling the girls wouldn't let up. She pointed to a dish that sounded amazing.

The waiter smiled and left.

"Now, I want to know, what *is* happening between you and George?" Piper asked. It was said in a friendly way, but Piper was expecting an answer. She grinned at Elle and Elle's annoyance melted away.

"I don't know."

"Do you like him?" Piper continued.

"Yes, he's very nice." Elle winced at the word. While she liked these women, she wasn't sure if everything she said would be reported back to George.

"Do you trust him?" Piper asked.

"Of course she does," Libby said. "Otherwise he wouldn't be babysitting Toby."

Piper opened her mouth to ask another question.

"Piper, we didn't invite Elle with us to give her the third degree," Imogen said.

Piper smiled. "Sorry, it's the reporter in me."

"Libby, I want to hear every detail about this Hollywood deal," Imogen said.

"Oh, yes," Piper agreed.

Elle was relieved the spotlight was off her and she settled back to listen.

***

Two and a half hours later, Elle was pleasantly relaxed. Her head felt lighter than it had in a long time, she'd eaten the best meal of her life, drunk two glasses of a very nice wine and was enjoying the banter between the women who were obviously best of friends. She'd always wanted friends like these, someone she could tell secrets or talk with about all manner of odd things and have such unconditional support. She'd had a friend in high school, Melanie, who had been her best friend but when she'd met Dean, they'd grown apart. If she was honest with herself, she'd probably neglected the friendship in favor of this new man who had swept her off her feet.

She'd been so blind.

"So Imogen, how much longer are you going to wait before Chris moves in?" Piper asked.

Imogen screwed up her face. "I promised myself six months," she said. "It's only been six weeks."

"You do spend almost every night together anyway." Libby pointed out.

Imogen sighed. "I know. I thought I needed some time to get to know me, to sort my life out, and it turns out, I can't imagine my life without Chris in it."

"Honey, you're the most sorted-out person I know, next to Libby," Piper said. "You've got a great job with a boss you love, you've got a gorgeous house wanting to be filled with children, a family who adores you, and a boyfriend who loves you. All you need to do is work out what you want."

"I want him," Imogen said.

Perhaps it was the wine that had relaxed Elle enough to say, "Don't let Chris take over your life. You need to be allowed to do things you want to do. If you're too crazy in love, you'll lose yourself and regret it afterward."

The women all turned to her with different degrees of surprise on their faces. She'd said too much.

"Is that what happened with you and Toby's father?" Piper asked, her voice gentle.

Elle felt like a deer caught in headlights. She shouldn't have opened her mouth. She didn't want these people to know about the mess she'd made of her life.

"You don't have to talk about it if you don't want," Libby said. "But I know what it's like to have a bad relationship."

"We all do," Piper said.

They were so sincere. Would they judge her for her mistakes? She closed her eyes. What the hell – if they were going to judge her it was better she found out now.

"Dean swept me off my feet," Elle said. "I was eighteen and was working in a diner when I wasn't at college. He was a script writer who used to work at a table all day and he called me his muse." It had made her feel so special. "He was a few years older than me." She glanced at the women, hoping they would understand. Imogen squeezed her hand.

"I gave up college for him. He needed me around so he could write. I continued to work in the diner and he was convinced he would soon sell his script and I wouldn't have to work any more." She sighed. That was Dean's constant mantra: soon, soon, soon.

"When I moved in with him my parents weren't happy. Then I got pregnant." She squeezed her eyes shut. "I was nineteen and terrified. We had so little money, and Dean was getting frustrated by the lack of success with his scripts." Elle glanced at them, willing them to understand. "Dean wanted me to get an abortion and my parents told me I had to keep it."

Piper's voice was soft. "It must have been awful for you."

Elle nodded. "James was the only one who told me to do what was right for me."

"That's your brother?" Imogen asked.

"Yes." Elle sighed. "I thought a baby would bring Dean and me closer together so I chose to have Toby. When he was born, he suffered from colic a lot and used to keep me up all through the night. Dean was angry all the time but I thought it was because of the lack of sleep. He said we were moving to his parents' ranch in Texas and his mother could help, so we did."

"What about your parents?" Libby asked.

"I didn't tell them how bad it was. I knew they didn't approve of Dean and I wanted to show them I could do it on my own. My mom and I had the worst fight." Elle hadn't heard from her since.

"What happened when you got to Texas?" Piper asked.

"We moved into the old ranch house and Dean's mother helped out. When Toby screamed at night, I'd take him for a walk around the ranch yard until he stopped crying." She remembered those nights when she'd jump at any sound, thinking a coyote was going to attack her from the darkness. The noises of the ranch were strange – it was a whole different world from the city.

"It must have been difficult for you," Libby said.

Elle shrugged. It had been but she'd brought it on herself.

Piper sipped her wine. "Things didn't get any better, did they?"

Piper must be one hell of a reporter. "No. Dean resented being in Texas, he hated the way Toby dominated my attention and he never let me leave the ranch on my own." Elle's tongue felt so loose; she wanted to tell them everything. "We had no money of our own so everything came from his parents. Dean only ever passed along enough for things I needed, like diapers. He controlled everything I did."

Imogen hugged her. "Why didn't you call your parents?"

"They never replied to the letters I sent."

"That you know of," Piper said.

"George said the same thing," Elle admitted. "I need to find time to see what James is doing now. Maybe contact him."

"So how did you get to Houston?" Piper asked.

"I told Dean Toby had a fever and I needed to get him to the doctor. Dean was waiting for a phone call from an agent and Dean's mom was away on a spa trip with some friends. None of the men could get away from the ranch, so Dean let me take Toby on my own. When I got to town, I went to the hospital there and asked where the nearest women's shelter was. They gave me an address in Houston and I drove there. One of the shelter employees drove the car back to Brenham and left it there so Dean's parents could have it back, and so they didn't know where I'd gone."

"You had nothing with you?" Libby was incredulous.

"I had grocery money because I told Dean I needed a few things but that was it." She hadn't dared to ask for too much money.

"Toby wasn't sick?" Imogen asked.

"No. Dean was too distracted to check." It was the only time she'd been pleased about his lack of interest in his son.

"You're amazing," Libby said. "I can't believe you did all of it on your own. And now you've got your own business."

Elle shook her head. She wasn't anything special. "It's not been easy."

"Of course not," Piper agreed. "But you've got us and George now to help you out. Call if you need anything."

Elle was silent. She wanted to tell them she wasn't amazing, she'd just been desperate – desperation could fuel all sorts of things. Instead she said, "Thank you."

They sat in silence for a moment and then Libby asked, "Does anyone want dessert?"

That lightened the mood.

"I have to," Piper said. "The food was so fantastic I need to taste the desserts."

Elle laughed along, relief that they supported her making her giddy. They ordered dessert and by the time they were finished she wasn't sure she'd be able to walk out – someone might have to roll her.

"Will the chef come out so we can thank him?" Piper asked the waiter.

"No, but I'll pass on your thanks. He's real busy." The waiter smiled as he handed Libby's credit card back.

"Are you sure? I could pop into the kitchen and tell him."

The waiter grinned at the idea. "No one but staff are allowed in the kitchen."

Piper opened her mouth to argue, but Imogen spoke.

"Piper, we're going dancing. You can chase up the elusive chef later."

"All right." Piper was quick to agree, but Elle suspected she *would* pursue the chef later. Her interest had been whetted.

On the way out to the limousine, Elle checked the time and called George.

"How's it going?" she asked.

"Absolutely fantastic. Toby's in bed and I've cleaned up the mess."

There was giggling in the background. "Is that right? Is he asleep?"

"Ah, well you didn't say anything about sleeping. You just said he needed to be in bed at seven-thirty."

Elle swallowed her smile, sure he'd be able to hear it in her voice. "If Toby is grumpy tomorrow, I'll tell Harry to drop him off at your place and then you can deal with him."

"Actually I was going to ask you if I *could* have him

tomorrow," George said. "Dad's doing some renovation work on a house and Toby might get a kick out of helping. There are a couple of small things he could do while Dad and I do the bigger stuff."

Elle was speechless. He wanted to spend more time with her son? "What time?"

"We'll start at eight and finish mid-afternoon. I can drop him off at the shop at whatever time suits."

"Let me think about it," she said. "But if he is going, he needs his sleep."

"Sure. Have fun. Don't be home too early." George hung up.

Elle tucked her phone into her pocket, still shaking her head.

"Anything wrong?" Imogen asked.

"George wants to take Toby to do some work with his father tomorrow," Elle said.

"That's so sweet," Libby said.

"Hank's a sweetheart. He did most of the work on my house," Imogen said. "They'll both keep an eye on Toby."

"But why would he want to? Toby's my responsibility."

"George loves kids," Libby told her. "He often calls Kate and takes her on an adventure somewhere. Sometimes I think it's because he's a big kid himself and it gives him an excuse to go to all of the fun places, but it's always genuine."

"I'm worried Toby will get too attached to him," Elle said. She wasn't used to having help with Toby, wasn't used to having a male interested in either of them. Dean's brothers and father were generally too busy, though they did take him riding on occasion. And she wanted to be clear in her mind as to where she and George were going before he and Toby got too attached – though maybe she was too late.

"You do like George, don't you?" Piper asked.

"Yes."

"Then what you need is to spend some time with him without Toby. When's your next day off?"

"I don't know. I don't really take time off."

"Honey, you need some time for yourself. Is there someone at the shop who can take over for the day?"

Nora could handle managing the café during the week, no question, but George worked. Elle wasn't sure if Drew was reliable enough – and the weekends were so much busier too. "I could train someone."

"When you're ready, I can take Toby for the day. I'm sure he and Kate will have a great time together," Libby said.

"Then you and George can have some get-to-know-you time." Piper winked and Elle blushed.

She wasn't sure she was ready to take the next step, wasn't sure she wanted to have another man in her life, but she did want to spend more time with George.

So maybe she was ready.

***

It was after midnight when she let herself into her apartment. The living-room light was on and George was stretched out on the couch asleep.

A twinge of guilt hit Elle. She shouldn't have stayed out so late. George couldn't be comfortable there and it was obvious he was tired. She closed the door behind her and George stirred at the sound.

"George, I'm home," she said not too loudly, hoping she wouldn't startle him.

"The phrase is, Honey, I'm home." He opened his eyes, and smiled at her. "Do I get a welcome kiss?"

Perhaps he hadn't been sleeping after all. She hesitated, blushed at the intensity in his gaze and quickly moved through to the kitchen to put her keys and phone on the table.

George followed her in.

"Did Toby behave?" she asked, filling the kettle with water, more for something to do with her hands than from a desire for a drink.

"He was fantastic. He's got a great imagination."

Elle smiled. "He does." She turned around to find George right behind her. Her breath caught but he didn't move forward or away, letting her decide what to do. She put her hands on the counter behind her, hoping to seem casual. "What time did he go to sleep?"

"A little after you called." He had the grace to look bashful.

"Have you decided if he can come with me tomorrow?"

"Won't he get in your way?"

"Nah. Dad used to take us with him when we were his age. There's always stuff to do."

"OK. If you think it's safe. If he's interested, he can go."

"He is." George ran a hand through his hair. "He overheard me on the phone."

Elle couldn't prevent the smile. "Fine, but when he's grumpy from lack of sleep, you can't bring him back."

"Agreed." George stepped closer, so he was only inches away but not touching her. "Now we have that sorted, you owe me a kiss."

# Chapter 11

George didn't wait for her answer: he stepped in and took. The kiss was scalding and his arms came around her, drawing her closer, enveloping her.

Elle stiffened for a second with a momentary sensation of being trapped, before the kiss swept her away. She answered his kiss with the passion she'd had pent up since he found her in her towel earlier in the day.

He trailed kisses down her neck and his hand drew up to cup her breast. Elle gasped at the tenderness, and the pulse of her body as his thumb ran over her nipple. The heat burned through her despite the layers of clothing.

"George," she whispered and brought his mouth back to hers. She wanted to taste him, needed him to make her *feel*.

His fingers went to the buttons of her shirt and undid them. Elle ran her fingers through his hair as her shirt fell open.

His fingers brushed her bare skin – and reality kicked in.

She pushed him back. "No."

What the heck had she been thinking? She couldn't do this. She was in her kitchen with her five-year-old son just down the hallway. He could wake up and walk in, and find them like this.

Her heart beat heavily as she crossed her arms. "I can't. Not here. Toby's asleep."

George stepped back, his eyes apologetic. "Sorry, too fast."

He ran a hand over her arm, stepped forward and kissed her gently. "I got carried away."

Elle closed her eyes on the kiss. Her throbbing body wanted her to continue but she couldn't. It *was* all happening too fast. She needed to think things through, decide what she wanted. She'd only ever had sex with Dean. Letting someone else in was a huge step.

One she wasn't sure she was ready for.

"I just –" She wasn't sure how to explain.

George smiled. "You're amazing," he said as he stepped away. "We'll go as slowly as you need."

Elle stepped forward and kissed his cheek. "Thank you." It was a relief he understood.

"No problem."

Elle wanted him to stay a little longer but she had to be at work early in the morning. And she needed to slow things down. "You'd better head off. We both need our sleep, you more so if you have to keep up with Toby in the morning."

"Good point."

At the door Elle said, "Are you free next Sunday?"

"Yeah, I'll be back from California on Saturday."

She took a deep breath, preparing for rejection. "If I can get the day off, would you like to spend it with me?"

George's grinned rivaled the Grand Canyon. "I'd love to spend the day with you and Toby."

"Actually, Libby offered to take Toby for the day."

He raised an eyebrow. "Sounds like a treat." He kissed her. "I'll pick Toby up from the café at eight tomorrow."

"See you then."

Elle shut the door behind him and locked it. Then let out a sigh.

It had been an amazing night.

She'd had a fantastic time with three women who she hoped would become her friends.

Then she'd been kissed almost senseless by a man who made her feel good about herself, who made her laugh and made her want. And who understood that she wasn't ready for more.

Her life was definitely looking brighter.

She couldn't have asked for anything more.

***

George couldn't wait to meet Elle the next morning. Despite the late night, he was awake early, already thinking about what they could do on their day together the next weekend. He wanted to woo her and turn the day into something special.

At half-past seven he walked into the café. Elle was making coffee for the line of customers wanting a take-out and his heart gave a little jump. She looked tired, her eyes weren't quite as bright as normal, but still she was gorgeous. He joined the line so he could get some coffee for him and his dad. Toby must be in the back room playing.

When it was his turn at the counter, Elle blinked.

"Morning, Elle."

"George, I didn't see you come in." She brushed back a loose strand of hair from her face and then smoothed down the front of her apron.

"Can I get a couple of lattes to go?"

"Sure. Why don't you go and get Toby and I'll bring them in?"

George handed over some money and Elle waved it away.

"No, you can have coffee on the house since you'll be with Toby all day. You'll need the fuel."

"I'm not taking free coffee, Elle." She needed the money more than he did.

"No." She gave him a look that said she wasn't going to argue.

George frowned and then spotted the tip jar. He slipped the money inside. "All right."

Elle glared at him but he smiled and wandered back to where Toby was playing in the room.

Toby didn't notice him at first and George stood at the door. The kid was playing with his horse and cowboy as usual.

"Come on, Cowboy George, we've got cattle to rustle."

At first George thought Toby had spotted him but then he realized he had named the cowboy figure after him. He rubbed at the pang in his chest. The kid was a lot of fun to be around and such a sweetheart. He was really looking forward to teaching him today. One of his favorite memories was spending days helping his father on a renovation, wearing his hard hat and safety glasses and digging in the sand or swinging a hammer on some section to which his father had deemed he couldn't do any damage.

He hoped Toby would have as much fun.

"Howdy, pardner," he said.

Toby looked up and his face lighted up. "Howdy, George!" He jumped up and gave George a hug.

Seriously, how could anyone not adore the kid?

"You ready for a day of construction work?"

"Sure am. Are we going now?"

"Yep; your mom's just making me some coffee to go."

Elle walked in carrying a tray with three take-out cups, two large and one small. She handed them to George. "I made Toby a hot chocolate," she said. "Let me grab my car keys and you can take the car seat out."

"No need. Adrian had Kate's old one still sitting in the garage so I've got that. I checked it out to make sure it's still in good condition."

Elle gave him a look that he couldn't decipher.

"I hope that's all right?"

"Ah, should be. I'll come out and check."

George didn't mind. He knew some parents were more protective than others and Elle had every right to be after what she'd been through.

"Toby, put your things in this bag." Elle held open a small backpack and Toby put his horse and cowboy inside. After it was zipped up, she helped him put it on his back.

Together they walked out to where George had parked and Elle checked the carseat.

"Looks good." She strapped Toby in, showing George how it was done, and then stepped back. "Toby, you need to listen to George and his dad today, all right?"

"Yes, Mom." Toby answered in a sing-song voice.

George swallowed his grin.

Elle turned to him. "You've got my cell number and the number of the café. Call if you need anything."

"Sure will. Don't worry, he'll be fine."

"I know." Elle sighed.

George drew her close to him. "I'll take care of him." He gave in to his desire and kissed her, savoring the taste of Elle, before drawing back. "Do you want me to call you at midday?"

Elle blinked, and then shook her head. "No, not if everything's fine." She glanced back to the café. "I'd better get back." She said good-bye to Toby and left.

George climbed into the car and glanced at Toby in the rearview mirror. "Ready, kiddo?"

Toby nodded slowly, but his forehead was furrowed. George started the car and set off. "Everything all right?" Perhaps Toby was a little unsure about being taken to a strange place without his mother.

"You kissed Mom." It wasn't an accusation, merely a statement with a hint of a question behind it.

George wasn't quite sure how to handle it. "Yes, I did."

"Miranda says only people who love each other kiss, but Mom kissed Dad and she doesn't like him very much."

Hell, how could he respond? He had to tread very carefully here, and he hadn't had his coffee yet.

"People kiss for lots of reasons," George said, hoping Toby would leave it.

There was silence for a moment and then Toby asked, "So why did you kiss Mom?"

He used to laugh when Kate would be tenacious about something with her father or Adrian, but it wasn't so funny when he was in the firing line.

He kept it simple. "Because I like her."

Another pause and then a quiet voice. "Don't you like me?"

George coughed. "Of course I do. There are different types of kisses and the kiss I gave your mom is different from the kiss I'd give you." He was digging himself deeper.

Sure enough, Toby asked, "Why?"

How the hell was he supposed to explain it? Really it should be Elle who had this conversation with him. But it was his own fault for kissing her in front of Toby.

"Well, you often like people in different ways." He wished the house they were heading to wasn't so far away. "You like Miranda in a different way than you like your mom, right?" He hoped he was right.

"Sometimes I don't like Miranda at all. She steals my horse."

Relieved to be on a safer subject, George said, "That's exactly right."

Toby was quiet and George congratulated himself on handling it so well, when Toby spoke.

"Should I kiss Miranda on the mouth?" He sounded a little disgusted.

George choked back a laugh. "No, I don't think so. There's love for family, which can be different from love of friends, which is different from love of …" What word could he use? "… partners."

"We're partners, aren't we, George?"

Bad choice of word. "Not that kind of partner." He needed to use something Toby would understand. Glancing in the rearview mirror, he spied the horse in the boy's hand. "You know how a stallion and a mare react when they get put in the same pasture?"

"You mean when they act all silly and the stallion tries to ride the mare." Toby laughed. "He's too big to get on top of her."

George was thankful Toby didn't understand precisely what was going on there. "Yes, like that. That's another kind of like."

"So you want to ride Mom and that's why you kissed her on the mouth?"

George swallowed his groan. He was digging himself deeper and deeper. He hoped to hell, Toby wouldn't repeat this conversation to Elle. There was no way he'd be able to explain it.

"Kind of."

Toby nodded and glanced out of the window. "Are we almost there?"

Relieved Toby was satisfied, George said, "Another five minutes, kiddo."

***

They arrived at the house George's father was renovating a few minutes later. Hank's truck was parked in the drive and there was banging coming from inside the seventies brick building.

George helped Toby out of the car, grabbed the coffees and walked through the front door toward the sound. "We're here, Dad."

George's mom appeared from one of the side rooms. "Good morning, darling."

George hugged her. "I didn't realize you'd be here."

"I can't let your dad have all the fun." She spotted Toby, who was standing behind George's legs. "You must be Toby. My name's Marla." She held out a hand.

Toby took it and shook it slowly. "Howdy, ma'am."

"Why don't you come through to the back? I brought some things you might need."

George and Toby followed Marla through to the kitchen, where George's father, Hank, was in the process of demolishing a wall. There was a fair bit of dust and Toby coughed and watched wide-eyed as Hank swung the hammer.

Another portion of the wall tumbled down and Hank grunted in satisfaction before pulling down his dust mask and turning to them.

"Howdy, folks." He took off his gloves and turned to Toby. "My name's Hank."

Toby took Hank's outstretched hand and shook it. "I'm Toby."

"I hear you're going to be helping out today," Hank said. He turned to the kitchen bench where a small hard hat and a pair of safety glasses sat. George recognized them from his youth.

"The first rule of the job is to be safe." Hank took the hard hat from the table and placed it on Toby's head. Toby's eyes were solemn as he gently touched the helmet on his head.

"You need to protect your head, your eyes," he handed Toby the glasses, "and your hands." From the bag on the table he drew out a small pair of gloves.

"Yes, sir," Toby said, carefully taking the items he was handed.

George remembered the pride he'd felt when his dad had handed him his first safety gear. He'd thought he was a grown up.

"But before we get started, I see you've brought refreshments." Hank grabbed a coffee from the tray George held. "Let's head outside and go over the plan."

Toby turned to George, but his hands were full of glasses and gloves.

"You can put those things down outside and get your drink," George told him and followed his father outside.

The yard of the house was a decent size but needed a bit of tidying. There were a few tall trees and shrubs to prune and the garden beds, though a respectable size, were covered in weeds. From the branches of one tree, a swing hung ready to be played with. George recognized his father's work. Hank had probably hung it there when he'd heard Toby was coming.

They sat on the steps of the porch and George handed Toby his drink. Then Hank took them through the work he wanted to get done.

George noted Hank had chosen a couple of small projects for Toby to work on; they'd keep him busy and out of the way of the big stuff. When he got bored he could play with his horse or on the swing outside. George's jobs were all in the back of the house, so he'd be able to keep an eye on the kid even while he helped his dad.

They got to work after they'd finished their drinks.

Toby's first job was to sand a small chest of drawers so it could be repainted. George showed Toby what to do and made sure he was doing it correctly. Then he helped his father demolish the kitchen.

It was dusty, dirty work but George loved using his muscles to rip the cupboards down and discard them in the dumpster his father had hired.

He kept an eye on Toby, who was quite content to do his task, or watch what he and Hank were doing.

It was just before lunch that George first met Cranky Pants.

Toby was playing with a hammer, randomly hitting things that George had told him he could, when there was an almighty yell. As George turned the hammer fell to the floor, Toby clutched his thumb in his hand and started wailing.

It was inevitable something was going to happen but George wasn't worried. He had a trick up his sleeve that had worked on every child he'd seen get hurt, every time. Placing down his own hammer he made the sound of an ambulance siren wailing and hurried over.

"Let's see what we have here."

Toby paused for a second and then wailed louder.

Damn. The siren usually shocked the child long enough that they forgot about the pain and started laughing. "It's all right, Toby. Let me check it out."

Toby shook his head and held his hand closer to his body, his wails getting louder and louder.

Surprised, George tried his no-nonsense voice. "Toby-boy, I need to check where you're hurt."

He reached out to take the injured hand and Toby screamed, "I want my mom!"

George closed his hand over Toby's and Toby flinched away from him. "No, no, no!"

George didn't have a clue what to do. None of his usual tricks were working. Flustered, he glanced up at his father, who stood by watching, not trying to help. He was waiting for George's reaction.

"Toby, please let me have a look."

"I want my *mom!*" Each word got louder and louder.

Marla hurried into the room, took one look and whispered to George, "Poor thing is tired." She swooped down and scooped Toby into her arms, murmuring, "Let Miss Marla kiss it better. I bet that hurt, didn't it?"

Toby's sobs subsided somewhat and he nodded.

"I remember George hitting his thumb like you did and boy did he caterwaul." She jiggled him up and down and smothered his cheeks in kisses.

Toby sniffed and let her kiss his thumb better.

George breathed a sigh of relief. He didn't want to take a screaming Toby home to Elle. And he couldn't say she hadn't warned him. A tired Toby was a grumpy Toby and George had kept him up past his bedtime the previous night.

"How about we stop for lunch?" Marla said, still with Toby in her arms. "George, the cooler is in the front room. Wash up and then bring it out back. Hank, grab one of the drop sheets and we can use it as a blanket." She swept out of the room with Toby in her arms.

George shook his head and breathed a sigh of relief. "She's

amazing."

"She sure is. Had lots of practice with you kids," Hank told him. "Trick is not to get flustered."

George rolled his eyes. "Thanks, Dad."

They followed Marla out to the backyard and Hank spread out the drop sheet like a picnic blanket under the trees. Marla sat with Toby still on her lap while Hank and George unpacked the cooler. Toby was a lot calmer now and his eyes were heavy.

"Let's get some food into us," Marla said and gave Toby a chicken drumstick to eat. Toby munched away quite happily while they all ate and George surreptitiously checked his hand. There was the faintest bruise on Toby's thumb he'd have to explain to Elle when he took him back. He hoped she'd understand.

When they were finished eating, Marla said, "Toby, why don't you go on the swing with George while Hank and I pack up?"

Toby nodded and stood up, walking over to George.

"Sounds like a great idea, kiddo," George said as he glanced over Toby's head at his mother who mouthed the word gently and then tilted her head to the side with her hands under it like a pillow.

George nodded as he got to his feet and walked over to the swing. He sat down and then pulled Toby on to his lap.

"Did you enjoy lunch?" George asked as he settled Toby back against his chest and began gently swinging.

Toby nodded.

Not wanting to keep him awake, George stopped talking and kept up a smooth, steady rhythm as his parents packed up the lunch together. When they finished, Marla looked over and smiled. "He's asleep. Lay him down on the drop sheet and let him sleep. I'll do some pruning out here and keep an eye on him while you two make noise inside."

George carefully stood and lay Toby on the sheet. He barely stirred. "Are you sure?"

"Course I am. It will give me a bit of peace too, and he's such a sweet child."

George looked down at Toby sleeping peacefully, slight tearstains still on his cheeks. "He is."

"Elle has done a wonderful job raising him."

He nodded. His mother didn't know the half of it.

"I hope you have a lot of patience, Georgie-boy," she said. "I can tell that girl has been through a lot."

It never failed to surprise George how much his mother saw and understood. He really should be used to it by now.

"For Elle, I do."

"Good. Now go and help your father and I'll watch the little man." His mother made shooing motions.

George hugged her and kissed her cheek. "Thanks, Mom."

Knowing Toby couldn't be in better hands, he went to help his father.

***

By the end of the day, George was pleasantly tired, Toby was well rested and back in good spirits and they'd achieved everything Hank had wanted to.

After Toby had woken up, he'd been happy as a clam for the rest of the day. He'd helped Marla pull weeds in the garden and then planted the few flowers she'd brought with her.

Toby hugged Hank and Marla and waved before hopping into the car to be strapped in.

George's thoughts turned to Elle and on a whim he called the café.

"Everything all right?" Elle asked when she heard his voice.

"Fine. We're on our way back. I'm calling to ask if you and Toby want to have dinner with me tonight."

In the back seat Toby yelled, "Yes!"

Elle laughed. "Are you sure you're up for more Toby time?"

"Absolutely." And he definitely wanted more Elle time. "I could grab some stuff to grill on the way over, or I could take Toby straight home and you could meet us there."

"If you're happy to have Toby, how about I meet you at your place? It will save you having to come this way."

"Sure. See you when you get there."

He hung up and turned toward the grocery store. "What does your mom like to eat?" he asked Toby.

"Chocolate, but only for special occasions 'cause we can't afford it every day."

George made a mental note to send Elle chocolates during the week when he was in California. She deserved to have chocolate whenever she wanted it.

"What else?"

"We have spaghetti a lot. I like it with cheese."

"What about sausages and steak?"

"Yep, with ketchup or barbeque sauce."

George parked and helped Toby out of the car. He took the boy's hand and together they went into the shop. George grabbed a basket and they walked up and down the aisles adding not only items for dinner but also the things Toby wanted to try. George couldn't say no to the kid. He wanted to spoil him.

By the time they arrived home, it was only a half hour before Elle would arrive. George threw together a marinade and added the steaks and then put Toby to work chopping tomatoes for the salad.

"I'm a good cook," Toby announced as he added the tomatoes to the bowl. "Mom and Memah taught me how to chop right and said I was a big help."

"You are," George agreed as he whisked together a dressing for the salad, and then passed Toby some cucumber to slice.

"Mom will like us cooking. Sometimes when we get home she is too tired to cook so we have leftovers or she cooks eggs."

"Does it happen often?" George didn't like prying Toby for more information but he'd noticed how tired Elle was.

"Nah, just sometimes."

The doorbell rang.

"Is that Mom?" Toby asked.

"Let's go check." George dried his hands on a dish towel and headed to the door, anticipation stirring in his veins.

***

Elle waited at the door as Toby's excited chatter came nearer. She'd dashed home to change after work and had slipped on her one summer dress. Now she straightened out the non-existent creases.

George opened the door and smiled at her, full and welcoming. Her heart did a little dance.

"Hi."

"Hi, Mom. Wait till you hear what I did today." Toby's voice was high with excitement. He grabbed her hand and tugged her into the house.

"Where's my hug?" Elle asked.

Toby leaped at her and hugged her legs.

Elle grinned and hugged him back. She'd not seen him so relaxed in a long time.

"Kitchen's this way."

Elle followed Toby down the hallway while George shut the door behind them. Toby had already launched into the tale of his day as he climbed on to a stool to cut cucumber.

Elle was aware of George's presence in the room but she focused on her son.

"Then I hit my thumb with the hammer but Miss Marla kissed it better for me." He held out the offending digit.

Elle made a show of examining it. There was the slightest hint of a bruise but it didn't appear too bad. "I bet it hurt."

Toby shrugged. "Not much."

George coughed as incredulity crossed his face. Elle grinned. She'd have to get the story from him later.

"But it was a friendship kiss, not a stallion kiss," Toby continued.

George cringed and Elle asked, "What do you mean, 'stallion kiss'?"

"Nothing," George said quickly. "Can I get you a drink?"

"Something cold would be lovely," Elle said and took a seat next to Toby. George hurried to make the drink, his movements jerky. There was something going on between the two of them.

"What's a stallion kiss, Toby?" she asked.

Toby concentrated on cutting cucumber as he spoke. "You know, Mom. There are different kisses depending on how you like people. There are friend kisses and family kisses and then there's stallion kisses. Like you and George. George explained it to me today."

Elle glanced up at George's pained expression and pushed further. "How about you explain it to me?"

"George wants to ride you like a stallion rides a mare," Toby said simply.

# Chapter 12

Elle's mouth dropped opened and George put up both hands facing outward.

"Hang on a second, that's not what I said."

"I hope not." She swallowed the laughter that was bubbling up inside. George was absolutely horrified, his face the color of radishes, and it was obvious Toby had misunderstood something.

Toby was oblivious to the stir he'd caused as he continued to chop his cucumber. "Stallions and mares like each other in a different way, like you and George," he explained. "You know when the stallion goes all funny and tries to ride the mare?" He glanced up then to check if she understood.

Elle had a suspicion of what was going on, but she looked at George for clarification.

"It kind of got lost in translation." George was mortified.

"So it seems. Do you want to translate for me?" She was trying her very best to stay serious because she'd never seen George in such a tither.

"Toby asked why I kissed you and I said you were my friend and then he asked if he and I were friends because we'd never kissed and I had to explain there were different types of likes and different kinds of kisses ..." He trailed off.

"So you compared our kind of like to horses?"

"I thought he'd understand. He made the connection between the 'riding'. I didn't realize he'd seen that." He squirmed.

He was so awkward and gorgeous standing there, pleading for her to understand. Elle couldn't hold it in any longer. She lost control of the laughter and it poured out of her, making her sides hurt.

The pure relief on George's face made her laugh even harder. She held her sides and shook her head when Toby asked her what was so funny.

George put a glass of iced tea in front of her and grumbled, "I'm glad you find it so funny."

Elle could imagine him explaining things to Toby. She knew a little of how Toby's mind worked and how he could jump to the strangest conclusions with his child's logic. She gasped for breath and slowly got the hilarity under control. She sipped her drink and calmed herself further.

"You're going to have to tell me the whole story later," she said to George.

He grimaced and nodded. "I'm going to start the grill."

Toby had finished chopping his cucumber so he and Elle joined George out the back. The backyard was as well tended as the front had been. There were a couple of large trees, one full of magnolia blossoms and the other with a swing underneath.

"Can I use the swing, George?" Toby asked.

"Sure, kiddo."

Toby raced over and, after a couple of attempts, managed to jump up into the seat. Then with a bit of effort, he started to swing.

Elle turned back to George. "So you got some tough questions today?"

George looked pained. "I'd hoped he'd forgotten about our conversation."

"I bet you did." She giggled.

"How the hell was I supposed to explain the difference between friendship and ..." He waved his hand between the two of them. "... this?"

"So you used horses."

"He'd been talking about stallions and mares when he

explained about foaling and while I knew he didn't quite understand what he was talking about, I thought he'd get the concept."

Elle decided to stop teasing him. He was obviously embarrassed enough. "Do I get my stallion kiss now?" she asked.

The grin flashed over George's face and he swooped her up with one hand, pulling her close. "Sure."

He kissed her hard and fast – not nearly long enough for Elle's liking, but it made her insides melt. She'd have to make do with that until later, because Toby's eagle eyes were watching them from the swing.

She stepped back and said, "So what about the thumb?"

George groaned as he turned the sausages on the grill. "Cranky Pants made an appearance."

Elle laughed again. "Told you so."

"I'm going to listen to your instructions in future," George promised. "He was screaming and I couldn't get through to him, but Mom swept in and soothed him without a problem. She said he was tired and after lunch he fell asleep in my arms."

Elle smiled at the image. "You've had a busy day."

George shook his head. "I don't know how you do it every day. I have no idea how my mother managed to raise so many."

"When you love them it's not as hard."

George made no comment, but removed the meat from the grill. "Dinner's ready," he called to Toby.

Toby jumped off the swing and ran across the lawn to them.

George placed the plate on the patio table. "We can eat out here. I'll grab the rest of the things."

Elle went to help but he stopped her.

"Take a seat. You've been on your feet all day."

So had he, but she did as he asked. It was nice to be waited on for a change. On the ranch she'd always waited on Dean and helped Lindsay cook the meals. After she left, there was only her to prepare the food.

In no time at all, George had brought out the salads and served Toby, cutting up his meat so he could eat it more easily. All Elle had to do was serve herself. After the long week she'd had, she appreciated it.

Perhaps that was the reason the food tasted so good. The meat melted in her mouth and the dressing on the salad had a lovely sharpness to it.

"This is fantastic," Elle told George.

"Thanks. I got the dressing recipe from the chef at the Wooden Spoon."

Elle eyed him. "Libby said you'd met him, but we were told he doesn't like to talk to patrons."

George grinned. "I didn't give him a choice. Plus it helps his brother is one of my artists."

"Really? Did you give me some of his music?"

"Yeah, he's booked to do a gig at your café next week."

"Great. Maybe the chef will come and I can thank him for the amazing meal we had there last night."

"Is that where you went?" George asked.

Elle blushed as she remembered they hadn't exactly spoken about her night when she arrived home. "Yes. Libby's treat. She was celebrating her new contract."

"It's great, isn't it? Adrian told me about it and the option."

Elle nodded and took a sip of her tea.

"George, can we play Go Fish after dinner?" Toby asked.

"Sure. Can you remember how?"

"Yep. Kate taught me good."

"Well," Elle corrected him.

"I'll teach you, Mom," Toby said.

They cleared the dishes and George found a pack of cards. After he'd dealt, they settled in to play a few rounds of Go Fish.

They slowed the game down for Toby, who took time examining each card to check if he had it. Inevitably he beat them at each game, though George gave him a run for his money a couple of times.

When Toby started yawning, Elle checked the time and said, "We should get going."

"Aw, Mom. Do we have to?"

"Yes. You had a late night last night."

Toby pouted but George smiled and got to his feet.

"I'm heading to California tomorrow but I'll call. I'll be home some time on Saturday."

Elle had forgotten he had to fly out for work. "I'm sorry.

Gosh, you probably still have to pack. We shouldn't have stayed so long."

George caressed her arms. "It's fine. It takes me about ten minutes to pack. I'll be done before you get home." His hands were warm and they slid down to take her hand. "I'll walk you out."

At the car, after Elle had strapped Toby in, George leaned in and gave him a loud kiss on the cheek. "See you later, Toby-boy."

"Bye, George. Thanks for having me today."

Elle smiled, pleased he'd remembered his manners.

George shut the car door and turned to Elle. "Brace yourself," he said. "It's stallion-kiss time."

Elle's smile was captured by his mouth and the kiss stole her breath. It was gentle, as though he were sweetly tasting her mouth, and she opened herself to him, letting herself feel.

Then he stepped back. "I'm going to miss you this week," he said, his voice quiet.

There was something in the way he said it that made Elle believe him. And she knew she'd miss him as well.

"Thank you for taking care of Toby today," she said.

"My pleasure. I'll take him whenever I can."

Elle couldn't quite believe she'd got so lucky. She got into the car and drove away.

***

The next morning Elle had her first meeting with the lawyer, Victoria, who Chris had recommended.

Elle liked her immediately. She was in her early thirties and had auburn hair and a bright purple suit that told people she was there to make waves. Elle needed a person like Victoria in her corner.

After Elle sat in the plush armchair across from Victoria, the lawyer said, "Tell me about your situation."

Elle put the box containing her diaries and photographs on the coffee table between them. "I need to make sure my ex doesn't get custody of our child," she said, cutting straight to the chase.

"A child has a right to at least see his or her father in most

151

cases," Victoria replied. "Why don't you tell me about your case?"

Elle nodded and proceeded to tell Victoria about how she met Dean, how he hadn't wanted Toby and then about the abuse she'd suffered. "Dean has never been affectionate with Toby and has never wanted to spend time with him."

"Why would he ask for custody then?"

"To have access to me." It sounded self-absorbed, so Elle explained. "He's convinced I'm his muse and that he can't write without me being around."

"You've got a restraining order. That means either someone would have to take Toby to Dean, or one of Dean's family would need to pick him up from you."

Elle nodded. "His parents love Toby and I hate to keep them apart, but I'm scared of what Dean would do. His mother, Lindsay, thinks he can do no wrong, but his father, Martin, is more sensible."

"Maybe we can make it a condition of his access – Martin must be present."

"I'd be happier with that." Though the idea of Dean being with Toby still didn't sit well with her.

"What about child support?" Victoria asked.

"Nothing. I don't want anything from him." Elle was certain. "He doesn't earn any money of his own anyway and taking money from his family would only tie me to him."

Victoria made a note. "I have all the information I need right now. I'll be in touch by the end of the week."

Elle stood, shook her hand and walked out into the lobby, feeling much more confident than she had in a long time. She had an hour before she had to be back at the café. Maybe she should drop by the library and research her family; she'd wanted to check out what James had been up to for over a week now – she wasn't ready to contact him, but knowing something about him was a step closer. If she went back to work she wouldn't get a chance or have any privacy.

She asked the receptionist where the nearest library was and drove over, familiar nerves starting to hum along her skin.

Luckily there was a computer available when she arrived. She gave the librarian her details and started searching.

First she checked her social media accounts. The first one wouldn't work but she could log in to the second one. She clicked on her friends list and found James. Holding her breath she clicked on his link.

His page was full of pictures and updates. Elle smiled at one photo of him goofing off in front of the camera. He was like that – a real dork.

She read through the updates. It sounded like he was happy at work, his social life was very active and he had dinner regularly with their parents. As she read, a new update came through.

*Got back from a week of backpacking and found an interesting email waiting for me. Need to follow it up ASAP.*

Elle panicked, remembering people could see who was online at the same time, and logged off. She took a deep breath as the login screen reappeared. She hadn't had a chance to scroll back to read what he'd written when she'd first left with Dean. Whether he'd been worried or asked others if they knew where she was. Perhaps he wouldn't have even written something like that in a public forum. She didn't know.

The question was, was she brave enough to contact him? Was she willing to risk rejection a second time if her brother wanted nothing to do with her? Was she strong enough?

The time at the bottom of the screen caught her eye. Whatever she decided, she didn't have time now. She needed to get back to work.

***

George sat backstage and monitored how Ophelia was doing on the talk show. She'd performed her single and had sounded amazing, but now it was time for the interview and, despite the training he'd given her, he wasn't sure how it would go.

He needn't have worried so much. Ophelia charmed the host, smiled for the audience and generally sold herself perfectly. As her segment ended, George breathed a sigh of relief.

When his phone vibrated, he answered it, seeing it was a private number.

"George, this is James Carter. I received an email from you

today saying you have information about my sister, Elle."

George sat down on the couch. He'd given up on getting an answer. "I sent that a week ago."

"I've been away."

He didn't know where to begin. "How do I know you're Elle's brother?"

"How do I know you really know her?" James countered, and then he sighed. "My sister has been out of touch with us for five years. I'm desperate to find out if she's all right."

"She is now," George said.

"Meaning she hasn't been in the past?"

George hesitated. "It's not up to me to tell her story. I wanted to find out whether her family wants to meet with her or if they disowned her when she left."

"We didn't disown her. She never responded to our attempts to stay in touch."

"She didn't get them," George told him.

"What?" James sounded shocked.

"I'm in LA at the moment. Your website said you live in the area. Perhaps it would be best if we meet."

"I'm free tonight at six. Name the place."

George told James where he was staying and hung up.

He stared at the phone for a minute longer. He'd been right about Dean. The asshole had kept Elle's family from her. But he'd wait until he'd spoken to James before he called Elle to tell her. He didn't want to get her hopes up.

Ophelia walked into the green room. "How did I go?"

"Great." George put aside his personal business and focused on Ophelia.

***

It was Tuesday before George called from California, but he had had the most decadent basket of chocolates delivered to her at the café on Monday.

The phone rang after Elle had put Toby to bed and had settled on the couch with a cup of tea and a book.

"Miss me yet?" George's voice asked when she answered.

Elle smiled and snuggled down on the couch. "Toby's been asking when he can see you again."

154

"And what about Toby's mother?"

"She knows you'll be back on Saturday." Elle chuckled at his growl of exasperation. "You have crossed my mind a few times since you've been gone." Then she added, "Thank you for the chocolates. You didn't need to do that."

"I hope there's something there that appeals. Toby mentioned you liked chocolate," George said.

"There's plenty to choose from. How's your trip going?"

"Really great. Ophelia is wowing everyone she meets."

They hadn't spoken much about George's work and Elle knew very little about what he did. "Tell me about her. What's the purpose of the trip?"

"Exposure," George said. "She's released a single and with her voice she could be big. I need to make sure people can find her, know who she is and buy her music. She's got a bunch of radio interviews and a couple of television appearances."

Elle knew more about the film industry than the music industry but she guessed getting air and screen time wouldn't be easy. "I'll have to keep my ear out on the radio. What's her song called?"

"'Once Upon A Time'. It's a soulful diva song. She can do amazing runs, especially for her age." George's voice was full of praise and Elle felt a twinge of jealousy.

"How old is she?"

"Eighteen, and believes she's entitled to everything, but she's been well behaved so far."

Elle relaxed. He didn't seem the least bit interested in Ophelia as anything but a client.

"There's a great restaurant you should try while you're there – Chuck's. I used to love eating there," Elle told him. As a child, when it had been her turn to choose where they went for dinner, she always chose Chuck's. It was quirky and had great burgers.

"Funny you should say that: I went there last night."

"Oh, did someone recommend it? It's off the beaten track."

George was quiet for a moment. "Your brother took me there."

Elle frowned. She couldn't have heard right. "What did you say?"

"I met your brother James last night. He took me there." George's voice was calm.

Elle's mouth dropped open and her skin erupted in goose bumps. "What? How?" This couldn't be right. George didn't know James.

"When we spoke last week about how Dean may have kept correspondence from you, I did a bit of research. I emailed the person I thought was your brother and he called me yesterday."

Fear, anger and hope warred inside her. She latched on to the easiest one to deal with. Anger.

"Why would you do that? I told you I'd get in touch when I was ready."

"I wanted to help." George's tone was cautious and a little surprised.

"No, you wanted to take control. You wanted to do what suited you and ignore what *I* wanted." She couldn't think rationally. What if James didn't want to get in touch with her? Her fear was suddenly too great to overcome.

"I'm sorry, Elle. I didn't think you'd be upset."

Had he really considered her feelings? No, just like the park, he'd done what he'd thought was best. "You should have known. I need to go." She hung up, her heart pounding and adrenaline pumping through her body. What had James said? She stood up, walked a few steps away and then turned back, reaching for the phone.

She stopped herself. No, she didn't want to know what George and James had discussed. It was between them. She would contact her brother when she was good and ready.

And not because George thought she should.

The phone rang. Elle checked the caller ID – George – and grabbed a cushion to put over the phone so the ringing didn't wake Toby. She wasn't going to answer it. She didn't want to talk to him.

What right did he have to search for her family? What right did he have to contact them, talk to them about her? Who knew what he told James? Had George told him about all of her failures? It wasn't right. She didn't want a man in her life who thought he knew better than she did, who made decisions for her without consultation. Damn it, she'd had that with Dean.

Were all men the same? Did they all believe they knew what was best or did she just attract that type?

She needed to make it clear to George she wouldn't stand for it. She wanted control of her own life, wanted to make her own decisions and wanted to make her own mistakes. Now he'd basically forced her hand. If he'd told James where she was, or given him her phone number, then James might contact her. And if he didn't, was it because he didn't want to talk to her or because George hadn't given him her details?

Damn.

She hated this. Hated not knowing what had been said, hated having the choice taken out of her hands. She'd been so close to contacting James on her own terms today.

Damn George.

Elle sighed and flopped on to the couch, putting her head in her hands. She took a couple of deep breaths, trying to calm herself down.

What was she getting so worked up about?

What was done was done. She had to decide what she wanted to do next.

Should she ask George what James had said?

No, that was the coward's way. Whether James wanted to see her or not, Elle had the right to have her own say as well.

So it meant calling him, if he still had the same cell number, or contacting him on social media.

She dug her phone out from under the cushion and stared at it for a long time. It would be easier to send a message via social media, less confronting.

She took a deep breath and dialed James's cell phone.

"James here." She smiled at the way he'd always answered the phone. His voice sounded the same and her eyes filled with tears.

"Hello?"

"James, it's Elle," she said quietly. She held her breath waiting for his response.

"Ellie? Oh my God, it's so good to hear your voice. Did George convince you to finally call?"

Elle scowled. "George has nothing to do with this. I don't know what you discussed and I don't want to know."

James chuckled – not the response Elle was expecting. "I've missed that ticked-off tone of yours. What did George do? I liked him."

"It doesn't matter." She didn't want to talk about George. "How are you?"

"I'm great but I've missed my baby sister like crazy. Tell me what you've been up to."

Elle was silent. "Where to start? How are Mom and Dad?"

"They're all right. They miss you too."

"Then why didn't anyone call?" Elle asked, unable to keep the sadness out of her tone.

"We tried. For six months we tried to call, email, write, but we never got any response. Dad and I even took a trip to Texas but the address wasn't right and no one knew of a Marshall family in the area. Then we got a letter from you saying you were happy and didn't want a family who didn't love Dean."

Marshall was Dean's pen name. She hadn't even realized it wasn't his real surname until she arrived at the ranch and discovered it was actually Williams. No wonder they hadn't found her. "I didn't send any letter."

"I guessed as much after talking to George. It was typed."

It had to have been Dean.

"Ellie, did he treat you badly?" James's words were cautious.

"Not at first." She didn't want to talk about it over the phone. She wanted to see her brother so badly, have one of his enveloping hugs. "And I have a beautiful son, Toby, because of him."

"Tell me about him." He sounded excited. "What is he? Five?"

Elle smiled. Her brother was never very good with dates, especially birthdays. "George told you how old Toby is, didn't he?"

There was a pause and then a guilty, "Yes. He sounds like a great kid. I can't wait to meet him. I've just got back from a vacation, but I could fly down on Friday evening, see you on Saturday. I've got to be back Sunday morning though."

"You don't need to do that. It'll be expensive to fly down for a day."

"I want to. I want to make sure you're all right."

Elle closed her eyes. She would like it, very much. "I'd love to see you, but I can't take any time out from work. My café has only been open a short time."

"I could help out, hang out, get to know Toby."

"That would be great. You could stay with me though I only have a spare couch. There might be a hotel somewhere nearby."

"A couch is good. Are you going to call Mom and Dad?"

Elle hesitated. Her relationship with her mom had been rocky before she'd left. "Do they want to hear from me?"

"Absolutely. We often talk about you and they always say a prayer for you at Thanksgiving and Christmas."

Elle closed her eyes. "I'll call them."

"Great. I'll let you know my flight details. Love you, Ellie."

"Love you, Jamie."

Elle hung up the phone and burst into tears.

She'd got her brother back.

***

George listened to the dial tone after Elle hung up. It was not the reaction he'd been expecting. He'd thought she'd be pleased, would want to find out James missed her and wanted to see her.

He'd thought wrong.

He redialed her number but she didn't answer.

Hell, somehow he'd messed up.

His cell rang and he answered it immediately, hoping it would be Elle.

"Hiya, Georgie-boy. How's California treating you?" It was Isla.

"Fine." He couldn't summon up his usual enthusiasm for talking to her.

"Well I don't believe you at all. What's up?"

"I don't understand women," he grumbled.

"No man can," she said. "Is Ophelia giving you trouble?"

"No, Elle."

Isla laughed. "What did you do?"

George was instantly defensive. "Why do you think it was my fault?"

"Because I know you, big brother. Now spill."

George grumbled but said, "All I did was arrange to meet

her brother yesterday."

"This is the brother she hasn't had any contact with for the past five years, right? You said something about her ex maybe keeping their correspondence from getting to Elle."

"That's right. I did an internet search, found a possible candidate and emailed him. He called me yesterday and we got together for a chat. When I told Elle, she got angry."

"Of course she did, Galahad. Did you not listen to anything I said last week?" Isla's frustration was clear in her voice.

"Aren't you supposed to be on my side?" he asked, annoyed.

"Not when you're wrong."

George couldn't prevent a smile. One of the things he loved about his sisters was they always told him straight. "So what was so wrong about contacting her family?"

"Did she ask you to?"

"No."

"Did she want to get in contact with them?"

"It was obvious from her tone that she missed them."

"Not the same thing." Isla sighed. "George, from what you've told me, Elle's spent the last five years with a man who controlled everything she did. Don't you think she'd want to take control of her own life from now on?"

"But I was trying to help."

"Perhaps her ex thought the same thing."

The reality of the situation struck him then. He had taken control of the decision to contact Elle's family. No wonder she was mad at him.

"When did you get so smart?" he asked his sister.

"I was born this way," Isla replied. "So tell me which celebrities you've spotted so far."

George laughed and regaled his sister with tales, while in the back of his mind he wondered how he could make it up to Elle.

# Chapter 13

Elle glanced up as the café door opened and then gaped as the biggest bunch of flowers she'd ever seen was carried in by a deliveryman.

"Delivery for Elle Carter," he said.

Elle came out from behind the counter and said, "That's me."

He handed over the flowers and she tipped him, then dug in to the middle of the bunch for a card to find out who they were from.

The card simply read:

*I'm sorry.*

*G*

Elle smiled. She couldn't stay mad at him. After she'd calmed down she realized he'd done it with the best of intentions and in the end everything had worked out. But she would make sure he understood why she'd been so angry, so he didn't do it again. She needed to make her own choices. She needed to be in control.

She carried the flowers into the kitchen and found a bucket for them to sit in out of the way. She'd take them home tonight and put them on her coffee table.

Elle sighed.

It had been an emotional twenty-four hours, what with her

argument with George and her reconnection with James. She couldn't wait to see her brother at the end of the week.

Her conversation with her mother had been as draining as she'd expected. They had always been such different people, and when Elle was younger she'd usually gone along with what her mother wanted to keep the peace. There'd only been two occasions when Elle had openly defied her, and one of those was Dean. Her mother was entitled to say I told you so. She *had* been right about him.

But through the whole conversation Elle could hear the relief in her mother's voice, the lift in her tone that said she was thrilled Elle had called. Unlike James, she couldn't get the time off to come to Houston straight away. Not that Elle minded. She didn't expect them to jump, just because she'd finally got into contact with them.

She hadn't had a chance to speak with her father yet as he'd been at work when she called. She would call again to speak with him as soon as she got Toby to sleep that night.

A yell from the front had Elle returning to the present. She had work to do.

***

That night, when Toby was in bed and asleep, Elle made a cup of tea and sat on the couch with a sigh. She checked the time and dialed her parents' number.

Her father answered after the first ring.

"Ellie, I'm so glad you called," he said.

Elle smiled as her heart swelled to bursting. It had been so long since she'd heard his voice. She hadn't realized she'd missed him so much. Suddenly it was difficult to talk.

Taking a breath, she kept her voice light. "How have you been?"

"Oh, same as always." Her father was so matter of fact. Nothing fazed him. "We've almost wrapped the new film."

"Is it any good?"

"This one's fantastic," he said. "Your Toby will be old enough to watch it."

"I'll have to take him when it comes out," Elle said. She'd been looking forward to the day she could take Toby to see her father's animation work.

They chatted for a while more about inconsequential things before her father asked, "Have you left Dean for good?"

The question took Elle by surprise, but then she grinned. It was her father's habit to lull her by talking about everyday things, before throwing in what he really wanted to know. She'd forgotten.

"Yes. About six months ago. I'm not going back."

"Your mother said something about you having a bookshop café?"

"It's only been open a few weeks, but it's doing well."

"Do you need any money?"

"No. I'm managing fine." It was the truth and she wouldn't take money from her parents anyway.

"You call me if I can do anything for you," he said. "I've got another few weeks of this project and then I'm due for some time off. I'd like to fly down to visit."

He didn't include her mother in the offer but she was fine with that. "I would love you to, but only if you don't have any other plans."

"Nothing as important as you."

The tears welled in her eyes. "Thank you, Dad." She managed to get the words past the lump in her throat.

"I'll call again soon," he said and hung up.

Elle disconnected and sat for a while. She'd missed her father. Missed his quiet strength and support.

She wiped away her tears and checked the time. It was still early in California and she should really call George to thank him for the flowers, though it felt rather awkward to call him after she'd yelled and hung up on him the night before.

She sighed. She needed to ignore her pride and do the right thing. She dialed his number and he answered it almost immediately.

"Elle." There was definite relief in his tone.

She should have called sooner. "Thank you for the flowers," she said.

"It was the least I could do. I made a mess of things. I'm sorry."

Elle shook her head. "I overreacted. It was a lovely gesture, but I needed to do it in my own time. I was scared."

"I understand now."

"Talk to me in future. Don't assume you know what's best for me. I can't stand it."

"Of course." Then he swore. "Hell, if we're being honest, there's something else you should know."

Elle frowned. "What?"

"Please don't get mad." He was prevaricating.

"George."

He sighed. "It's about the family lawyer dealing with your case – Victoria."

"What about her?" Anxiety began to crawl over her skin. Was he going to tell her Victoria had been disbarred, or that she wasn't really a family lawyer?

"Imogen and I are paying her bill."

"No, she's doing it pro bono," Elle said.

"She *does* pro bono work, but she had a full case load. We wanted you to have the best so we decided to pay her bill ourselves."

Elle stared at the coffee table. Was she some kind of charity case now? "How much?" she said, her tone flat.

"That doesn't matter."

"It does to me. How much?" She wasn't sure how long it would take her to pay them back but she would do it.

He named a figure and her jaw dropped.

"I'll work out a payment plan," she said.

George hissed in frustration. "You don't need to. We're doing it because we care about you and Toby. We don't want Dean to come anywhere near you. We don't want anything from you but your safety."

"It's still my problem. I got myself into the mess."

"Sure, you chose Dean. You were young and naïve and the asshole hid his real side from you until you were trapped. If you'd known what he was really like, you wouldn't have gone with him, would you?"

"Of course not."

"Then stop blaming yourself. You have friends now who want to help, you're not alone, you don't have to do it all yourself."

His words made her stop. He was right. She *wasn't* alone any more. In the space of a few weeks she'd reconnected with her family and found some wonderful friends who had helped her out time and time again without wanting anything in return.

She wasn't used to it.

For so long she'd had to rely on herself for everything. She'd always felt obligated to pay back any money they'd taken from Lindsay and Martin, not in cash but in work. She regularly cleaned the ranch house or fed the chickens and collected the eggs. She'd even spent time grooming the horses, mucking out their stalls and feeding them.

All while Dean wrote his next unsellable masterpiece.

She wasn't used to taking something for nothing.

"Are you still there, Elle?" George's voice in her ear brought her back to the present.

"Yes. It's a lot of money."

"Not to me and not to Imogen. We want to help."

Dare she just say "thank you"? What if George used it to ask for more than she could give?

Even as she had the thought she dismissed it. George wasn't like that.

She sighed. "Thank you."

"You're not mad?"

Was she? "No. Surprised, uncertain, but not mad."

"Good." His relief was clear.

"I called my brother after we spoke yesterday," she said.

"Great! What did he say?"

"You already know what his reaction was. You spoke to him yourself."

"Right." The bashfulness was back. "When's he going to Houston?"

"He's going to try to get a flight Friday night."

"Wow. That's fantastic. How are you feeling?"

"Overwhelmed. A little uncertain. It's happening so fast." She ran a hand through her hair.

George's tone turned compassionate. "I can only imagine. I wish I was there so I could give you a hug."

"So do I." It was true.

"I'll be back in a couple of days. Are we still on for

Sunday?"

"I'm not sure. It depends on when James flies out."

"Perhaps we can do something all together. I'm easy."

He sounded it as well. He didn't seem disgruntled that their first solo day together might be hijacked by family.

"I've got to run. I have a dinner meeting in ten. I'll call you tomorrow."

Elle hung up and smiled. Maybe they could all do something. She hadn't been to the movies since she lived in California and Toby had never been. She stood and went into the kitchen to go through the community newspaper that had been delivered earlier. It usually had a movie section in it. If there were a children's movie showing, she was sure Toby would get a kick out of it.

There were a couple to choose from and after reviewing the synopses she narrowed it down to one.

A knock on the door had her frowning. It was late for someone to visit. Perhaps Nora needed something.

Elle checked through the peephole and frowned. She opened the door to find Chris and Imogen on her doorstep. "Hi."

Chris grinned at her, and shuffled his feet. "Hi. Today I'm playing the stand-in for George. Imogen is here so you don't freak out. I'm under orders to give you a hug."

Elle stared at him for a second while what Chris said computed, and then she laughed. "He didn't call you," she protested.

"He did," Chris confirmed. "I'm under strict instructions not to enjoy it though."

Elle shook her head. George never ceased to surprise her. She opened her arms. "All right then."

Chris stepped forward and gave her a big hug. It wasn't anywhere near the same as how she felt with George's arms around her but it was nice nonetheless.

When Chris stepped back, Imogen stepped forward. "I need to apologize. I shouldn't have paid for the lawyer without asking you first. I was so angry when you came home with those bruises I had to do something."

"I appreciate the gesture," Elle told her. "As long as you're sure you can afford it."

"I can," Imogen said. "It's my turn for a hug now."

Elle hugged her friend. "Thank you."

"You're welcome." Imogen glanced at Chris. "We should go and let you get some sleep."

Elle closed the door and locked it. She smiled and picked up her cell. The text message she sent to George said *Thank you.*

A minute later came the response. *You're welcome. As long as you didn't like it too much.*

She chuckled and went to sleep, still thinking of George.

Chapter 14

After dinner on Friday, Elle put Toby into the car to drive to the airport to pick up James. Toby was a bouncing bundle of excitement, more to do with seeing the airplanes than meeting a new uncle.

James was only staying twenty-four hours, flying back Saturday night, and she wanted to make the most of their time together. She'd tried to arrange the whole day off work, but her other waitresses had plans.

They arrived in time to watch a couple of planes land and then Elle took Toby to the arrivals section to wait for her brother. When the passengers began to walk through, Elle scanned the faces of each one, her chest tight.

Then she spotted him.

Elle stood where she was and examined her brother. He looked a little older than he had, wore a designer stubble beard and his usual board shorts and top.

He smiled as he walked up to her. "Don't I get a hug, Ellie?" he asked, a little uncertain.

Elle launched herself at him and flung her arms around his neck, and he picked her up and swung her around. Elle's eyes filled with tears as he put her down again.

"It's so good to see you," she whispered.

"That's my line," he said.

"Mom. Are you all right?" Toby's voice was worried, next to her.

"Of course I am."

"But you're crying." He stared accusingly at his uncle.

"Happy tears, Toby-boy. I haven't seen my big brother in a long time."

Toby screwed up his face in a frown.

"Toby, this is your Uncle James."

James crouched down to Toby's level. "Pleased to meet you," he said holding out his hand.

Toby shook it. "You can't make Mom cry again," he said, his voice cross.

James laughed. "I'll do my best not to."

On the drive back to the apartment, they chatted about James's work and the flight. When they arrived home, Toby was asleep in his car seat. Elle woke him up to get him inside and into bed, where he promptly fell back asleep.

She hurried back to the living room where her brother was standing, examining the place.

Elle prided herself on keeping her little furnished apartment clean and tidy, but nothing could change the fact all the furniture was old and worn. She had saved a lot of money not having to buy everything herself – in fact if she'd had to, they'd be living on cardboard boxes and the floor.

"Can I get you a drink?" she asked.

"Got any beer?"

Elle shook her head. "I don't drink much. Tea, coffee, juice."

"Coffee would be great." He followed her into the kitchen and sat at the table, making himself at home. Elle still couldn't quite comprehend that her big brother was in Houston with her.

She made the coffee and sat down next to him.

"Have you lived here long?" he asked.

"Since I left the shelter," Elle replied.

Her brother put his mug down with a bang, slopping coffee over the sides, and stared at her, horrified. "What shelter?"

Elle swallowed. She hadn't meant to mention that. Briefly she debated making something up, but she knew James would push until she told him the truth.

"When I left Dean I had no money. Toby and I had to stay in a women's shelter until I could find a job bussing tables and earn enough to put together a deposit."

"What happened to you, Elle?" His voice was quiet, his gaze direct.

She sighed. "Dean kept me on the ranch and his parents paid for us. I wasn't allowed to go into town by myself so I couldn't work. When I'd had enough, I had to leave with nothing."

"Tell me the rest." He wasn't buying it.

"I was so stupid," she said to her brother. "I thought Dean loved me and that he would love our son, but he didn't. He barely tolerated Toby in the same room and often made me take him to Lindsay to babysit while he wrote. He didn't mail the letters I wrote to you and then told me you didn't love me enough, that you didn't want me any more. I was so alone and desperate for Toby to have a father that I stayed."

"Why didn't you call?"

"We didn't have a phone. Dean told me his parents were already giving us so much I couldn't ask to use the phone as well. I was trying so hard to make it work." She'd done whatever Dean had told her, trying to please him. It made her sick with shame to think of it. "After a couple of years, it no longer occurred to me."

James swore. "What made you leave?"

Elle looked down at her hands, clenching them together. "He started hitting me."

James pushed away from the table and paced the small room. "If I could get my hands on that son of a bitch ..."

Elle stayed where she was, unused to seeing her brother so angry. "It's over now," she said quietly, trying to soothe. "When he hurt Toby I left."

"Does he know where you are?"

She shook her head. "Martin, Dean's father, has my cell number and they know I'm in Houston, but that's it."

"Good." He stood behind his chair, hands on the backrest. "Why didn't you contact me after you left, Elle?"

She felt his pain. "I wasn't sure what reaction I would get and I was too fragile to deal with another rejection."

He swore again, but under his breath.

"I had to protect Toby and I needed a job and a place to live. That was my focus. It wasn't until George asked about my family and suggested Dean might not have sent the letters that I began to reconsider."

"Remind me to give the man a medal," James said.

Elle smiled. "I don't think he'd accept it," she said. She yawned. "It's getting late and I need to start early in the morning. Why don't you have a shower and I'll make up the couch?" She couldn't deal with any more tonight.

James nodded and Elle breathed a sigh of relief. He wasn't going to push any further. He gave her a hug. "You're so brave, little sister," he said.

Elle blinked and said, "Let me show you the bathroom."

***

The next morning, James was up, dressed and ready to go when Elle was. He'd given Toby an astronaut toy when Toby had got up and Toby was happily playing with it instead of eating his breakfast.

"You don't have to come to work with me," she said.

"We've only got the day," he said. "Plus I figured you could do with an extra pair of hands."

"All right." Pleasure lightened her mind. She wanted to spend more time with her brother though she was nervous about how he would react to her café.

But when they arrived, James broke into a big grin. "This is fantastic, Ellie." He walked over to the book area, running a hand over the tables. "The design is perfect."

Elle smiled. "I remembered some of the design tips you told me about while you were studying," she said.

"You've done so well. Where would you like me to start?"

"Why don't you play with Toby while I organize everything? I'm sure he'd like the company."

Toby nodded.

"Does Toby play here every day?" James asked, making himself a coffee.

"I share a babysitter with Nora, one of my waitresses," she said. "It's only until school starts – they'll both be going in the fall. I needed to get the café started as soon as possible."

"Must be hard," James said and took his coffee and a hot chocolate for Toby into the playroom. "Come on, Toby. How about a game of chutes and ladders?"

"All right!"

Elle smiled and began the morning preparations.

***

By the time Harry arrived at ten, the café was packed. With Toby gone, Elle handed James an apron.

"How are your cleaning skills?" she asked with a grin. "Clear the tables and I'll show you how the dishwasher works."

He winked at her. "Yes, ma'am."

It was amazing to have her brother there.

After lunch, the singer arrived: a Native American by the name of Adahy. Elle showed him where to set up and got him a drink. "George said it's your brother who owns the Wooden Spoon," she said as she put the glass of water on a stool next to him.

"Sure is." Adahy grinned.

"I went there the other night. Please tell him the food was amazing."

"You can tell him yourself if you like. He's right over there." Adahy pointed to a man sitting by himself in the corner. He had brown skin and dark eyes and his dark hair hung to his shoulders. There was something intense about him: everything about his body language said he didn't want to be disturbed.

"Maybe later."

Adahy laughed. "He won't bite."

"What's his name?"

"Taima." Adahy strummed a few chords, made an adjustment to the note.

"Let me know if you need anything else," Elle said and moved away to let him begin his set.

While Adahy was open, smiling and friendly, Taima was the polar opposite. Noticing his cup was almost empty, she took a deep breath and walked over to him.

"Can I get you something else to drink?"

"No."

Adahy had begun to sing and his tone was rich and full. "Wow, your brother is amazing," Elle said.

Taima looked at her then. "He is." There was pride in his voice.

Pleased he wasn't quite so hostile now, she said quickly, "I really enjoyed eating at your restaurant the other day. I've never had food so good."

There was a small smile. "Thank you."

A hand came around Elle's waist and she jumped: it was George. Her heart leaped and she turned into his arms.

"You're not chatting up my girl, are you, Taima?" George asked, giving Elle a quick kiss.

Elle blushed and glanced around the café to check who might be watching.

James stood there with raised eyebrows.

Elle cringed.

"Never dream of it," Taima replied with a bigger smile.

"Mind if I join you?"

Taima indicated the chair. "Fine by me."

George turned his attention to Elle. "I missed you." He kissed her again, this time slower, more intensely.

Elle melted against him. To hell with her brother. She'd missed George too. She deepened the kiss and then, before she got carried away, stepped back.

George's eyes were hungry. "Wow."

Elle grinned. "I've got to get back to work. You staying for long?"

"A while." He winked.

Elle laughed and went to make his drink.

"George told me you were friends," James said, coming over to her.

Elle ducked her head. "We are."

"My female friends don't kiss me like that."

She sighed. "Not now, James, please."

He put a hand on her arm. "I'm worried for you."

"I know." She patted his hand and got back to work.

*** 

George ended up staying for Adahy's whole set. He chatted with

Taima, who had relaxed and seemed more approachable. Perhaps that was George – he did seem to put people at ease.

Then after Adahy had packed up, the three of them sat and chatted for longer.

It was after three when Toby marched in to the café, closely followed by Harry.

"Did you have a good day?" Elle asked, giving him a hug.

"Yeah." He spotted George. With a five-year-old's sense of entitlement he walked over and George pulled him up on his lap.

"George, can people have happy tears?" Toby asked.

George glanced up and smiled at Elle. "Sure they can. Why do you ask?"

"Mom cried when she saw Uncle James. He seems nice but I wanted to check."

"No, kiddo. Everything's fine."

"Good, cause I like him."

James laughed, next to her. "That's one hell of a kid you've got there." He swung his arm around her shoulders.

"Yeah. I should go and rescue George."

"Doesn't look like he minds."

It didn't. George was continuing to chat with Taima and Adahy while Toby openly stared at the two men.

Elle knew instantly he was going to say something inappropriate. "I'll be right back," she said to her brother.

She was two steps away from their table when Toby asked, "Are you real Indians?"

Elle winced.

"The term's Native American, kiddo," George said. "These are my friends, Taima and Adahy."

"Hello," Toby said. "Can you ride horses bareback like they do in the movies? I can. My Pepah taught me."

Adahy laughed. "Can't say I can."

Toby pouted. "What about shooting with a bow and arrow? I wanted to try but Mom won't let me."

"Nope, but I can play guitar."

"Cool." It was a suitable alternative to Toby.

Before he could say anything else, Elle stepped in. "I'm sorry. Let me take Toby so you can finish your conversation."

"He's not doing any harm," George said.

"Though you may want to update his knowledge on *Indians*," Taima said, his voice on edge.

Elle flushed. "I'm sorry. He's only watched the old movies his grandparents showed him."

"Maybe you should educate him further."

Elle nodded. She didn't know much about Native American history herself, only that some lived on reservations. She would have to do some research.

"You can leave Toby here," George told her. "You've got catching up to do." He raised a hand to greet James, who was still standing across the café.

"All right."

The café was quieter now. She checked Drew and Mary-Beth had things under control before she sat down with James.

"Toby is comfortable with George," James commented.

"He is. Watching him stand up to Dean helped," Elle said. "Plus George is so good with children." She wasn't sure if she wanted to go into their relationship right now.

"You've seen Dean recently?" her brother asked.

"Lindsay came into the café one day and found me. When we arranged to meet so she could play with Toby, she called Dean."

"Didn't she know what he did to you?" The disbelief was clear in his voice.

Elle shook her head. "He was good at hiding it, so she didn't believe me when I told her."

"You two ever get married?"

"No. I've got a lawyer working out a separation agreement, though, and she believes I can get full custody."

"Good. Now what's between you and George?"

Elle sat straighter in her chair. "That's none of your business."

"Elle, you've only just broken up from a bad relationship. Is it wise to get involved with someone else so soon?"

She hissed out a breath, reminding herself James cared for her. "It's not what you think. I've told George I'm not interested in a relationship. It's all very casual."

"Doesn't seem that way."

"Appearances can be deceiving," Elle said.

James opened his mouth to say something else, and then closed it. He changed the subject and Elle was more than happy to let him.

***

At closing time, she let Drew and Mary-Beth run through the routine. They knew what to do now and they were proving to be responsible. George locked the door behind Taima and Adahy and came over to greet James.

"Nice to see you again," George said, shaking James's hand.

"Likewise." Though James was studying George closely.

Elle stood and said brightly, "We should go. Drew and Mary-Beth are going to lock up. What time is your flight again, James?"

"Nine. We could grab some dinner before I have to be at the airport. Do you want to join us, George?"

Elle knew what he was doing. He wanted to scope out him some more. "George is probably tired. He's been in California all week."

"I'm fine. I'd love to. There's a nice steakhouse around the corner."

Elle wanted to swear. They were sizing each other up. This was ridiculous.

"Great."

Before Elle could argue she couldn't afford the steakhouse, the two men were out of the door and walking down the street.

She pushed down her irritation. Her brother was leaving in a few short hours and she wasn't going to let them part on a sour note.

She sighed. "Come on, Toby. It looks as though we're going out to dinner."

***

George walked along the pavement, waiting for James to speak. He'd known an inquisition was coming from the moment he'd seen James's raised eyebrows when Toby had climbed into his lap.

He also knew what he wanted to say.

"You weren't quite honest when you said you were 'a friend' of Elle's," James said.

George glanced behind and saw Elle and Toby were far enough back not to hear their conversation. "I am her friend."

James pressed. "There's more to it though."

George grinned. "If you want to know what my intentions are toward your sister, you just need to ask."

James grunted. "What are your intentions?"

It was a question he'd been asking himself since day one. "I'm not sure. I'm not out to hurt her. I'm not sure she's ready for anything too serious. It's only been a few months since she left Dean."

"You never did say why."

"You'll have to ask her." He wasn't going to share Elle's secrets with him.

"What about Toby?" James asked.

"What about him? He's a fantastic kid. Wait until you get to know him."

"I'd like to. He seems fond of you."

"We're pardners." George grinned at James's frown. "He'll get you to play cowboys with him. Though after meeting Adahy and Taima he might want to add some Indians in." That had been interesting. Toby had the curiosity of a child and Adahy hadn't minded. It was Taima who'd been touchy, but that was normal as well. After their conversation Toby would probably cast the Native Americans as the good guys.

They arrived at the steakhouse and were shown to their seats.

James sunk into the chair with a groan. "Geez, Elle. I don't know how you do it. I thought I was fit but being on my feet all day is tiring."

Elle smiled. "You get used to it."

"I must say I was surprised when you said you owned a café. I always figured you'd go back to college." He turned to George. "She was a straight-A student."

Elle flushed. Her brother knew why she hadn't gone back to college. She had to care for Toby and find a job. What was he getting at?

"Impressive," George said, winking at her.

"Yes, well it was a long time ago."

The waiter came and took their order. Elle ordered the cheapest thing on the menu and a kid's burger for Toby. Before she could choose a safe topic of conversation, James had already asked George about his job.

The two of them spoke quite happily but Elle knew an interrogation when she heard one. Luckily George seemed to be enjoying himself.

Elle barely ate a thing. She hated being in the middle of this – two of her favorite men sizing each other up. What if they didn't like each other?

Should she listen to James if he warned her away from George? She hadn't listened to him about Dean and it had ended badly. Perhaps her brother had a better sense about men than she did.

Finally it was time to take her brother back to the airport.

James insisted on paying and George walked them all back to Elle's car. James shook his hand and got into the car.

"What time shall I pick you up in the morning?" George asked.

Elle had almost forgotten about their date. She glanced at James, but really it didn't matter what he thought. "Libby is going to pick Toby up at nine," she said.

"I'll drop around about then," he said. "Are you happy for me to plan the day?"

She checked Toby was strapped in properly and then turned. "No. I've got everything under control."

"Oh really?" He raised his eyebrows. Elle guessed he was used to organizing everything.

Well she wasn't like other women.

"Don't have breakfast," she warned him. Then she kissed him and drove off before he could ask for more details.

***

They were halfway to the airport before James said, "I like him."

Elle didn't ask who he was referring to. The smallest fluttering of relief swept through her. "He passed your interrogation then?" Her tone may have been a little bit tart.

"Yep. Just looking out for my baby sister. I'm a bit out of

practice."

She couldn't be angry at him. She'd missed him and she knew he was worried for her. She wished he could have stayed for longer.

"Thank you for flying out," she said as she pulled into the airport.

"I needed to make sure you were all right."

"Did I pass your test?"

"It's not a test. I was so worried, but I should never have doubted you'd make it on your own." He got out of the car. "Don't come in. I can find my way." He got his bag out of the trunk.

Elle and Toby climbed out as well.

"Nice meeting you, Toby. I hope to see you again soon."

"Bye, Uncle James."

Elle turned to her brother, her heart tight. She gave him a big hug. "I'll miss you."

"You promise to stay in touch this time?" James asked.

She nodded.

"Good. Otherwise I'll be forced to fly out again."

Elle waved him goodbye as he was swallowed by the airport doors.

She pulled Toby closer to her and hugged him. "We've got our family back, Toby-boy," she said and smiled.

***

Elle overslept. She woke on Sunday morning to sunlight streaming through her window, much more brightly than it normally did. Checking her clock she saw it was seven.

She never slept that late.

Fear gripped her. Where was Toby? He always woke her at dawn.

She leaped out of bed, straining to hear the murmurs that accompanied his solo playtime. Nothing.

She rushed to his bedroom but stopped short at the door.

He was fast asleep.

Quietly she walked over to check he was still breathing, and that he didn't have a temperature.

He was and he didn't.

He was still asleep.

Now her heart rate could return to normal, she crept out of his room. The excitement of the last few days had obviously exhausted him. She'd let him sleep longer because he was likely to have another full day today.

Elle slipped in to the shower. As she considered her day, nerves prickled her skin.

It was the first time she would spend so much time with George without anyone else around.

She wanted to get to know him more, figure out what it was about him that tempted her to risk her heart again.

In line with that idea, she didn't have a whole lot planned, despite what she'd told him. She hadn't got past brunch and a movie, but she figured they'd be able to wing it from there.

Elle browsed her wardrobe. It was past time she took herself clothes shopping. She didn't need too much – just a couple of nice tops for days when she could go out with friends and maybe a dress or two. The Texas heat meant she didn't need much more than that at any time of the year. It was quickly creeping toward mid-summer and the humidity was already hideous.

By the time she was dressed, Toby was stirring. Seven-thirty, a new record.

She made him breakfast and listened to his excited chatter as he talked about what he was going to do that day with Kate.

She packed his backpack with the things she thought he would need.

"What about your bag, Mom?" Toby asked.

"I'm not coming, sweetheart."

"Why not?"

"I thought it would be nice for you to spend some time with Libby and Kate." Liar.

"You can come too."

"I've got other plans." Hoping he wouldn't ask what they were.

No such luck. "What?"

"I'm going to go out with George."

Toby brightened. "Can't I come?"

"Not today, Toby."

He pouted.

"You'll have so much fun swimming in the pool and playing Go Fish."

"I'll be the best swimmer ever, one day."

"I'm sure you will."

The knock on the door prevented her having to answer any more questions. She went to answer it and Toby tagged along.

Libby and Kate stood there. "Ready to go?" Libby asked Toby.

Toby looked up at his mother and then nodded.

"We'll have a great time today, Toby," Kate said.

Elle was sure Kate was right, but she felt nervous all the same. "You have my cell number, don't you?" she asked as she grabbed Toby's backpack from the sofa.

"Yes and I have George's too," Libby told her.

"Toby's not a strong swimmer. He's only been swimming once, so if he goes in the pool, you need to keep a close eye on him."

"I will," Libby said and smiled at her.

Relaxing a little, Elle handed Libby the backpack. "Toby's got a change of clothes, a towel, sunscreen and water. Do you need any money for entry fees? Meals?" She wasn't sure what their exact plans were.

"No, we're good." Libby took the pack.

Kate held her hand out to Toby. "Come on, Toby."

Toby took Kate's hand.

Elle stopped him and gave him a kiss. "Have fun today."

"Bye, Mom," he said and walked away with Kate and Libby without looking back.

Elle's heart panged. Mentally she knew Toby was getting older, that he was going to kindergarten soon, but emotionally she wasn't sure if *she* was ready for the separation. He'd been her focus for so long. It was hard to let go.

Footsteps on the stairs had her coming back to the present. It was George, looking delightfully casual in black cargo shorts and fitted blue T-shirt. Elle smiled as he walked closer, her heart fluttering a little.

"Waiting for me?" he asked.

"Toby just left," she said.

"You OK?"

Elle sighed. "Yes. He's growing up."

"Kids tend to do that," George told her and pulled her into her arms.

Elle hugged him back, drawing comfort from him. She'd forgotten over the years with Dean how lovely a hug could be.

When George drew away she smiled up at him, shifted up on to her toes and kissed his mouth. "Thank you."

George gave a wicked grin and said, "No, thank *you*." He bent his head and took possession of her lips.

Possession was the only word for it. Elle clung to him as he deepened the kiss, sliding his tongue over her lips and parting them. He tasted like coffee and strength. Perhaps it should have scared her but it didn't. She felt safe and desired – a heady combination. Her skin tingled and warmed and her head felt light as she matched him kiss for kiss.

When they broke apart, George was breathing as unsteadily as she was.

"The plans you had were for staying in, right?" he asked, his tone light but his eyes intense.

Plans. That's right, they were going out. She shook her head. "Don't think you're going to get out of taking me on our first date," she said, keeping the tone equally light. "Give me a second." She left him at the door so she could grab her purse, then checked she had her keys and locked up behind herself.

He took her hand as they walked down the steps to the parking lot.

"My car or yours?" she asked.

"Mine. I'm always afraid something is going to fall off yours."

"So am I," she admitted. The car had been given to her by the brother of one of the waitresses she'd been working with, after he'd won a brand new one. She'd been lucky to be in the right place at the right time. The shelter-associated mechanic checked it over because it did look like it was about to fall apart, and he'd assured her it was in good working order.

George's car on the other hand was shiny and silver. He held open the door and she slid on to the leather seats, breathed deeply and smiled. It still had the new-car smell, along with a subtle hint of George.

"Where to?"

She gave him directions and he pulled out.

In the close confines of the car, she suddenly wasn't sure what to say. It was just the two of them, not separated by a telephone line, or with a child in the next room, or with others around them.

"What time is Toby due back?" George asked.

"Around five." A whole eight hours. What were they supposed to do for eight hours? Her mind flitted to the bedroom but she blocked the thought.

"He seems to be getting along well with Kate."

"Yeah, he is." Glancing out of the window she said, "Pull over here."

George did as he was told and they got out.

"It's down this way," Elle told him and took his hand to lead him into an alleyway.

"Where are you taking me?" George asked checking over his shoulder.

"To brunch." She rounded the corner and tucked into the space was a café she'd discovered when she'd been researching what to do with hers. She'd read the menu, checked out the décor and the atmosphere, and taken notes.

"How did you know this was here?" George asked surprised.

"Research," she said. Hoping there was a table free, she walked in.

The aroma of coffee and freshly baked pastries hit her first. She breathed deeply and headed for a table for two in the back corner. "This way."

There was something cozy and secretive about the café. It had blue-green tones on the walls and the temperature was a good deal cooler inside than out. Some country music played softly over a speaker and voices spoke quietly.

"This place is fantastic," George said as he took his seat. "I can't believe I didn't know about it."

Elle grinned at him. "When I was checking out all the cafés in Houston I came across this one. It was marked as a best-kept secret. I promised myself I'd come back and eat here when I could afford it."

George frowned. "I can't begin to understand how hard it must have been for you. You had nothing when you left him."

Elle shook her head. "I don't want to talk about me. I want to know about you. Tell me about George Jones."

# Chapter 15

George sat back, surprised. "What do you want to know?" He wasn't used to talking about himself. He spent most of his dates finding out about his date. They were never really interested in him, except for finding out what Adrian was really like.

"Why talent management?"

He grinned. "That was easy. Adrian was so damn good and he needed help getting out there." Adrian's crippling anxiety had been one hell of an obstacle but between him and Adrian's brother, Daniel, they'd managed it.

"But what about you? What did you want to do?"

The question stopped him for a moment. "Really the first time I heard Adrian belt out a Foo Fighters tune I knew he had what it took to make it big." He smiled. "We were fifteen and were stuck inside because of the rain. My sisters decided we should put on a concert and insisted Adrian and I take part." He could never say no to them. "Adrian hated the idea but Rose could always convince him. He chose 'My Hero', and he rocked it. It was just the stereo and a cheap microphone that Rose had, but by the end of the song we were all blown away." The picture was so clear in his mind even now. "I grabbed the guitar I never played and gave it to Adrian. Within weeks he had mastered it and was putting together his own tunes. We started making plans for him to perform and that was my focus from then on."

"How did you know what to do?"

George grinned. "I made it up as I went along." Though the internet had been a big help. "Myspace was a big thing back then."

"And you never thought there might be something else you'd like to do?"

"No." He shrugged. "I didn't really have any other career aspirations." He'd liked school and girls, but hadn't begun to think about the rest of his life.

"So was it after Adrian made it big you started representing others?"

"Yeah. I had all these people contacting me and wanting my help, plus I had enough cash to set up, so I thought why not?" He liked helping others; it made him feel good about himself.

"How do you choose who you represent?"

He'd never analyzed it, but that answer interested him as well. Reviewing his list of artists, he realized that stylistically they were all different. Some wanted regular gigs and a half-decent income and others wanted fame, fortune and all that came with it.

The one thing they all had in common was they loved music.

He told Elle.

"What about Ophelia? Didn't you say she could only sing and wasn't interested in anything else?"

"She lied to me." It still grated on him. "Said she was a singer/songwriter, handed me a list of songs she'd paid someone to write for her and gave me a down-on-her-luck story."

Elle watched him steadily. "You do like to help people, don't you?"

"Sure. Doesn't everyone?" He was a little uncomfortable with the way she was watching him. It was as if she was trying to work him out. No one had looked at him like that before.

"No." She smiled then. "When you've saved them, do you go on to the next project?"

George wasn't sure what she was getting at. "They're all still my clients."

The waitress came and took their orders.

When she left, Elle asked, "Have you always got along well with your family?"

Relieved with the change of subject, he said, "Of course."

"Never squabbled, or stopped talking to them?"

She was genuinely interested. "We argue occasionally but it never lasts more than a day." Tired of talking about himself, he asked, "What about you?"

She dipped her head, acknowledging she should answer some questions too. "James and I were always close. Dad works long hours and Mom often fretted about how people perceived us. James could always calm her down and make things better."

"So you and your mom didn't get along?" Elle hadn't said much about her.

"She wanted me to be one of the popular girls and that was never going to happen. They were nasty and mean." She sighed. "When I refused to go to prom, she didn't speak to me for a week."

He raised his eyebrows. "I thought all girls wanted to go to prom." He and Adrian had taken to hiding out in Daniel's apartment in the weeks leading up to any big dance. There was always the drama of the dress, or the boy who'd asked someone else.

Elle shook her head. "Not me. I wanted to have a party at my house for my friends. Mom would have nothing of it. She bought me a hideously low-cut, black dress that was far too sophisticated for me, hired a makeup artist and drove me to the dance herself."

"Did you go in?"

"I pretended to and then caught a cab home. I arrived not long after she did, and luckily Dad arrived home at the same time. He sided with me."

"No interest in boys?"

Elle groaned. "They were all so juvenile." She grimaced. "It's probably one of the reasons Dean found it so easy to sweep me off my feet."

George was quiet, waiting for her to go on.

"The older man, the struggling *artiste*, the loner. I got all three clichés wrapped up in one." There was self-recrimination in her voice.

"You were looking for maturity."

"And intellect."

"You were a good student." James had said as much the night before and he'd seen Elle a fast learner with the café.

"Yes, teacher's pet."

"I can imagine." George sipped his coffee. "So what did the young Elle want to be when she grew up?"

Elle was silent for so long George thought she wasn't going to answer. "A scientist."

There was a big difference between a café owner and a scientist. "Which field?"

She shrugged. "I hadn't decided. I was considering medical research and renewable energy."

"Would you consider going back to college?"

Elle sighed. "I'm not sure. Right now my focus is on providing a safe home for Toby. If the café is successful, I might take night classes when he gets a little older." She frowned at him. "How did we get talking about me?" She smiled at him. "So tell me, did you get crowned Prom King?"

He laughed, letting her turn the conversation back to him. "Of course."

They continued to talk, but George made a mental note of the information she'd given him. He wanted her to achieve all her dreams.

***

It was close to midday when they left the café. Elle held her stomach and groaned. "I ate way too much."

"I noticed," George said.

Elle glanced at him. He was grinning. She swatted his arm. "That's no thing to say to a lady."

"You're right. I should apologize, particularly because you paid." He drew her close and kissed her; it was quick and casual, but it still sent a thrill through her.

She was pleased he'd let her pay. They'd argued about it but in the end she'd simply handed over the cash before he could.

"Where to now?" he asked as they got into the car.

They still had five hours before Toby was due home. "What would you recommend is a must-see in Houston?" she asked him.

"Indoors or outdoors?"

Elle paused. Rain clouds were forming and she suspected they'd have an afternoon shower. "Indoors." Then she remembered what she wanted to do. "Can we go to the movies?"

George looked amused at her enthusiasm. "What do you want to watch?"

"Something light – a comedy maybe."

George tapped into his smartphone and pursed his lips. "There's not a lot on. Why don't we go to my place? I've got a home theater, popcorn and soda, and lots of movies to choose from."

Elle hesitated. It meant they would be alone together. Was she ready? She glanced at him and he was watching, waiting for her decision. Letting her choose.

"That sounds great."

George flashed her a grin and started the car. "So what was the last movie you watched?" he asked.

Elle had to think about it. "Possibly something Dad worked on." She named the last one she could remember.

"That was years ago," George commented.

"I haven't been to the movies since I moved to Texas."

"Dean never took you?"

She shook her head. "There wasn't a theater nearby and he didn't want to contaminate his own writing." How had she not recognized how self-absorbed he was?

"Well then. I'll give you the full movie experience," George said.

He pulled into his garage and the automatic door lowered behind them. There was a clang as it hit the ground and suddenly Elle was transported back to the ranch, back to the time Dean had locked her in the pantry.

Her breath restricted as she remembered the tight, enclosed space, recalled banging on the door, using her shoulder to try and force it open, all the while terrified as to where Toby was. She fumbled with her seatbelt, her heart racing and her skin prickled and hot. Finally she forced open the car door and climbed out, looking for the exit of the garage.

"This way," George called. If he noticed her panic, he didn't comment on it, just led the way to the door into the house.

Her heart rate began to slow. She wasn't trapped. She was with George and she was safe.

"Theater room is here." He flicked on the lights and Elle's mouth dropped.

The room was almost as big as her whole apartment. A huge screen and projector hung from the ceiling. Massive, overstuffed armchairs and sofas lined the opposite wall, some with drink holders in them. It was luxury.

"DVDs are over there," George said. "You can choose something. They're ordered by genre and then alphabetically."

Elle took a deep breath, rubbing her arms and calming further, and walked up to the cabinet George had opened. It contained row upon row of movies. It was incredible.

"Would you like popcorn and soda?"

Elle cleared her throat but her voice was still a little hoarse. "Yes, please."

George left the room and she stepped forward to browse the titles. There were many there she recognized, classics from her childhood and even later, and plenty she'd never heard of before.

It had been a long time since she'd had a panic attack, months in fact, and she didn't know why she would have one here with George. She'd thought she was over them, that she'd stopped looking over her shoulder to see if Dean was following her.

Perhaps she'd never fully be over her ordeal. She'd always remember it – that was certain. Taking another breath, she read the spines of the DVD covers. She was determined to enjoy herself with George. A panic attack would not ruin her day.

A title caught her eye and she smiled. She hadn't seen the movie since she was a teenager but it was a favorite of hers. She drew it out and went in search of George. Following the scent of popcorn she found him in the kitchen and he glanced up as she walked in.

"That was quick."

She held up the movie and he nodded in approval. "Classic." He poured two huge glasses of soda, adding straws to them both, before turning and retrieving the popcorn from the microwave. He poured it into a bowl and turned to the pantry to take out a huge packet of chocolate candy.

"Fancy some?" he asked.

"Absolutely." She tucked the DVD under her arm and picked up the bowl of popcorn and one of the drinks.

Together they went back to the theater room and Elle settled on one of the sofas, putting the popcorn bowl between them, while George loaded the DVD.

"This is amazing," she said, snuggling down into the chair.

"You ain't seen nothing yet," George said as he sat next to her and then pushed a button on the side of the chair.

Elle gasped as the chair started moving, slowly tilting her back and lifting her legs up. By the time it was finished she was lying almost horizontal, but was able to see the screen fine.

"I might never leave," she said.

"Fine by me."

Elle's head whipped around to check if he was kidding, but he was adjusting something with the remote. The lights dimmed.

What the heck did he mean by that? The words implied commitment but they'd not spoken about anything of the sort.

Hell, they hadn't even slept together yet. Were they words thrown out without thought or was he hinting at something?

"Movie's about to start," George said, glancing at her and then indicating the screen.

There was nothing in his look or in his tone that suggested it was anything but a throwaway comment, so why was she so uptight?

Elle swallowed her groan and turned her attention to the screen. She would think about it later.

***

George waited for Elle to turn away and settle in to her seat before he quietly let out the breath he'd been holding.

Where the hell had those words come from?

He'd noticed her panicked glance, as he'd noticed her panic earlier when he'd closed the garage door behind them. Then, as now, he pretended to be oblivious until she'd relaxed.

But now the lights were down and the movie had started, he could concentrate on what he'd said. He took a handful of popcorn, using the movement to glance at Elle, but she was either engrossed in the movie or studiously ignoring him.

Either way suited him.

As he'd said those words, he felt like he'd been hit over the head with a two by four. Dazed and confused. Now his head had cleared and he could focus.

It felt right having Elle next to him in the room. He could picture them cuddled up on the couch together on a stormy spring night or with Toby watching the latest blockbuster animation.

She'd seemed at home in his kitchen, picking up the popcorn and drink, wandering back to the theater room.

They'd known each other a month. He'd been in casual relationships for longer than that, but none of them had ever given him this sense of fulfillment. He'd brought none of those women to this house, the one he'd renovated himself. The place he called home.

But it felt right with Elle.

He loved spending time with her, learning about her life, her hopes, her dreams. When he got her to laugh, it was a rich, unfettered sound that made him smile. He loved hearing it, loved he could make her laugh, loved her.

He loved her.

The realization didn't hit him with a bang, didn't shock him or worry him. It made sense of everything, made him relax, made him smile. And he loved Toby as well. The kid was so inquisitive and so full of life. George wanted to be a part of both their lives.

He reached out and took Elle's hand, entwining their fingers.

She glanced at him and he smiled, turning back to the movie.

She wasn't ready to hear he loved her. He understood that, even though he wanted to tell her over and over again.

It would be hard. He'd never hidden how he felt with anyone, had always been open and honest.

With Elle he had to take it slow.

He had to remind himself constantly of what Isla had told him. Elle was still working out what she wanted, who she was as a person and what she wanted out of life. If he tried to push her a certain way she'd push back.

But he could wait. She was worth waiting for.

****

When the movie ended, Elle was still holding George's hand. She'd dismissed what he'd said as a flippant comment and had relaxed to watch the movie she'd loved as a child. She stretched, breaking contact.

"That was fun," she said.

"It was," George agreed, moving the chairs so they sat upright again. He checked the time. "You've got a couple of more hours before you have to be home. What else would you like to do?"

Elle wasn't sure. She stood, grabbed the half-empty bowl of popcorn and her drink and said, "Shall we clean up?"

"You can leave it," George said, but Elle was already out of the door.

Why was she so twitchy all of a sudden?

Placing her cup and bowl on the table she glanced out of the kitchen window at the rain falling in sheets. Hopefully Toby wasn't still outside. She checked her phone to make sure she hadn't missed any messages from Libby.

Nothing.

George came into the room and loaded their dishes in the dishwasher. "Coffee?"

"Sure." She couldn't sit still so she stayed standing. "Lucky we stayed indoors," she commented, wincing at the mundaneness of her words.

"Always lots of rain in June," George replied as he got the coffee things together. When the coffee machine was humming, he walked over. "What's wrong?"

What could she say?

She'd really enjoyed the morning, learning more about George. But listening to him talk about his clients made her uncertain. Was she his latest project, his latest damsel in distress? Elle had decided if she was, she'd enjoy it while it lasted, not get too caught up in it, focus on protecting Toby and herself.

But then he'd thrown out the comment about her staying. It didn't gel with everything else.

Perhaps she was overthinking things. She and George were friends who were attracted to each other. He'd made her feel things physically she'd never felt before and she was woman enough to admit she wanted to experience those things again.

Could she get more intimate with the man without wanting more? Did she even *want* more?

George complicated matters.

She'd become used to it being her and Toby. She enjoyed the freedom of being able to make her own choices and live life her way. So what choice did she want to make about George?

Elle looked into his eyes and saw the concern, saw the caring. She wanted that. Even if it was for a brief moment in her life, she wanted to be cared for, desired, and to feel like every fiber in her being was alive.

Stepping closer, she wrapped her arms around George's waist, bringing him closer. "I was debating what else we had time for," she said, those nerves twitching in her stomach again. She'd never instigated sex before. With Dean she'd been too young and uncertain at first. Later, she'd done everything she could to keep him uninterested.

George's eyes darkened but he made no move. "What are the options?" he said, his voice low.

A little braver now, Elle nipped his bottom lip and then kissed him, quick and hard. "You haven't shown me the rest of your house," she said, sliding her hands down his back and over his bottom.

He tensed. "Which room would you like to see first?"

She kissed him again, longer this time, closing her eyes when his lips moved over hers, drawing her deeper. The sensations floated through her body were slowly drugging her. She wanted this. She wanted him. "Which way to the bedroom?" she murmured against his lips.

George groaned. "Down the hall," he said, but still didn't move.

Elle smiled and took his hand. "This way?" she asked as she

led him down the corridor.

He nodded. "Last door on your right."

Anticipation and nerves sparked as Elle reached the room. It was almost as large as the theater room, and held the biggest bed she had ever seen. It had to be at least twice the size of her double bed at home.

A little uncertain, she turned to George and kissed him. It was all she needed to reassure herself she was making the right decision.

When she broke the kiss, George said, "This is my bedroom." He smiled at her, and trailed kisses down her neck, soft, slow and sensual.

Elle lifted her chin to give him better access and ran her hands up through his hair. She'd never realized her neck was so sensitive. Tingles went through her body wherever his lips met her skin. She moaned, moving her hands to grip the bottom of his T-shirt and then slide her hands underneath.

George hissed and brought his mouth back to hers, while his hands slipped under her top too.

She was too hot. There were too many clothes between them. Moving away she stripped off her top, toeing off her shoes too, and then reached for George, pulling him closer to the bed.

She slipped her hands back under his shirt, feeling the muscles shift in his abdomen as she ran her fingertips up his chest and slipped his shirt over his head.

George watched her. He was holding back, she knew. Letting her take charge, letting her be in control.

She reveled in it.

Pressing up against him, she kissed him. His hands brushed over her back, pausing over her bra strap.

"Undo it," she said.

Nimbly he unclasped her bra and she shrugged it off. Then it was skin against skin. George slowly lowered his head to take her nipple in his mouth.

Elle forgot to breathe and her legs went weak. She clung to him as his tongue danced and he sucked. Her eyes rolled back in her head.

"You're so perfect," George murmured as he drew back.

Elle was too aroused to be embarrassed by his gaze. She reached for his belt, running her hand briefly over the bulge in the front of his pants.

George moaned as she unzipped his shorts, pushing them and his boxer briefs to the floor. She gazed at his body, his subtly defined muscles, his gorgeous thighs and the more than impressive indication he wanted her as much as she wanted him. It was a heady sensation. She was in charge.

Unbuttoning her own shorts, she wiggled out of them and stood naked in front of him.

"You're killing me, Elle," he said, his eyes raking her body, but still he stood where he was.

She took his hand, led him over to the bed and gently pushed him on to it. Then she climbed up after him.

***

George pulled Elle close to him, needing to hold her.

He'd not been expecting sex – he hadn't thought she would be ready – and she'd particularly surprised him with her take-charge attitude. It had been difficult controlling himself, letting her set the pace.

He brushed her nipple, fascinated by her body, not wanting to let go. She sighed, long and satisfied, and George felt himself stir.

She was truly amazing. He wanted to touch, taste and explore every inch of her. He nuzzled her neck in the spot he'd discovered she liked. She turned her head toward him and he captured her mouth, kissing her gently, trying to express how he felt through the kiss alone.

He loved Elle.

If he hadn't realized it earlier, he would have known for sure now, seeing her in his bed, wanting her there forever.

He brushed his fingertips over her side and she leaned in to him. "You're amazing," he said, kissing her mouth, her cheek, her earlobe.

"I feel amazing," she said with a grin.

Her eyes lit up when she grinned. He kissed the creases at the side of those eyes, unable to keep from touching her. She stretched, arching her back and moaned.

George wanted her again.

"This bed is phenomenal," she said. "I never knew they came this big."

"Isn't that what you're supposed to say about me?" he asked, keeping things light when all he wanted to do was ask her to marry him.

She smirked, glanced down at the appendage he was referring to, and stroked it.

It immediately responded.

"It does appear to be getting bigger," she said.

"Give me a minute, honey."

Elle sighed and snuggled in. "What time is it?"

He glanced at the clock across the room and wished she hadn't asked. "Almost four."

"Oh, I need to go soon," she said, sounding disappointed.

He didn't want to let her go. "How about a shower?"

"Sure."

He led her into the master bathroom and turned on both showerheads. When he turned back, she was staring around the room, her eyes wide.

"It's a bit decadent," George admitted. When he'd renovated the house, he'd planned it for his future family. The shower had lots of space for the two rainfall heads and there was a huge bath, big enough for two, beneath a window looking out over the garden.

"A bit," Elle agreed. "Imagine lying in a bubble bath on a cold day with a good book."

He could visualize her there, but in his imagination he was in the bath with her, trying to distract her.

She stepped past him into the shower and George closed the door behind them. He reached for the soap, lathered up the sponge and began to wash her back.

"Mmm, I could get used to this," she said, turning so he could wash her front as well.

George didn't comment. He didn't want to freak her out again.

Instead, he continued his steady strokes, lathering up her body and trying to remember she had to leave soon.

"My turn," she said when he was finished, and took the

sponge from him, adding some more soap and rubbing his back.

George closed his eyes and let himself enjoy the sensation. How long would it take for him to convince her they needed to be together? How could he make her come around?

When she'd finished washing him, he rinsed then turned off the shower, handing her a towel.

She buried her head in it. "So soft."

He'd come to take the luxury he'd surrounded himself with for granted. He'd never been poor. His father was a successful builder and his mother ran the business side of the company. There had been plenty of food to go around, and always money for school excursions and clothes.

He'd been careful to hide it, but Elle's apartment had been somewhat of a shock to him when he'd first visited it. Second-hand, worn furniture, stained ceilings and so small you could be talking in the kitchen and someone could hear you down the hall in the bedroom.

He wanted to provide her with luxury. He wanted to take care of her, shower her with gifts – not to buy her love, but because she deserved the finer things in life.

Concentrating on drying himself, he followed her back into the bedroom as she dressed.

"You might want to put on some clothes if you're going to drop me off," she said.

He wasn't ready to let her go. "Why don't you call Libby and get her to drop Toby off here?" he suggested. "You could stay for dinner. I'm sure I've got something in the freezer." If not, there was a supermarket down the road.

Elle hesitated. He wished he could tell what she was thinking. "I'm not sure," she said.

Though disappointed, he didn't want to push. "No problem. I'd better get dressed then." He dressed quickly, and then drew Elle in for another kiss. "When can I see you next?"

Elle sighed, resting her head against his chest. "I'll call you."

Don't rush her. "Come on. I'll take you home."

He kept up a light conversation on the drive back to her apartment, talking about his plans for the week. She was the most relaxed she'd been since he'd met her. Maybe that's what great sex did.

He parked and accompanied her up to her apartment. The neighborhood wasn't the worst in Houston but he wanted her somewhere else – preferably his place.

"Thank you for a lovely day," Elle said, when she'd unlocked the door and pushed it open.

"I should be thanking you. You planned it."

"Yes, I did, didn't I?" she said, smiling.

He grinned. "I'll call you tomorrow." He kissed her long and slowly.

Too soon, she drew back on a sigh. "I look forward to it." Still smiling, she closed the door.

George turned and walked slowly back down to his car. He was determined to win Elle's love, but for the first time in his life, he was uncertain. It meant too much to fail. He had to take it slowly.

There was one person who might be able to help him work out what to do.

He got out his cell and dialed a number. When it was answered, he said, "Hi Mom. Can I get some advice?"

# Chapter 16

Elle closed the door behind George and sat on her sofa. She'd lied to him. It hadn't been a lovely day: it had been the best day she'd had in years.

She'd learned more about George, had completely chilled out watching one of her favorite movies, and had incredible sex with a man she cared for.

Her cheeks warmed. Sex had never been like that for her. She'd always felt helpless: Dean had controlled every touch, every movement. She'd never known she could feel so in control.

George had let her take charge.

She'd been so tempted to accept his offer of dinner, to stay longer, but she didn't want to get too comfortable being at his place. Not until she figured out where this was going.

She was already looking forward to their next encounter, which she acknowledged was likely to be some time away. Checking the time she sighed. Her day for herself was almost at an end. She had to find something for dinner.

Searching through the freezer she had just found enough ground beef to make enchiladas when Toby burst through the front door.

"Mom, Mom, I'm home!"

Elle hurried out of the kitchen and opened her arms wide

for a hug. When he ran over, she enclosed him in her arms. She loved him so much.

"What did you get up to today?" she asked as she stood and smiled a greeting at Libby and Kate.

"We went swimming, and played Go Fish and chutes and ladders."

"That sounds nice. Did you thank Kate and Libby for having you?"

"Yep, lots of times. And then we went to the Space Center!"

The twinge of envy was immediate. She'd been planning on taking Toby to the Space Center soon, when she took her next day off.

"Were you well behaved?" she asked.

"Course," he said and grinned at her. "There were astronaut suits like the toy Uncle Jamie gave me!" He hurried over to his backpack to get it out.

"Thank you for taking care of him," Elle said to Libby.

"He was no trouble at all. He's so well behaved and polite. He and Kate had a great time making each other laugh. We're happy to have him any time."

Elle smiled at her. "Thank you."

"No problem. We'd better get going. Adrian's cooking dinner and it will be ready soon."

The expression on Libby's face when she mentioned Adrian was beautiful. She smiled and got doe-eyed.

"I'll talk to you later," Elle said and closed the door behind them.

Would she ever get doe-eyed over a man again?

***

The next day the phone rang and Elle answered it, hoping it would be George.

"Elle, it's Imogen. Do you and Toby want to come to the Fourth of July party I'm having at my place?"

Elle checked the calendar out of habit. The café would be closed as all her staff had plans. "We'd love to come."

They arranged the details, then Elle hung up and started drying the dishes. It would be another day she could be with George. Were they spending too much time together? What they had together wasn't serious, they'd already agreed to that. But she did like hearing his voice and being with him. She gave in to temptation and called George.

"Hi, Beautiful. I was hoping you'd call."

Elle smiled at his voice. It was calming and sexy at the same time. "What have you been up to?"

"Wrangling artists." He sounded tired.

"Ophelia again?"

"Among others. What about you?"

"Same as usual, though my stamina is improving."

"And it's already impressive."

Elle laughed.

"Are you going to Imogen's on Friday?" George asked.

"Yes. Toby will be counting the sleeps when I tell him."

"That's great." There was a pause and then he asked, "Can I drop by the café some time tomorrow?"

"Sure. Why?"

"Because I miss you."

Elle smiled. She missed him as well. "I'll see you then." She hung up and hugged herself.

Tomorrow seemed a little bit brighter.

***

George timed his day to make sure he got to the café by ten, when he knew things quieted down a bit. He took his laptop with him so he could sit and do some work until Elle needed the table.

Elle came out of the kitchen and spotted him, her smile instant. He grinned back at her. He liked the fact she smiled now when he came in. He walked over and pulled her into his arms. "Morning."

"Morning," she said and kissed him.

It was brief and he wanted more, but he would make do for now.

"Take a seat and I'll make you a coffee. Toby's still in the playroom if you want to say hello."

George moved straight to the playroom. He'd missed Toby as well as his mother. When he ducked his head through the door he found Toby and Miranda playing with an astronaut and cowboy – there was some kind of space cowboy thing happening. He grinned.

"Hey, kiddo."

Toby looked up and a big smile crossed his face. "Hi, George." He got to his feet and ran over to give him a hug.

George's heart melted.

"Uncle Jamie gave me an astronaut." Toby showed him the doll.

"That's pretty neat," George said.

"It is," Toby agreed. "I want to be an astronaut when I grow up."

"It's a cool thing to be. Hey, Miranda." She'd come over as well.

Nora dashed into the room. "Harry's here. Grab your backpacks."

George followed Nora back out into the café and together they said goodbye to the kids as Harry took them out for the day.

He sat down at his table and took his coffee from Elle. "Have you got time to sit down?"

Elle glanced around the shop. "Maybe five minutes." She pulled out the chair across from him and sat down. "What are you working on?" She indicated the laptop George had yet to set up.

"Marketing and promotion." Along with a whole heap of other things. "Are you free for dinner?" He was trying not to push, but damn he wanted to see her more.

Elle smiled. "That would be great. What time?"

"Come over after you lock up." Toby would be hungry.

She nodded and stood up. "I'd better get back to work."

She walked over and greeted a customer, showing her to a table.

His heart always felt as if it was twice as big whenever he was around her. Smiling to himself, he booted up his laptop, but instead of starting work, he went to some recipe websites to decide what he could make to impress his future family.

***

Elle pulled into George's driveway and wiped her sweaty palms on her jeans. She wasn't sure why she was so nervous. She'd had dinner with him before and it hadn't been a big deal.

She helped Toby out of the car, then they walked up to the house and knocked on the door.

George opened the door, wearing an apron and holding a wooden spoon. "Come in. Close the door behind you." He dashed away toward the kitchen.

Toby giggled. "George is wearing an apron."

"He sure is." Somehow he made it look sexy. "He's in the middle of cooking dinner."

They walked into the kitchen to the aroma of spices, white wine and something else. "Smells divine," Elle said. "What are you making?"

"Risotto," George said, stirring the pot. "Sorry, it requires constant stirring. Help yourself to some wine. There's juice in the fridge for Toby."

Elle got them both a drink. "Can I do anything to help?"

He looked slightly frazzled. "Should we eat inside or outside?"

"Inside." The weather was sweltering. "Do you want me to set the table?"

"Please."

Elle stepped over to him and ran a hand down his back. "Don't stress." She kissed his cheek.

George grimaced. "I wanted to impress you."

Ridiculously pleased, Elle kissed him again. "You do, just by being you." Toby was looking out the back door, holding his glass of juice. He was happy so she left him there while she got cutlery out of the drawer and went to set the table.

In the dining room, her steps slowed. George had already put a white tablecloth on the table and a vase with flowers in it. He'd gone to a lot of trouble for what she had thought was a simple dinner. Was there something more to it?

She hoped not.

Determined to be casual about it all, she set the table and returned to the kitchen, where Toby was now at the stove, standing on a chair, stirring the risotto.

"How's it going, kiddo?" George asked from where he was slicing up vegetables for a salad.

"It's dry."

George went over and poured more liquid into the pan. "Good job. Keep stirring and tell me if you're getting tired."

Elle's heart swelled at the lovely domestic scene. Toby often helped her in the kitchen and here George was, letting him help too. George would make a great dad.

She froze. Where the hell had that thought come from? She shouldn't be thinking like that. She wasn't searching for a father figure for Toby any more than she needed a husband for herself.

No, she'd rushed into her last relationship and she wasn't going to make the same mistake again. Perhaps she should cool things with George for a little while, or reiterate she didn't want a relationship. Or was it too late? If Piper had spent this much time with a man, Elle would have classified it as a relationship.

So, how the hell had that happened?

Her heart was beating rapidly and she slid into a chair, taking a sip of wine.

"Are you all right?" George asked.

She forced a smile. "Yes. Just resting my feet."

George held her gaze for a moment longer before continuing his salad preparation.

There had to be some way to slow down what was happening, to stop it getting out of control. She wasn't ready to trust herself yet, not when she'd made such a huge mistake the last time. She couldn't afford it.

*** 

Elle got a call from her lawyer on Wednesday morning.

"Dean wants a meeting with you to discuss matters. He said if you can come to an agreement, he won't take it to court."

Elle closed her eyes. As much as she didn't want to see him, she didn't want the matter to go to court either. "What do we do about the restraining order?"

"I'll sort it out," Victoria promised.

"All right then. Tell me when."

"He wants it tomorrow morning."

Of course he did. Dean was never good at waiting. "I can do three o'clock." She wasn't sure how long the meeting would take and she couldn't leave the café over the lunch period. There wasn't enough time to get a replacement, not with a lot of people heading out of town for the Fourth of July weekend.

"I'll call you back to confirm." Victoria hung up.

Elle took a seat in the café. She wanted time to plan what she was going to say to Dean; figure out how she could convince him she wasn't going back to him. But she didn't want to anger him enough that he'd fight to get Toby away from her out of spite. She had no doubt Lindsay would advise him to get custody, promising she would take care of the boy.

But it wasn't how it should be. Sure, Toby needed his grandparents, but not as stand-in parents. Dean wasn't interested enough to fill a parental role. George had done more in the month she'd known him than her ex had during the whole of Toby's life.

She sighed.

First thing was to find someone to babysit Toby while she was at the meeting.

"Elle, can I get some help?" Nora called.

She got to her feet. Her worries would have to wait until later.

***

The next day at five to three, Elle walked into Victoria's office. She was dressed in her suit and was determined to keep the whole matter as business-like as possible. Toby was her primary concern – she had to make sure that whatever was decided was right for him. She'd spoken to him the night before about whether he wanted to spend time with his father and he'd been adamant he didn't.

The court wouldn't necessarily listen to a five-year-old if it came to that but hopefully she could get Dean to come to his senses.

Sarah had picked Toby up from the café after collecting her own children from school and taken him back to the apartment building where they both lived.

Victoria came out and greeted her with a hug. Her suit today was a sunny yellow and she looked fantastic. "Are you ready?" she asked.

Elle nodded. "I'd like to get this resolved as soon as

possible."

"I know. Come on through; they're waiting in the meeting room."

Victoria led the way to the room and as she and Elle entered both Dean and his lawyer stood up.

Dean was wearing an ill-fitted black suit that probably belonged to one of his brothers. His gaze at Elle was intense.

She nodded a greeting and went to the opposite side of the table to take a seat. She didn't want to encourage him by smiling, or shaking his hand.

"Elle, you look amazing," Dean said, giving her a head-to-toe appraisal.

Elle's skin crawled. "Thank you." She would be polite but no more.

"Let's get straight to business," Victoria said. "My client has separated from Dean Williams and seeks full conservatorship of their son, Toby."

Dean's lawyer held up a hand. "Now, wait a minute. There's nothing to say the separation is permanent. It's one of the issues Dean wanted to discuss today."

Elle's spine went rigid. "Let me assure you, sir, there is no way I will ever go back to Dean. The separation is definitely permanent."

"Now, Elle. Don't be so hasty. We had an argument and you got your feelings hurt. It doesn't mean we can't make up."

Had Dean always been this delusional? Considering their time together, Elle realized, yes, he had. This meeting could be more difficult than she'd expected.

"My client has no desire to reconcile," Victoria said.

"Let Elle speak for herself," Dean snarled.

Elle sat straighter in her chair. She stared directly at Dean and said, "I am not coming back to you, Dean. I refused to be abused, controlled and manipulated any longer. I don't like you, I don't want you and I don't need you."

Dean sat back as if she'd struck him. "You can't mean it. You're my soul mate. We're meant to be together."

It was the puppy dog look that had sucked her in so many times before. It wasn't going to this time. "No we weren't. I've moved on, Dean, and it's time you did too."

"There's another man, isn't there? The asshole in the park." Dean's face went red and his fists banged on the table as he stood and leaned over. "Have you fucked him yet?"

Elle didn't answer but she held his gaze. She didn't care if he took it as a sign of aggression or assertion. She wasn't going to be cowed by him any longer.

"You have, you whore. You'll pay for cheating on me."

"That sounded like a threat, Mr. Williams," Victoria said calmly. "Please note it is on record."

The other lawyer put a hand on Dean's arm and whispered in his ear.

Dean snatched his arm away but sat down again. "I don't know what I ever saw in you. You're a naïve, frigid bitch and you got yourself knocked up to keep your claws in me."

Elle wasn't sure why she was so surprised by the words coming out of his mouth. He had never been the most rational of people.

"I never wanted you anyway."

His tune had changed but Elle was fine with that. If she could convince him she was the enemy, he'd stay away from her.

"It is clear to me the separation issue has been resolved," Dean's lawyer said. "Miss Carter no longer wants to be in a relationship with my client. We should now discuss the matter of the child."

"Who cares about the fucking kid? He's nothing but a whiny pain in the ass. Why should I be stuck having to look after him?"

Elle's heart hurt for Toby, and that his father could speak about him in such dismissive terms, but the logical part of her rejoiced he was admitting it in front of the two lawyers.

"Then we have agreement that Miss Carter will gain full conservatorship of Toby Carter?" Victoria asked.

"God, yes," Dean said. "Where do I sign?"

Victoria pushed over the legal forms that Elle had asked her to prepare, explaining what each one meant. Dean grabbed a pen and his lawyer put a hand on his arm once more.

"Don't be so hasty. You should read the forms and make a decision when you're feeling calmer."

"Fuck off," Dean snarled. He scrawled his name on the

signature page and Victoria pointed out the other sections he needed to sign. Then she passed the document to his lawyer to witness.

The man sighed and added his signature.

Elation bubbled up inside Elle, threatening to burst forth in a scream, but she controlled herself, clenching her hands together to prevent fist bumping the air. The forms were just the first part of the process – it still had to go to court – but Dean had signed the waiver and agreed to the terms of the order. He'd basically given Elle sole custody of Toby.

"Thank you, gentlemen," Victoria said. "I believe we're finished here." She stood up and walked them out.

Elle got to her feet, too elated to sit. She paced up and down the room until Victoria returned.

"We did it," Victoria said. "We've got that asshole out of your life."

"He can't claim he signed under duress?"

"Hell, no. His lawyer advised him to read it first and he didn't. I'll let you know when the court hearing is, but it should just be a formality."

"Thank you." The words came out as a whisper and the relief flooded out of her body in the form of tears.

Victoria hugged her. "It was you who took that first step. You achieved this," she said. "If you have any other worries, you come back and talk to me."

Elle found a tissue in her bag and wiped her eyes. "I appreciate all your help."

"I know, honey. Now why don't you go home and tell your little boy the good news?"

Toby.

She wasn't sure he would fully comprehend what had happened today, but it would be enough for him to understand he didn't have to go back to his father again.

Elle would decide what to do about his grandparents at a later date.

***

Her phone rang as she walked out of Victoria's building.

"Elle, it's Sarah. Toby left his astronaut toy at the café and he's pretty distraught. Are you able to pick it up on your way home?" In the background Toby was sobbing.

"Of course. I'm on my way home now."

She drove straight to the café, picked up Toby's toy and continued home. Sarah's apartment was on the ground floor, so she stopped there first to pick up Toby.

"How did it go?" Sarah asked.

Elle had told her what the meeting was about. "Perfectly," Elle said. "Dean agreed to me being the sole managing conservator of Toby."

"Congratulations. I hope you and that spunky George celebrate with champagne tonight."

Elle hadn't had a chance to tell George about it. He'd been busy arranging a show for a client the night before and she hadn't spoken to him since.

Toby clutched her hand and said, "Can we go?" His shoulders were drooping and he was obviously tired.

"Sure. Thank Sarah for having you."

"Thank you, Sarah," he said.

Sarah smiled. "You're welcome."

When Elle got into her apartment she sat on the couch and pulled Toby on to her lap. "How was your day, Toby?"

He shrugged. "OK."

"Did you do anything nice?"

"We helped Harry pack for his vacation. He's going to …" He screwed up his face, trying to remember.

"Florida?" Elle suggested, knowing that's where Harry was headed.

"Yep. Is it far?"

"It's a ways," Elle told him. She jiggled him on her lap so she could see his face. "Toby, I met with your dad today."

His eyes widened and he bit his bottom lip.

"We had a meeting with some lawyers. They're people who help solve arguments."

"Do they stop Dad hitting you?"

"In a way. They've made sure we don't ever have to visit him again if we don't want."

Toby sat bolt upright. "Really?" There was so much hope on his little face.

"Really. If you meet your dad you don't have to go with him and you don't have to speak to him. But," Elle had to add, "if you change your mind and want to see him, you need to tell me, all right?"

"Does it mean I don't have a dad any more?" He frowned.

"No. He'll still be your dad. You just don't have to live with him again."

"Oh. I thought maybe George could be my dad then."

Elle froze. That was not good. She knew Toby liked George but she hadn't realized he'd got so attached. She and George were nowhere near making that kind of commitment. She didn't *want* that kind of commitment: not yet anyway. Elle wasn't sure what to say so she shifted Toby off her lap and stood up. "How about we get take-out for dinner?" Sarah was right. The day deserved celebrating. Maybe she should call George and see if he wanted to bring over a bottle of champagne.

She groaned. Hadn't she just decided she didn't want a commitment? That she wanted to take things slowly? So why was George the first person she thought of when she had good news?

Oh hell. She didn't want to think about it now. She wanted to enjoy this victory and if George were available, she'd celebrate with him.

"Yay. Can we get Chinese?" Toby asked.

"Sure."

Her phone rang as she was about to call George.

"I was going to order some take-out and thought if you haven't eaten already, you might like some too." It was George.

Elle smiled. "Funny, I had the same thought. There's a Chinese restaurant around the corner that Nora says is good."

"Why don't you order and I'll pick it up on my way over?"

"Any preferences?"

"Just you," he said.

He made her smile with his silly comments. "Can you pick up a bottle of sparkling wine as well?" she asked.

"Are we celebrating something?" George asked.

"Yes. I'll fill you in when you get here."

"I'll be there as soon as I can."

She hung up. "George is coming around."

"Yippee."

Elle knew Toby wouldn't mind but she was still a little concerned about how he'd latched on to George. Perhaps it was normal for a child who hadn't had a father figure to put any kind male in the role.

She placed her order and wondered how she should raise the subject. Or perhaps she should ignore it. When Toby went to school at the end of the next month, he'd be surrounded by other people to admire.

She was probably getting worried over nothing. Today wasn't a day for worrying – it was a day for celebrating, and so she would.

***

When she opened the door to George a little later, she flung her arms around him and kissed him. He took half a step back, wrapped his free arm around her and slid his tongue between her lips, deepening the kiss.

Elle broke away and smiled at him. "Hi."

"Hi, yourself. If that's the greeting food gets me, I may bring take-out every time I come over."

Elle laughed and gestured him inside.

He put the take-out on the table and Toby got them plates without having to be asked.

"What are we celebrating?" George asked, holding up the bottle of champagne and a bottle of soda. "For Toby," he said at Elle's look.

It warmed her heart that he would consider Toby as well. "Freedom," Elle told him, searching for glasses. The champagne would have to be drunk out of their plain tumblers. With a shrug she put them on the table.

"Whose?"

"Ours," she said. "Toby and mine."

"What happened?" Serious now, he handed her a glass of champagne and Toby a glass of soda.

Elle was too excited to sit. She dished up Toby's meal and then her own. "I met with Dean today."

George frowned. "Why didn't you tell me? You could have been hurt." He took one of her arms and examined it.

She pulled back. "It was at my lawyer's office." With some of the elation seeping out of her, she said, "Victoria called yesterday to say Dean wanted a meeting today. We got together, I made it clear I wasn't coming back and he was so angry, he signed the necessary forms for me to get sole custody of Toby."

George's jaw dropped. "Really?"

Elle nodded. "Yep. His lawyer witnessed the document. Victoria said it would be hard to fight it in court."

"Did he understand what he was signing?"

"I really don't care. His lawyer advised him to read it and he ignored the advice." A gleeful giggle escaped. She hadn't been sure Dean would sign, but she wanted all the necessary forms filled in just in case. Taking a sip of the champagne, she finally sat and let the bubbles lighten her head.

Dean had always thought she was unintelligent. She was a little bit worried how he might react when he realized the extent of what he'd signed away but hopefully he'd be back at the ranch by that time. Unless his lawyer *had* insisted on explaining the whole document to him after they'd left.

Either way it didn't matter. Dean didn't know where she lived or worked, and she had no reason to agree to meet him again.

She was free.

Taking another sip of champagne, she decided it might be fun to get a little bit drunk. It was Independence Day tomorrow, the café was shut and they'd be going to Imogen's about mid-morning. She had the opportunity to indulge and she deserved to.

***

George read Toby his bedtime story and when he was asleep he returned to the living area, where Elle was reading a book of her own. She stood, took his hand and led him into her bedroom.

She closed the door behind them and slipped her arms around George's waist. "You can stay a bit longer, can't you?" she asked.

George's heart contracted and he smiled at her. "You've had quite a bit to drink," he said. She had a slightly tipsy looseness about her muscles, and it was quite adorable. If he'd known she had such a low tolerance, he wouldn't have kept topping up her glass.

"I have, but I feel fine. You can make me feel better." She took his hands and put them on her breasts.

Maybe she was more than a little tipsy. He ran his thumbs over her nipples and she groaned. He had to be careful: if she made too much noise, she might wake Toby and that wasn't a situation George wanted to be caught in.

He backed her over to the bed, kissing her lips and neck as he did so. When she hit the bed, she unbuttoned her shirt and flung it over her shoulder, before freeing her breasts from her bra.

George's good intentions of getting her into bed so she could sleep it off faltered. He bent his head to suck on one of her sweet nipples as she wiggled out of her skirt.

She was killing him.

There she was, lying fully naked on her bed, silently begging him to touch her. He kicked off his shoes, ignoring the throbbing down the front of his pants, and laid next to her.

She flung her arms around his neck, pulling him in until her lips met his, demanding to be kissed. He gave in to the demand, indulging himself by tasting her, and teasing quiet moans from her.

"George, you make me feel so free," she whispered.

Moved by an admission she probably wouldn't have made if she were sober, he continued his exploration of her body, kissing, caressing it, and discovering what she liked the best.

When he touched her between her thighs she arched upward and grabbed on to his hair, pulling hard.

Aroused by her response, he focused on giving her as much pleasure as possible.

"George, now," she begged.

He stopped and looked up at her and her eyes cleared. She frowned.

"You're wearing too many clothes."

Quicker than he expected, she sat up, pulling him up with her, and slid his shirt over his head. Then she reached for his belt.

"Honey, you're drunk," he said, trying to resist her.

"I don't care," she said, her gaze sharp. "I want you." She struggled with his zipper and gave a cry of success as it slid down, along with his shorts. She reached for him and he was lost.

This beautiful goddess wanted him. The passion exploded and they fought to touch and kiss each other all over. George ended up on his back with Elle straddling him, such an expression of triumph on her face that his heart flipped over in his chest.

As she lowered herself on to him, he lost himself inside her.

***

The shrill ring of a phone woke Elle. Fuzzy headed and confused, she reached for it, coming fully awake as she realized it was still dark outside.

Good news didn't come at this hour.

Her heart pounded in her chest. "Hello?"

Next to her a body stirred and with a start she remembered it was George and that they were both still naked.

"Is this Elle Carter, owner of Eat, Drink, Read?" a voice asked.

"Yes." She sat up, pulling the sheet up to cover her, and waited for the bad news.

"Ma'am, it's Ally Cooper, from Bobcat Security. I'm sorry to inform you your café has been broken into."

Chapter 17

"Broken into?" No, this had to be a dream. She pinched herself and it hurt. George got up, turned on the light and started to dress. Elle blinked at the brightness and concentrated on what she was being told. "I'll be there as soon as I can," she said.

When she hung up, she turned to George. "Someone's broken into the café. There's a lot of damage and the security company doesn't know if anything's been stolen. They've called the police but aren't sure when they'll arrive. I need to go and check things out. Can you stay with Toby?"

To her surprise, George shook his head. "You're not going down there alone," he said. "Give me a minute to call Chris." He walked out the door before Elle could protest.

Quickly she dressed and followed him out to the living room, where he was talking on his phone.

"You can't expect them to come out at this hour," she said.

George hung up. "Imogen and Chris are both coming. They'll be here soon."

Elle ran a hand through her hair. "George, this is my problem. If you'll stay here with Toby, I'll deal with it."

"Please. Elle. I don't want you going out alone." He walked into the kitchen and poured two glasses of water. "Besides you did have a bit to drink last night, and it might not be out of your system yet."

That made her pause. "You're right." She gulped down the water George had handed her. "But it's not fair to ask Imogen and Chris to come around. Imogen has her party tomorrow. I can take a cab."

George frowned at her, came closer and put his hands on her arms. "Please, let me come. I won't go back to sleep until you get home safely and you might need me when you see all the mess."

Elle sighed. She couldn't think about that yet or she'd imagine the whole building – and her life – in shards. "Fine. You'd better brush your hair if you're coming with me," she said and went to check on Toby.

He was still sleeping soundly.

It was two o'clock when Imogen and Chris knocked on the door. Elle let them in. "I'm so sorry for waking you."

"It's no problem," Imogen assured her. "We'll keep an eye on Toby until you get back. Don't worry about anything."

She would worry, but they were here now, and she needed to go and assess the damage.

George drove the short distance and pulled up across the road from the café. A police car was already there.

The first thing Elle noticed was the gaping hole in what had been her front window. It had cost her a fortune to get the shop's name decoratively written on that enormous pane of glass.

She reached out and took George's hand. His other hand ran up and down her arm.

"It will be all right," he said and she relaxed her grip a little.

Taking a deep breath, she walked over to one of the police officers, who was getting something out of the car.

"I'm Elle Carter, the owner," she said.

The officer checked his pad. "Evening, ma'am. If you just wait here a moment, please." He carried a kit inside and gave it to another officer.

Elle got her first glimpse inside her café. The lights were turned on, illuminating what had happened. Tables were overturned, chairs were broken and the cabinet that held her cakes was smashed.

Her heart sank; she turned to the book area and froze.

George swore.

Nausea rose so fast in her stomach she had to put her hand over her mouth to stop herself retching. Spray-painted in large, red letters over one wall of books was the word *WHORE*.

Elle swayed and George's arm came around her, holding her steady. She leaned in to him, drawing from his strength.

"Miss Carter, I'm Officer Oslow." The man who had been at the car returned. "This must be very distressing for you. Have you got any idea who may have done this? Anyone who might have a grudge against you?"

It was the word painted on the wall that made it personal.

"My ex, Dean Williams, called me a whore today and said I'd pay for rejecting him."

"But he doesn't know you own this place," George said.

He was right. Elle retraced her movements that afternoon and groaned. "After the meeting I came here to pick up the toy Toby forgot," she said. "He could have followed me." More nausea rose as she realized something else. "And he could have followed me home," she said, turning to George. "You need to call Chris. You need to make sure Toby is all right."

George already had his cell phone out and was dialing.

There was no telling what Dean might do to make Elle miserable.

"Chris, we think Elle's ex may have done this and may know where she lives. Can you take Toby to my house?" He was silent as Chris said something. "Toby's been to my house and he knows Imogen. If he wakes up, call me and he can speak to Elle." Another pause and George nodded in response to something Chris said. "Make sure no one follows you."

Elle wanted to leave, to go to Toby, and make sure he was fine. If he woke up, he'd be confused and maybe scared.

"He'll be all right," George said, hugging her.

"Ma'am, would you like to explain what is going on?" Officer Oslow asked.

Elle told him about the meeting, told him about the restraining order and the other run-ins with Dean, and that she'd left in the first place because of years of physical and emotional abuse. She'd repeated the story so many times of late that it was as if she were reporting something that had happened to someone else. All the time he took notes.

"Your ex has never been to the café?" he asked.

"No. His mother came, but I didn't tell her I owned it. I said I was visiting a friend who worked there."

When he finished asking questions he said, "I'll let the special victims unit know about the break-in. Right now I need you to come in and check the place out, tell us if there is anything missing –" he gave a wry smile "– if you can tell with all the mess – or if there is anything the perpetrator might have left behind. We're dusting for prints now."

"I'm coming too," George said.

The officer shook his head. "I appreciate your concern for the lady," he said, "but the fewer people who contaminate the area, the better. She'll be fine with me."

George protested and Elle turned to him, putting a hand on his chest. "I'll be fine." She gave him a small smile. "We want to make sure it's easier for the police to do their work."

George frowned but nodded. "Be careful."

Elle followed Officer Oslow into her café. Glass crunched under her feet and she winced. She wasn't going to be open on Saturday.

"Take a good look around," Oslow said. "Does anything seem odd to you?"

Elle took her time, shutting off the part of her that wanted to weep at the destruction, and examined it as thoroughly as she could. Not all the tables and chairs had been disturbed: only the ones on the path to the cake display cabinet and those to the book area. She walked slowly, careful where she stepped, trying not to move anything.

The smell of fresh paint was in the air – it probably hadn't had time to dry yet. She wanted to check, and then if it was still wet, wipe it all away, but she didn't bother asking if she could. It was evidence.

As she sniffed, she caught the smell of something else. She inhaled again. The slightest hint of cigarette smoke.

"Can you smell cigarettes?" she asked Oslow.

He sniffed and nodded. "Harlam, did you light up?" he asked the other officer, who was dusting for prints.

Harlam shook his head.

"Keep an eye out for ash or a cigarette butt," Oslow said. He turned to Elle. "Does your ex smoke?"

"When he's stressed."

She continued her walk through. The spray-painted books –

a whole wall's worth – were ruined. She wouldn't be able to sell them and she couldn't return them. Her stomach squirmed and she crossed her arms over it. How much would her insurance cover? She felt sick and violated. She'd built a safe world, and in an instant it was destroyed. All of the hope and effort she'd fed into her café was for nothing.

Behind the counter, the cash register lay on the floor. The doors to the kitchen and the playroom had been forced open and Toby's books had been ripped apart.

Elle shook her head, shock and anger warring with each other. It was so senseless.

In the kitchen, cupboards were open and their contents had been pulled out over the floor. Food was squashed and there was a partial footprint on the floor in a pile of spilled hot chocolate powder.

The door to her safe had been spray-painted but not opened. He wouldn't have found much money in there as Elle had been to the bank the day before, but she was glad he hadn't managed to damage it.

"Notice anything else?"

Elle shook her head. "It's all my stuff," she said.

"Thank you." He directed her out of the café.

As she reached the door, Harlam said, "I've found it." He held up a bagged cigarette butt.

"Great," Oslow said. "We'll check it for DNA back at the lab," he told Elle.

She hoped they found some and were able to find who did this.

"Miss Carter, it's going to take us a little longer to finish up here. You'll need to arrange to make the café secure."

Of course. She had to get the glass window fixed, but she doubted any glass company would have the right size in stock.

George walked over. "I've found a twenty-four-hour glass company," he said, showing her the website on his phone. "Do you want me to call them?"

"Yes. Please." The quicker it was done, the better. She turned to the officer. "I wasn't going to open today," Elle told him. "Can you tell me when I'll be able to start cleaning up?"

"As soon as we're finished here." He glanced inside. "We'll

probably be another twenty minutes."

Elle's mind was already planning what she needed to do. "Can I get a copy of your report when it's done? I'm sure the insurance company will want it."

"Sure. Why don't you both take a seat over there? Officer Harlam has finished that section." He pointed to the opposite side of the café from the broken window and then walked back in to help his partner.

She rubbed her arms to ward off some of the chill that was creeping in. It was such an awful helplessness – utter vulnerability, like she'd had at the ranch.

She couldn't let it overwhelm her.

George took her hand. "Chris called to say they're at my house. Toby woke but he calmed down when he recognized Imogen."

"They didn't see anyone?"

"No. No one followed them."

Elle breathed a sigh of relief. She took a seat at one of the tables and George sat next to her.

"The glass company will be here in about an hour," George told her. "They're not sure they'll have a pane big enough, but if not, they'll board it up."

It was one less thing to worry about. She took out her phone. "I'll call the insurance company, check what they need from me." She had to do something; she couldn't just sit still.

After a long conversation with the insurance company they said they'd send someone out on Monday to assess the damage. Elle argued with them for another ten minutes that she needed to clean up everything so she could reopen as soon as possible. Monday wasn't good enough. In the end the person agreed the police report and photos would be sufficient evidence of the damage.

As she hung up Officer Oslow came over. "We're finished here. Have you got someone coming to fix the window?"

"Yes." She checked the time. "They'll hopefully be here in about half an hour."

"Great. I don't think the perpetrator will be back tonight. He did what he wanted." He handed her a card. "Call this number if you have any questions, and we'll send you a copy of the report."

Elle nodded. "Thank you. Can I start cleaning up now?"

"Sure. Just be careful of the glass. You don't want to cut yourself." Both officers said goodbye and left.

Elle didn't know where to start. It all seemed too much.

It had to have been Dean. There was no one else. No disgruntled customer, no staff member who was pissed off, no one she'd had an argument with since she'd come to Houston.

Only Dean.

She hadn't asked the officer what time the break-in had occurred. The only thing that surprised her was that Dean had had the patience to wait until dark … though if she thought about it he did have a way of stewing over things for hours until they burst out of him.

She looked around at the destruction of her shop. All of her hard work damaged, though not beyond repair. She desperately tried to hold onto that little thread of hope, because right now defeat was her reigning emotion.

She'd been helpless to stop it. The bastard still had the power to hurt her, hurt what she'd fought so hard to build, hurt what she loved. She'd thought after her success yesterday that she'd dealt with him, that he was out of her life, but it wasn't true.

Would she ever really be free of him?

"Do you want to talk about it?" George's voice sounded loud in the silence.

Elle sighed. "There's so much damage. Where do I start?"

"We'll make a list, be methodical. I'm sure once we get started it won't be so bad, and everyone will help." He got to his feet. "But there's not much point getting stuck in tonight. Let's just sweep up the mess in the kitchen so it doesn't attract any vermin. By then hopefully the glass company will be here."

He was right. She didn't think she had the strength to focus on more than that tonight. Her mind was heavy with despair and fatigue.

She grabbed her broom and walked into the kitchen. She couldn't believe how much mess had been made so quickly. Containers of food from the refrigerator had been dumped on the floor, boxes had been sliced open and their contents spilled, and half of her plates were lying shattered on the floor. She squeezed her eyes shut to stop the tears. They wouldn't help. Not now.

With a sigh, she started sweeping.

When the man from the glass company arrived he decided he would have to manufacture a new pane. With George's help, he quickly removed the remaining shards and covered the opening with wooden panels. Elle gave him her contact details so he could call as soon as he was able to replace the glass. As she shut the door behind the man, George came out of the kitchen.

"The food has been swept up," he said. "Let's go home. We'll come back in the morning after we've rested."

Home. Would she ever have a safe place she could call home? Her apartment suddenly seemed too/ vulnerable. She squeezed her eyes shut. She had to see Toby, to hold her child, to make sure he was all right. "Let's go."

George called Chris to tell him they were on their way.

When they pulled into his garage the lights were on inside the house and Chris's car was parked out front.

Elle hurried in to the kitchen where Chris was making coffee. He smiled. "He's sleeping in George's bed. Imogen's with him."

Elle turned and went to George's room. There was a lamp on, giving enough light to see Toby was buried under the covers with just his head showing. Imogen was lying next to him, watching him, and she got up when she saw Elle.

"He was a little worried when he woke but as soon as he got here and under the covers, he fell back asleep," she whispered and left the room.

Elle nodded and sat down on the bed, brushing her hand over Toby's forehead. He was safe. Mentally she'd known he was but seeing him sleeping soundly gave her the peace of mind she needed. She laid down next to him and pulled him close, needing to be near her baby.

Toby stirred. "Momma?"

"It's all right, Toby. I'm here now."

He snuggled closer. "George's bed smells like him," he said and promptly fell asleep again.

Elle smiled. Toby was right. There was definitely the masculine scent of George in the sheets.

Not willing to let go of him, she stayed where she was until George appeared at the doorway.

"How is he?" he asked.

"Sleeping," Elle said, getting up off the bed. "Safe." She wrapped her arms around him and hugged. "Thank you for going with me." It had been easier with George there. Without him she might have fallen to pieces. "I should go and thank Imogen and Chris."

"They've already gone," George said. "You'll be able to thank them later today."

"Oh, they must think me so rude," she said. "They came to my aid and I haven't even thanked them."

"What they think is you're a wonderful woman and friend who needed their help. They understand your first priority is Toby." He kissed the top of her head. "Do you want a cup of something?"

She nodded. She was too wired for sleep. Her body was still a little jittery and now she'd seen her son was safe, thoughts of what to do next kept pouring into her head. She needed to get some of it down on paper.

Following George to the kitchen, she asked for some paper and began to make a list of all the people she needed to call, while he made her a cup of tea. Not much would be open because of the holiday, but hopefully a few places would be.

"When it gets light we can get some supplies and start cleaning up," George said.

It was Independence Day. Imogen's party was today and Toby had been so looking forward to it. "You've got other plans," she said. "Maybe you could take Toby to Imogen's party for me, while I clear up."

George handed her a mug and sat down next to her with a frown on his face. "You don't have to do this on your own," he said. "I'm right here with you, every step of the way."

He was so serious, so earnest.

"I don't want you to feel obligated," she said, not quite sure how to explain it. It was such a commitment and she wasn't promising anything in return – couldn't promise anything.

Toby was her only focus.

George swore. "Damn it, Elle. I … care for you." He took hold of her hand, squeezing it. "It killed me to watch you walk into the shop, looking so afraid and cut up. I wanted to be by your side, holding your hand, being there for you." He pulled her closer and wrapped his arms around her. "The police will find out who did it and punish him and we'll rebuild it, back to how it was. Together."

It was all too much for Elle. In under twenty-four hours she'd swung from elation to devastation and now to – well she didn't quite know how to describe the swirly, warm, smothering feeling now covering her. All she knew was she had to be by herself.

Pushing him gently away, she brushed a kiss over George's cheek. "I need some sleep," she said, hoping he would understand, and fled to his bedroom.

***

George resisted the urge to call after her or follow her. There'd been so much confusion in her eyes, but it wasn't all bad. She'd kissed him before she ran.

He sighed, rested his head on his hands on the table. He'd nearly told Elle he loved her. Judging from her reaction, that would have scared her even more.

She was pulling away from him, ever so slightly, and it was her bastard ex's fault.

George was sure it had been Dean who had trashed the shop. He'd obviously been mad enough to follow Elle home.

Had he waited, seen George arrive? What if he'd been watching, waiting for George to leave and had finally given up? He hated to consider what the asshole would have tried if he hadn't fallen asleep at Elle's apartment. The very idea of Dean forcing his way into the building had nausea rising in his stomach.

He had to convince Elle to stay with him, at least until Dean was caught. And if he couldn't do that, he'd teach Toby how to dial his number in case anything happened.

But the real question was: how could George convince Elle that he loved her, that he wanted to marry her – that he wasn't like Dean?

It was only sensible for Elle to be reluctant to dive straight into another relationship, but hell, he didn't want her to be sensible. Not about this.

He pushed himself to his feet. There was still an hour or so before the sun would come up. He should get some sleep so he could face the day ahead.

Moving toward his bedroom he stopped. Elle and Toby were in his bed and while there was plenty of room for the three of them, he wasn't sure how either of them would react if he tried to join them.

Changing direction he moved to the spare room, where he always kept a bed made up.

He doubted sleep would come.

***

"Mom." Toby's voice was a loud whisper in her ear.

Elle opened her eyes, smothering the groan she wanted to let out. It felt like she'd just gone to sleep.

"Mom, where are we?"

Elle sat up and recognized George's room, and the events of the early morning came back. "We're at George's place," she said. "This is his bedroom."

"Wow, it's so big," Toby said as bounced up and down on his bottom. "Where's George?"

It was a good question. They'd effectively kicked him out of his own bedroom so he must have gone to sleep elsewhere. Surely there was another bed somewhere in the sumptuous house. She hoped so.

"Give me a minute to get dressed and we'll look for him." She slid into her jeans and slipped on her bra, before taking Toby's hand and heading out of the room.

She wasn't sure what reaction she was going to get from George. She'd freaked out the night before, become too overwhelmed by his support, and he probably thought her ungrateful.

Following the scent of freshly brewed coffee, they found George in the kitchen, sitting at the breakfast bar, drinking a cup.

"Morning, George," Toby said brightly.

"Morning, kiddo."

Elle examined him. He was dressed casually in shorts and T-shirt and his hair was damp and freshly combed. He was ready for the day, but looking closer, his eyes had that not-enough-sleep look to them.

"Did you get much sleep?" she asked.

"Some," he said, getting to his feet and pouring her a cup of coffee. "Do you want some juice, Toby?"

"Yes, please." Toby clambered onto the stool next to where George had been sitting.

George poured him a glass and then got out a bowl and poured some cereal. Elle stood where she was and they casually chatted – as if this kind of thing happened every day.

She smiled. It would be nice to wake up to George every day.

The jolt of the thought had her carefully lowering herself into a chair.

What was she thinking?

She didn't want another man in her life, no matter how nice he was, or how he made her smile, or how well he got along with Toby. She'd sworn off relationships – had made that clear to George at the very beginning.

George placed her mug of coffee on the table in front of her and she automatically lifted her lips for a kiss. He complied with a half-smile. Wrapping her hands around the mug, she ignored the skip in her heart caused by the kiss and stared at the freshly brewed drink.

What was happening to her?

Perhaps it was the lack of sleep or the stress from last night. She still had all the mess to sort out and her brain knew George would help her. *No.* She wasn't going to rely on a man again. She had proven she could do things on her own and she would do it again.

Taking a sip of the coffee, she tried for casual. "When we've had breakfast, could you take us home? I need to start making calls and we both need a change of clothes."

"Sure. What would you like for breakfast?"

She didn't want to put him out. "Coffee's fine. My stomach

hasn't woken up yet."

George opened his mouth, then closed it again.

Elle drank her coffee as quickly as she could while Toby and George kept up an easy conversation about what the day would bring. Toby was incredibly excited about Imogen's party and the opportunity to play with Kate again.

She didn't want to tell him they probably wouldn't be going. "Toby, I need to tell you something," she said, getting to her feet and going over to him.

"What?"

"Last night someone broke into the café and they smashed a lot of things."

Toby's eyes widened. "Why?"

"I don't know. The police are looking into it. What it means is I'll have to clean up the mess. I'm not sure if we'll be able to go to Imogen's party."

"But you said we were going." The disappointment was clear on Toby's face.

God she hated to disappoint him.

"Why don't you wait until you've made a few phone calls before you decide?" George suggested. "There may not be a lot you can do today."

She sighed. "All right. Could we go back to my place now? I really need to get started." It was time she got her life back on track.

***

George drove them back to the apartment and came upstairs to ensure Dean hadn't been there in their absence. Nothing appeared to be out of place.

Elle didn't want to throw George out straight away, so she left him to keep Toby amused while she dug through her business records and found the receipts for her furniture and cake display. She tried both numbers but they had recorded messages to say they were closed for the day.

She checked the time. They were supposed to be heading over to Imogen's soon but it was the last thing she wanted to do. Her brain wasn't functioning at full capacity and there were a million items she needed to organize. Quickly she called Nora,

Drew and the rest of the staff to tell them what had happened. She wasn't able to tell them when she would reopen, but promised it would be as soon as she could.

She jotted several items down on a notepad and went searching for Toby and George. They were playing in Toby's room. Toby had changed out of his pajamas and was ready to go.

"How did it go?" George asked.

"I couldn't get through to anyone." Elle sighed. "I should go to the café and start cleaning up. Can you take Toby to Imogen's?"

"Mom, can't you come too?" There was such a hopeful look on Toby's face. "Please?"

She was exhausted, but how could she say no to him? It was supposed to be a day of celebration, of family, food and festivities.

George stood up. "Why don't we go to Imogen's for a couple of hours, have something to eat and then go together to clean up the café?"

She really didn't want to have to do it all herself. She was running on empty. "All right," she agreed. "Let me have a shower and then we can go." She walked out.

Behind her George said, "Wait here a minute, kiddo."

As she went to close the bathroom door, George stopped her. "You've forgotten something."

Elle closed her eyes, not wanting to play games. "What?"

"This." He stepped closer and pulled her into his arms, kissing the top of her head. "You haven't had your hug today."

Despite her efforts not to rely on him, she found herself leaning into the hug, wrapping her arms around him and drawing strength from his embrace.

"Imogen's got a great guest room and she won't mind if you disappear for an hour or two to take a nap," he said when he stepped back. "I'll keep an eye on Toby for you."

It sounded very enticing. "We'll see," she said. "Now, if we're actually going to get there, you need to let me have a shower."

George's eyes twinkled and she shut the door before he could follow up on his thoughts.

Standing under the warm spray, she closed her eyes. Her whole body was wound tight, her head thumped a techno beat and she felt like one wrong word and she might fly apart at the seams. There was too much happening too fast, and while George's kindness helped one aspect of it, it only added to her worries of getting involved too soon.

What was she going to do?

***

The party was in full swing by the time they arrived. Imogen's house was an old nineteen-twenties house, two stories high, and looked like it had been recently renovated: everything was in pristine condition. The wood siding was painted a pale blue, the front porch was in good repair and the garden was beautifully manicured.

Imogen greeted them at the door and within seconds Toby had sought out Kate and the two of them had disappeared out into the backyard with some other children. Elle called out to him, but he either didn't hear, or ignored her.

"There's nothing for them to damage out there," Imogen said. "The backyard is fully enclosed and in fact we'll all head out there shortly. What can I get you to drink?"

Elle asked for a cola, hoping it would energize her. Glancing around she noticed Libby and Adrian chatting to Chris; George's parents, Marla and Hank, talking to an older man, stylishly dressed; and a bunch of other people she didn't know.

Imogen returned with the drink. "Any news about the break-in?"

"The police found a cigarette butt and they're going to test it," Elle said. "Can we not mention it to anyone today?" she asked. "I don't want to spoil the mood." Or be continually asked about it.

Imogen bit her lip. "I've already told Libby and Adrian and they're ready to help when you need it," she said. "But I won't tell anyone else."

Damn. Wanting to change the subject Elle asked, "Where's Piper?"

Imogen frowned. "Hot on the trail of a story," she said. "That girl works too hard."

"Didn't you tell her it's illegal to work on Independence Day?" George joked.

Imogen laughed. "You know Piper, nothing gets in the way of the story." She glanced toward the door. "I've got to go. My grandma just arrived." Imogen left them and George steered Elle outside.

Toby was running around the backyard, chasing Kate. The temperature was already high and promised to get hotter and stickier as the day progressed. Elle walked over and, after a couple of attempts, managed to get her son's attention.

"There's water in the bag when you get thirsty," she said.

"Thanks, Mom," he said and raced off again.

Elle sighed. She wasn't sure he'd actually heard what she'd said.

Turning to the back deck she saw George had claimed one of the two-seat couches positioned there in the shade. He gestured her over and patted the empty spot beside him.

Elle smiled.

She joined him on his couch and he put his arm around her shoulder, drawing her closer.

"I thought you might like to relax a little," he said. "But if you like, I can introduce you to everyone."

It felt right to rest her head on his shoulder so she did. "In a minute. I need to give the caffeine a chance to hit my system."

Her eyes were so heavy she had to fight to keep them open. She wasn't sure if she even had the mental capacity to manage small talk today and she didn't want people to think she was rude.

"How are you feeling?"

She yawned so widely she risked dislocating her jaw.

George laughed. "You don't need to answer," he said.

Elle smiled. "It was a long night."

Marla spotted them as she came out of the house and waved. "It's lovely to see you, Elle," she said and she bent down to kiss George on the cheek. "How's the café going?"

Elle hesitated. She didn't want to ruin the happy vibe, but she didn't want to lie either. "I had a little trouble there last night."

George coughed.

"Oh, I hope it's nothing serious." Marla sounded concerned.

"Nothing that can't be fixed," Elle said, reminding herself it was true. Dean might be trying to hurt her but she wouldn't let him succeed.

"That's good. Tell me if there's anything I can do to help."

Elle was amazed. George's family and friends barely knew her and they were all so willing to help. She wasn't used to that at all. In LA her mother never would have shown she needed help, let alone asked for it, and no one would have offered.

She'd always thought most people were too caught up in their own lives to bother helping another.

"Thank you," she said.

"George, we haven't had dinner in a while. Why don't you, Elle and Toby come on Sunday night?"

"Sounds great, Mom," he said and then asked Elle, "Are you free?"

Pleased he wasn't taking her for granted she said, "That would be lovely." It was going to be hard work cleaning up the café over the weekend and not having to worry about dinner on one night would be a relief.

Marla spotted someone else she knew across the deck and waved. "I'll talk to you later," she said and walked off.

"Your mother is so sweet," Elle said.

"I think so," George answered with a smile. "Though she can be fierce when she needs to be. If we were naughty as kids, it was Mom we tried to hide it from." He chuckled at the memory.

It was nice he had so many fond memories of his childhood.

She leaned her head back on to his shoulder and closed her eyes.

"Elle, honey," George murmured, rubbing her arm.

"Yes?"

"We need to find you a bed before you start snoring."

Elle sat up and blinked. There were more people out on the deck than there had been a minute earlier. But she'd only briefly closed her eyes. "Did I fall asleep?" she asked, brushing her hair off her face.

George nodded and helped her to her feet. "Come on, let's

go find Imogen."

He was right and she was too tired to argue. A glance at the backyard showed Toby was still happily playing. "Will you keep an eye on Toby for me?"

"Of course."

They had a brief chat with Imogen, then she showed them to a spare room on the second floor. Elle slipped off her sandals and sat on the bed. "Don't let me sleep for more than an hour," she said.

"I'll wake you when lunch is ready," George promised. He waited until she had lain down and then kissed her softly.

Already sleepy, the kiss drugged her further. She fell asleep before he left the room.

***

George stood watching Elle sleep. She was exhausted and hadn't been able to keep her eyes open. She slept, curled on her side, hands under the pillow and her face relaxed so the worry frown she'd been wearing all morning smoothed out. He wanted to stay but he'd promised to watch Toby.

He turned and walked down the stairs.

Chris was in the kitchen pouring some drinks when George walked in. "How is she?"

"Mostly tired, but she's uptight as well. She won't talk to me about it."

"It's a lot to deal with. Some people have to work stuff out on their own before they talk to others."

George nodded. It didn't mean he had to be happy about it.

"Any sign of the ex?" Chris asked as Adrian walked in. Adrian grabbed a drink from Chris and perched himself on one of the stools to hear the answer.

"Not so far. The cops found a cigarette butt they're testing. I hope they put him behind bars."

"Is he likely to go after Elle?" Adrian asked.

George rubbed his eyes. He was more used to late nights than Elle, but he was tired too. "I hope not. I'm going to ask her to stay with me until it's sorted out, but I'm not sure she'll agree." He felt so helpless. If only she would trust him and trust herself.

Adrian watched him for a moment. "You're really serious about her, aren't you?"

"I'd marry her in a heartbeat if she'd have me."

Chris whistled. "Congratulations, man."

George scowled at him. "It would be better if she loved me as well."

"What's not to love?" Chris asked. "You'll win her over in the end. Look at me and Imogen. I'm wearing her down day by day. I'll have her agreeing to marry me by the end of the year."

George couldn't help smiling at his friend. At least Chris knew Imogen loved him. Her issue was she wanted a little bit of independence before she committed. Not that she and Chris didn't spend almost every night together anyway.

George paused.

Maybe that's what Elle needed as well. Some time to show herself she could make it on her own. But damn, she'd left Dean six months ago and she was doing fine.

He followed his friends outside, pausing at the door to adjust to the wave of humidity that struck him. He put his cold drink to his forehead and looked around for Toby.

The boy was still running around but his face was as bright as a tomato.

Grabbing a bottle of water from the ice tub, he trotted down the steps. "Toby!"

Toby didn't hear him.

George moved to intercept him. "Hold on a second, kiddo," he said, grabbing Toby and motioning for Kate to stop.

Toby blinked and brushed his sweaty bangs back. "I'm playing, George."

"I know, but you need to have something to drink before you keel over." He uncapped the bottle and passed it to Toby.

Toby took the bottle and drank half of it in a couple of gulps. He handed the bottle back to George and made to run off again. George stopped him.

"It's time to play quietly for a while," he told both Toby and Kate. "It's too hot to be running around like this."

"All right, George," Kate said. "Come on, Toby, we'll do something else."

Toby took a couple of steps toward Kate and then stopped,

swaying. "I don't feel so good," he said and promptly threw up.

Chapter 18

Fear choked George's heart. He put his hand on Toby's back to find the kid's shirt was soaked with sweat.

And his forehead was hot to the touch.

"Kate, go and ask if Imogen has a thermometer," George barked, running his hands over Toby's arms. They were dry.

"My head hurts," Toby whimpered. He started shaking as if he was crying but no tears came out.

Hell. George had seen these symptoms at Adrian's concerts when fans had overheated in the crowd. Heat stroke. He needed to get Toby cool.

Quickly he swept the boy up in his arms and hurried him inside. "Wake Elle," he told Imogen as she handed him a thermometer.

In the bathroom he placed Toby on the ground and put the thermometer under his tongue. "Keep it there for a minute, kiddo," he said, then grabbed a hand towel and soaked it in water. He ran the towel over Toby's arms, neck and forehead and then checked his temperature.

A hundred and four.

George turned on the shower and lifted Toby under the cold water. The boy didn't protest.

Elle rushed into the bathroom. "What's going on?" She took one look at Toby and demanded, "What happened?"

Toby reached for his mother and sank to the floor, weak.

George heart raced. "We need to get him to the hospital," he said. He grabbed Toby out of the shower, wrapped a towel loosely around him and carried him to the front door. Luckily there was no one parked behind them.

"What happened?" Elle asked again, her voice frantic.

"Heat stroke. He's been running around since we got here," George said as he opened the car door and put Toby on Elle's lap. He raced around the other side of the car and started it. "I gave him something to drink and told him to take it easy but he threw it up."

Hell, he should have stopped him sooner. It was hideously hot today. He should have considered something like this. How could he be so stupid?

He drove in record time to the nearest hospital and parked in front of the emergency room, Elle nursing Toby on her lap.

Together they raced inside and, after explaining to the triage nurse, were rushed straight to a bed. The nurse packed cold packs around Toby's groin and under his arms while another tried to get him to drink something. He refused.

Calling over a doctor, they arranged some IV fluids.

Elle held Toby's hand while George stood back helplessly. It was his fault. He should have been keeping a closer eye on Toby. He'd promised Elle he would.

She hadn't so much as glanced at him since they came in.

He wanted to wrap his arms around her and tell her he was sorry, tell her it was going to be all right, but every ounce of her body language screamed *leave me alone* and he honestly wasn't sure if Toby would be.

The boy lay limp in the bed, his skin was flushed and he was panting.

The nurse checked his temperature. A hundred and two.

It was coming down.

Slowly.

The nurse had turned on a fan and was alternating between spraying him with a mist of water and wiping over his arms and legs with a damp cloth.

A few minutes later the nurse checked his temperature again. A hundred and one.

"Toby, how are you feeling?" the doctor asked, checking his responses.

"My head hurts," he whimpered.

"We'll get you something," the doctor promised. "Can you drink something for me?" He held up a cup with a straw in it.

Elle took the cup from the doctor. "Here you go, Toby. It's even got a straw for you."

Toby opened his mouth and let Elle put the straw in. Then he sipped the drink.

"Good boy. I'll get you something for your head now." The doctor injected something into the IV fluids.

The nurse checked his temperature. Ninety-nine.

George heaved a sigh of relief.

Turning to Elle, the doctor said, "He's going to be fine. You did the right thing by getting him to the hospital so quickly. I'd like to keep him for a little longer for observation."

"Thank you." Elle's face was blank with relief.

The doctor left the cubicle and the nurse removed the ice packs from Toby's underarms and groin. Elle picked up the damp cloth and wiped his face.

"Feeling any better, Toby-boy?" she asked softly.

"A bit," he said.

George stepped up to the bed. "You gave us quite a scare," he said, running his hand over Toby's arm. His skin was so much cooler.

Toby closed his eyes.

Alarmed, he said, "Toby-boy, don't go to sleep."

He opened them again and frowned. "I'm tired."

"You need to wait until the doctor says it's OK to sleep."

He pouted and George was pleased to see it. It meant he was feeling better.

The nurse came back in and checked his vitals.

"Is he allowed to sleep?" George asked.

"Sure. We'll need to wake him to check his vitals, but if he's tired he can rest."

Toby snuggled down in his bed. "Night, Mom. Night, George," he said and went immediately to sleep.

Elle turned to him for the first time. "There's no need for you to stay, George," she said, her voice cool. "We'll be fine now. You should go back to the party."

Fear gripped George. He had never heard such a tone from her. "I'm happy to stay," he said. "I care for him too."

"I don't want you here," she said.

The look she gave him pierced his skin, made panic rise in his chest.

"Please, Elle. I'm so sorry. I love Toby like he was my own. I never meant for anything to happen to him."

Elle flinched.

Hell, he hadn't wanted to tell her like this but he would. He had to make her understand. Taking a step closer to her, he said, "Elle, I love you. I love you and Toby so much. It's killing me to see him like this."

Elle gaped at him and then shut her mouth with a snap. "You need to leave."

She'd shut down completely, blocked him out with words and actions.

He hadn't realized it could hurt so much. "Please."

Elle turned away.

He wanted to take her into his arms, shake her, demand she listen to him, but it would only make matters worse. He ran his hand over Toby's forehead, then bent down and kissed Toby's forehead. "Get better soon, kiddo," he said.

Then he turned and left the hospital, leaving his heart behind.

***

Elle didn't watch him go. Her whole body was stiff, and tingled as if an army of ants were crawling over her skin.

George said he loved her.

How could he say that, *use* that, when her baby had almost died? Did he think she would fall for his lie and it would make everything better? What a time to say it, when her mind was a whirl of fear. He couldn't possibly mean it. She'd made it clear she didn't want a relationship, that Toby was her priority.

Damn, she couldn't deal with that right now.

She turned back to her baby, who was sleeping peacefully, though still a little flushed. The IV stuck out of his arm, reminding her of what had happened.

She'd been so stupid. She'd left Toby in George's care while she'd *slept*. It had been selfish of her. She should have taken care of her boy, rather than giving in to her exhaustion.

She shouldn't have left him alone.

The terror of seeing her baby wet and weak under the shower still encased her heart, no matter what the doctor said. She wouldn't fully relax until Toby was running around again, demanding to play with his cowboy.

She pulled up a chair to the bedside. She held his hand, and stroked his hair. She had to touch him to convince herself he was still alive, that he was cooling down.

Elle didn't move from his side. Her little boy was so small in the bed, so frail. She'd been woken from the deepest sleep, then left hurrying to keep up, to figure out what the hell had happened while she'd been out. All she really knew was Toby had been fine when she'd left him.

And needed the emergency room when she returned.

How could that be love?

***

George arrived back at Imogen's house but hesitated at the door. He didn't want to face anyone, didn't want to deal with the festivities – he just wanted to curl up and forget about the world for a while.

But he needed to be sensible, sort things out. That was his role in any crisis. Firstly he had to get Elle's things for her. They'd driven off in such a hurry she'd left her bag behind.

While he stood deliberating at the front door, his mother came into the house from the backyard and saw him standing there.

She hurried toward him. "Is he all right?" She opened the screen door and put a hand on his arm.

All of the fear he'd been holding inside broke free at her touch. "He's going to be fine," George whispered as the tears ran down his face.

"Oh, my poor boy. It must have been terrifying for you." She bustled him into the living room and made him sit on the sofa. She sat next to him and pulled him into a hug.

For the first time since he was a child, George cried in his mother's arms.

***

It was some time later that the sound of a phone ringing brought George back. He wiped the tears from his face and sat up.

It was coming from Elle's bag.

He grabbed the cell and answered it. It was the guy from the glass company.

"We've found a panel of glass in the warehouse that will fit the shop front. Would you like us to come and install it now?"

George needed to do something, anything to rid himself of this hollow ache inside. "That would be great. I'll be there as soon as I can." He hung up.

"What was that about?" Marla asked.

"Elle's shop was broken into last night. We think it was her ex. He made a real mess of the place and broke the front window. That was the glass company. They came out and boarded up the window last night, but they've found a piece of glass that will fit and are willing to come and do it now." He found the café key in Elle's bag.

Marla patted his hand. "Your father and I can meet them there. You should be with Elle and Toby."

George ached. "She doesn't want me there." His voice was dull.

His mother gaped at him. "Does she blame you?"

"I was supposed to be watching him. I should have stopped him running sooner."

"Any one of us could have stopped him. None of us realized how hot he was getting. It is *not* your fault and I won't have you taking the blame for it. It's bad enough Kate thinks it's her fault. I explained it to her like I'll explain it to you. It was an accident. It happened very quickly."

George would have loved to believe her, but he couldn't. "I'd better go and talk to Kate."

"Wash your face first," his mother said. "Then we'll work out what we need to do next."

***

George took a deep breath before he went outside. His mother had already been out to tell everyone Toby was fine.

Imogen came up to him and gave him a hug. "Is there anything we can do?"

George didn't want to spoil her party. "I was going to ask Libby to drop Elle's bag off at the hospital. I'm going to meet the glass company at the café."

"Are you going to clean up?"

He nodded. Hopefully Elle wouldn't mind, hopefully she wouldn't see it as him taking control again. He just *couldn't* sit around doing nothing.

"I'll come and help," she said.

"Imogen, you're in the middle of a party."

She shrugged. "No one will mind if I duck out for an hour or two."

"You don't need to."

"I want to," she said. "Elle's my friend too. Besides, weren't you the one to suggest the demolition party for me?"

When she'd first bought her house it had been in need of some serious renovating. He'd suggested a demolition party and Chris had arranged it, with a whole heap of people coming over to help rip out and clean up what needed to be done.

Before he could protest further, Imogen clapped her hands together. "If I could have everyone's attention for a minute," she said. "As Marla mentioned, Toby is now fine. What you don't know is, last night Elle's café was broken into and damaged quite badly. The police have cleared her to go in and clean up, but she's obviously going to stay with Toby. George and I are going to go over there and make a start. Help yourself to food and drink and we'll be back in a couple of hours."

"Can I come?" Kate asked, glancing at Adrian and then George.

George could tell from her expression she was still upset and worried about Toby, but he wasn't sure the café was the right place for her. "I was going to ask Libby if she could take Elle her bag. Maybe you could go with her."

Libby stood up. "Sure."

"I'll help you clean up," Adrian said and Chris agreed.

"So will we," Marla said speaking for her husband.

In all six people decided to help clean up the café, including some of Imogen's cousins. If they could get everything cleaned before Toby got out of the hospital it would be one less thing for Elle to worry about.

And another way to apologize for his mistake.

***

"How are you?" The quiet question caused Elle to look up from Toby's sleeping face. Libby and Kate stood there with her bag.

Elle forced a smile to her face. "I've had better days."

"Is he OK?" Kate asked, staring wide-eyed at her friend.

"He's going to be fine," Elle told the girl.

Tears welled up in Kate's eyes. "I'm so sorry, Elle. I didn't know that could happen. I should have made him stop running, or got him a drink – like George did. I didn't mean to hurt him."

The sorrow on the young girl's face was heartbreaking. Elle stood and hurried over to give her a hug. "It's not your fault, sweetheart. It wasn't your responsibility." It had been George's.

"I should have noticed he was getting hot." The words were muffled against Elle's chest.

"No one noticed," Elle said.

"Except George," Kate said.

Elle stepped back, frowned. "What do you mean?"

"George stopped us playing, made Toby have a drink. When Toby was going to run off again, he said we had to stop running and do something quiet in the shade. That's when Toby threw up and he carried him inside."

Elle sat back down again. Had she been too quick to blame George? Was it her own guilt about not being there that made her lash out at him?

"The glass company called," Libby said, giving Elle her bag and a hug. "George has gone to the café to let them fix the window."

The café. She'd forgotten all about it.

"He didn't need to do that," she said. They'd said they didn't have glass the right size.

"George needed something to do. He was pretty shaken when he got back to Imogen's," Libby told her.

Elle closed her eyes. She hadn't given a moment's thought to how George might feel – she'd been so caught up in her own fear. She'd lashed out and been cruel to him. He didn't deserve it.

He'd said he loved her and she'd ignored him, kicked him out.

She wasn't sure how she could make it right. "I'll call him later," she said.

Toby stirred then, and when he opened his eyes and saw Kate, he woke straight up. "Hi, Kate! What are you doing here?" He pushed himself up in bed and Elle had to stop him from jumping out.

"No you don't. You haven't been well," she said, putting a firm hand on his arm.

"I'm fine now."

He looked fine as well. His skin was a normal color and wasn't too hot or too cold. Kate walked closer to him, on the other side of the bed from Elle.

"Gosh, you scared me, Toby," she said. "I'm so glad you're all right." She gave him a hug.

He grinned and hugged her back. The two of them starting chatting and Elle closed her eyes. He really was going to be fine.

Libby put a hand on her arm and leaned down to hug her. "It was pretty scary, huh?"

Elle nodded, blinking back the tears. There was no need for them now.

"Do you want us to stay for a while? Or is there anything else you need?"

"You can stay."

"Mom, I'm hungry," Toby complained.

"I'll go and find a nurse," Libby said and Elle smiled her thanks.

She sat back in her chair, listening to Kate and Toby chatter.

Toby was going to be fine.

***

It didn't take long for the glass to be replaced. The company arrived just after George, and was finished in about half an hour.

244

Inside, Imogen swept the floors while Chris cleaned up the remaining mess in the kitchen with Imogen's cousin, Sadie. Adrian and Cece, Imogen's other cousin, cleared up the playroom.

Hank examined the damage to the tables and chairs while George worked methodically, taking notes of what was needed.

Elle would have to get a new cake display and all the food inside needed to be replaced. He wrote down what was in there before throwing the whole lot into the trash.

He examined the coffee machine, but couldn't tell if it had been damaged. He ran a hand through his hair, trying to put a lid on his frustration. Imogen came behind the counter to empty her dustpan and start sweeping up the glass from the cake cabinet.

Hell, he hated this. He hated that the bastard could do this to Elle. Dean had obviously never loved her. He knew if he met Dean again, in his current mood, he wouldn't be responsible for his own actions.

He picked up the cash register and heaved it back onto the counter, connecting it back to the power. His movements were jerky and the anger seeped into his muscles. He glanced up at the books. The word *WHORE* leaped out at him.

He had to get rid of it.

Now.

He stormed over to the wall and started pulling books off the shelf, throwing them on to the floor. Inside his head he raged.

A hand on George's shoulder had him spinning and his fist rising – until he recognized Adrian.

Panting, George lowered his hand.

"Let's take a walk," Adrian suggested.

George stared at him. What the hell? "There's work to be done here."

"You're making it worse," Adrian commented mildly.

George looked around. He'd covered the floor in books. He swore, and then headed for the door.

***

Adrian caught up with him outside and they walked in silence,

George's stride eating up the pavement.

Suddenly he stopped and turned to Adrian. "This is bullshit."

"What is?"

"This whole mess. We know it was Dean: the police should arrest him and throw his ass in jail."

"They need proof," Adrian reminded him. "I understand how helpless you're feeling," he said, putting a hand on George's shoulder. "I remember what it was like with my dad and being powerless to stop him. If someone was doing this to Libby, I'd be furious."

"Yeah, well, I am."

Not that it helped.

"Have you spoken to Elle about staying at your place?" Adrian asked.

George shook his head. "I'm not sure she'll want to. She hates me right now. I can't blame her. I almost killed Toby." His voice cracked and he kept walking.

God, shouldn't there be a limit to the amount of guilt and anger you could feel at once? He was being weighed down by it; he was drowning in it.

"Don't be stupid." The harsh tone Adrian used was so unlike him that George stopped walking.

"You're meant to be the sensible one out of the two of us, the one who's got his head on straight. I can't believe I'm hearing this shit from you."

George gaped at him.

"It is not your fault Toby got heat stroke, just like it's not Kate's. They hadn't been playing very long at all. If you put your normal rational hat on, you'd see it. From the time you took Elle upstairs to going back outside was maybe ten minutes. Don't fool yourself by thinking you would have noticed it any sooner than you did. What you did do is save the kid's life. You knew exactly what to do and you got him straight to the hospital."

It wasn't often Adrian got mad. It wasn't often he spoke so much all at once. Those two facts squeezed through George's self-loathing.

"I don't know how to make it right." The admission helped.

"You'll talk to Elle," Adrian said. "That's what you do best.

And together you'll work it out."

George raked a hand through his hair.

"Besides, you're helping to clean up the café – when you're not throwing books on the ground – so that's got to count for something."

Maybe it would. He didn't know any more.

"Come on." Adrian slapped a hand on his shoulder. "It's too hot out here to argue. We can do that in the air-conditioned comfort of Eat, Drink, Read."

Some of the anger dissolved. Adrian was right. It wasn't like him to wallow. He was better when he was fixing things.

He turned around and followed Adrian back to the café.

# Chapter 19

It was a couple of hours before the doctor came around again to check on Toby and gave him the all clear to go home. Elle chatted to Libby to keep her mind off what had happened, while Kate kept Toby amused.

When Toby was discharged, Libby took them home. Elle was glad she didn't have to drive. Her brain was sluggish and the exhaustion that followed such fear was setting in.

When they pulled up in front of Elle's apartment, Libby asked, "Do you want us to come in?"

Elle shook her head. She wanted to sit on the couch with a cold drink and rest. "Thank you for your help."

"That's what friends are for," Libby said and smiled at her.

Elle climbed out of the car and took Toby's hand. He was beginning to flag now, his short nap not quite enough to carry him through the rest of the day. The doctor had recommended more fluids and had given Elle some electrolytes to put into water to further hydrate him.

She waved goodbye to Libby and Kate and took him upstairs to the apartment. Once inside she settled him on the couch with a book and went into the kitchen to get them both a drink.

She'd just nestled in next to Toby on the couch when someone knocked on the door. She must have left something in

Libby's car. She answered it without checking the peephole.

Dean stood there, one hand on the doorframe, the other holding a cigarette.

He'd been watching the apartment.

A chill ran through her body.

She had a weakened child sitting on the couch who couldn't run from danger if he needed to. Anger rose and burst out of her. "What the hell do you want?"

"Now, now, Elle. That's no way to greet me. Aren't you going to invite me in?"

"No." She stepped forward to block the entrance. What she really wanted to do was slam the door in his face, but she controlled the urge. Somehow she had to get through to him that they were over, that he had no right over what she and Toby did for the rest of their lives.

Dean took a drag on his cigarette and blew the smoke in her face. Elle blinked but didn't back up. "You need to come back to me, Elle. I haven't been able to write since you left."

There was no "I miss you" or "I love you": it was all about the writing. That's all it had ever been about for him.

It had taken her so long to realize it.

Being calm and rational wouldn't work with Dean. Being nice in hope he would leave her alone was pointless. The only thing he would respond to was danger to himself.

"No." She reached into her pocket and pulled out her cell. She was sick of this, sick of him. "I will never come back to you, and you will never be part of my or Toby's life." She dialed nine one one. "I'm calling the police. You're breaching your restraining order."

Dean gaped at her and his expression switched from calm to furious in an instant. "You're not getting me arrested, bitch." He stepped forward and grabbed her arms.

Elle saw red. She kneed him in the groin, and felt immense satisfaction as he grunted in pain. Using all her weight, she shoved him so he fell backward away from the door and slammed it, locking it. She focused on the phone in her hand. "I need the police. My ex is breaking his restraining order. He's here at my house – he grabbed me." She gave them her address.

Outside Dean cursed and then suddenly he started banging

on her door, screaming obscenities at her.

"Mom?" Toby's frightened voice came from the couch.

"It's OK, baby. The police are on their way." She could hear the sirens in the distance, but she wasn't willing to leave the door to comfort him. She didn't know how sturdy her locks were. The door vibrated behind her.

Toby was still wobbly on his feet, she knew, but she needed him out of the room in case Dean broke through. "Why don't you go and lie in bed and I'll get you when the police arrive?"

Toby shook his head. He stood up and came to stand next to her, his back against the door. "I'll help."

Elle closed her eyes as she fought her panic. She didn't want her baby to be hurt. She needed to get rid of Dean.

She raised her voice. "You can find a new muse in jail," she shouted at Dean.

The pounding stopped as the sirens got louder.

"I'm not going to jail for you. You can't prove anything."

"You broke into my café," she yelled. "The cops have evidence."

Dean swore and then there was the sound of pounding feet, a curse, a scuffle and then silence.

Elle peered out the peephole but couldn't see anything.

"I think he's gone, Toby-boy. Why don't you go over behind the couch?" She needed to get him somewhere safe.

A knock on the door made her gasp. She checked and saw a police officer outside. Relief flushed through her and she opened the door.

"Miss Carter?" he asked.

She nodded.

"We caught Mr. Williams downstairs. Are you all right?"

"Yes." Her heart might still be racing, but she was unhurt.

"I'll need to get your statement."

"Of course." She stood back and let him in and then picked up Toby and hugged him. "It's back to the couch for you," she said, her voice as cheerful as she could make it, carrying him to the couch and handing him his drink. "Drink up." She was trying so hard to hide her fear from him.

She went back to close the door and noticed the squashed cigarette butt on the ground. Officer Harlam had found a butt in the café. Elle hurried back inside, grabbed a plastic sandwich bag from the kitchen, and carefully flicked the butt into it and zipped it up.

If they could match prints or DNA to this one, they could prove it was Dean.

She shut the front door, her limbs shaky.

"Are you all right, ma'am?" the officer asked, having settled himself on a kitchen chair with his notebook on the table.

"There was a break-in at my café last night. They found a cigarette butt. I think it was Dean – and he was smoking when he was here." She held out the bag.

"Which officer was assigned to the case?" the police officer asked.

"Officers Oslow and Harlam."

"I'll see that they get it."

The officer asked her some questions and Elle answered as accurately as she could. When it was done, she walked him out.

Shutting the door, she breathed a sigh of relief.

She'd stood up to Dean, she'd protected her son and, if the DNA turned out to be a match, he might just be out of her life forever.

She hoped so.

***

The next morning, Elle slept late again. When she woke she heard Toby playing quietly in his room. Quickly she got up and went to check on him. He was sitting on the floor in his pajamas and from what she could gather his cowboy had been injured and was in hospital.

"It's all right, Cowboy Chris," he was saying. "Astronaut George got you to hospital in time."

George.

Elle had avoided thinking about George and what he'd said. It had been too much to deal with yesterday, but today was a new day, and Toby was perfectly fine.

"Morning, Toby-boy. Do you want some breakfast?" she asked.

Toby turned. "Morning, Mom. I've already had some, thanks."

Elle frowned. "Who got it for you?"

"I got it myself."

Elle put a hand on his forehead to check his temperature. "How are you feeling?"

"Good." He pushed her hand away and continued his game.

The residual worry melted away. He was back to normal. Elle walked into the kitchen to find the box of cereal on the table with a few flakes next to it. Toby's empty bowl was also there, surrounded by a puddle of milk.

Her little boy was definitely growing up. She'd have to teach him how to clean up after himself next.

She wiped up the mess and poured herself a coffee. She didn't want to eat.

The insurance policy documents on the table reminded her of the café. She had to go and clean up, make sure everything was all right.

She shouldn't put it off. It wasn't going to go away and it meant she could avoid thinking about George for a little longer.

The last thing she wanted was for Toby to see the mess, but she wasn't ready to be parted from him yet.

"Toby, let's get ready to go out. We need to go to the café."

***

An hour later they were standing outside the café. The boards had been replaced by a new, clean window and someone had put a sign on the door to say closed until further notice.

Elle sighed, and unlocked the door. She flicked on the lights and stared. She blinked a few times just to make sure she wasn't seeing what she wanted to see.

There was no glass on the floor.

The broken chairs and tables had been neatly stacked and the spray-painted books were gone, leaving gaps on the shelves.

Toby pushed past her and headed for the playroom, bringing Elle back to the present.

"Wait a second, Toby," she said taking his hand. She wanted to check everything out first.

Together they walked to the back of the shop. The cake display was empty – all the broken glass had been removed and it had been cleaned – the cash register was back in place on the

252

bench and there wasn't a bit of mess anywhere.

In the playroom, there was a box containing the ripped-up books but everything else was tidy.

"Mom, what happened to my books?" Toby asked.

"The person who broke in tore them up, Toby-boy. We'll get new ones." She gave him a hug. "Can you play here for a bit while I look around?"

He nodded.

In the small kitchen everything had been put back, though she did notice one or two things in the wrong spot. She fixed them, still trying to work out what had happened.

Over on the bench top there was a sheet of paper. She immediately recognized George's writing. It was a list of all the things that needed replacing, including a list of the damaged books with publisher, author and title in columns.

Her hand clenched, scrunching the list a bit. Her head swam.

Pulling out one of the chairs in the café, she sat down, still staring at the list. George had come here, after he'd left the hospital, after the way she had treated him, and had cleaned the whole café.

She closed her eyes.

Why would he do that?

He loved her.

He'd told her but she hadn't believed him. All this proved it.

Actions spoke so much louder than words. Why else would someone do this, come and clean up the mess, after the way she'd treated him, if it weren't for love? Could it be guilt?

Elle shook her head. She was searching for a different explanation, but in her heart she knew the truth.

So if George loved her, where did that leave her?

She hadn't let herself think about him, think about how she felt, what she wanted. Hadn't wanted to. The idea of another relationship, of being trapped like she had been with Dean, still scared her. But to compare George with Dean was like comparing a Ferrari with a Smart car.

George was so much more in every way. She sighed. One thing she knew for certain was she needed to apologize to him.

Wanting to find out more about what happened, Elle called

Imogen.

"How's Toby?" Imogen asked when she heard it was Elle.

"It's like yesterday didn't happen," Elle said.

"I'm so glad."

"Imogen, I'm at the café. Who did all this work?"

"George went down to let the glass people in and a few of us went to help clean up. I hope that's all right?" Imogen sounded concerned.

"It's amazing," Elle told her. "I was expecting a mess, so it was lovely to find everything tidy."

"I'm glad."

After thanking her and hanging up, Elle made her own checks of the café. George had been thorough. There wasn't anything she needed to add to his list.

She began making phone calls, arranging a new cake cabinet and ordering chairs to replace those that had been broken. She also placed a new order for cakes and cookies to be delivered during the week. The break-in wasn't going to stop her for long.

With that done, she called out to Toby. She crouched down so she was at eye level with her son. "We're going over to George's house," she said.

"Yes!" Toby said.

Elle needed to be clear with him. "I need to talk to George about a couple of things. Do you think you could play on his swing while I do that?"

"Sure, Mom. Then can I tell George how you beat up Dad?"

She swallowed a smile at his exuberance. "If you want."

She took his hand and they headed to George's house.

***

Elle wiped her sweaty palms on her shorts and stared at George's front door, working up the nerve to knock. She still had no idea what she was going to say to him, but she knew she had to apologize.

"Aren't you going to knock?" Toby asked.

"Of course." Before she could talk herself out of it, she knocked loudly.

There was no noise from inside. What if he wasn't at home?

She hadn't wanted to call before she came, wasn't sure what she'd say over the phone.

As she was debating whether she should knock again, she heard footsteps coming to the door.

She wiped her hands again and clenched them together, then decided it looked stupid, and put them by her side as the door opened. George stood there.

He looked exhausted.

His normally deep blue eyes were dulled with deep circles under them, and he stood as if his body weighed a ton.

When he saw Elle he straightened. "Elle." He reached out to touch her and then stopped, putting his hand down again.

She hated that she'd made him hesitate. George's little touches were what made her feel loved.

*Loved.*

There was no doubt George made her feel special, made her feel wanted, made her happy. But how did she feel about him?

"Howdy, George!" Toby said.

The smile that broke out over George's face was beautiful. "Toby." He squatted down and held his arms out. The kid dived into them and gave him a hug.

George closed his eyes and held Toby tightly.

Elle rubbed her chest as her heart swelled.

"How are you feeling?"

"I'm great. Can I play on your swing?" George glanced up at Elle. She nodded. "Sure."

Toby ran past him and down the hall.

"Can I come in?" Elle asked, the nerves building again now they were alone.

George nodded, gestured her inside and closed the door behind her. She walked through to the backyard, where Toby was swinging, and took a seat at the outside table.

George hesitated and then sat on the chair across from her.

Her heart pinched. She'd made a mess of things with him and she wasn't sure how to fix it.

"George, I need to apologize," she said, wanting to reach out and touch him but keeping her hands in front of her. "I was so upset yesterday and I blamed you, but it wasn't your fault. It could have just as easily happened while I was there. If you hadn't known what to do, things would have been a lot worse." She didn't want to consider the other possibilities.

"I was supposed to be watching him," George said, his voice quiet.

She couldn't stand the distance between them, the hurt in his voice. She leaned forward, placed a hand on his arm. "It wasn't your fault," she said, her voice stern. Somehow she needed to convince him. "And Toby's fine today."

She smiled at Toby, who was singing as he swung.

George just looked at her, his eyes sad.

Silence fell between them. She needed to fill it. "I was at the café this morning," she said, starting with the easiest. "I really appreciate you cleaning up."

"I had help," he said and gave a small smile. "Imogen left her party to come."

"I know. She didn't need to do that." Elle closed her eyes. She'd been a burden to them all.

"She wanted to," he said simply.

And wasn't that the key? Elle had friends who wanted and were more than happy to help, who liked her and her son and welcomed them into their group. She didn't know how she'd got so lucky.

"Thank you," Elle said, wanting to move closer but not risking it.

"You're welcome."

"Your lists were great and I've called a few places and made arrangements for replacements this morning."

"I'm glad."

It was getting awkward, but still Elle didn't have the courage to address the whole love issue. "Dean came by last night," she said instead.

George sat up straight, reached out to her, and dropped his hand. "He didn't hurt you?"

Elle shook her head. "I called the police and he was arrested."

"Really?" George raised an eyebrow. "That's fantastic."

She nodded. "I realized he'll never let it go. I couldn't reason with him and now hopefully he'll be out of our life."

"I'm happy for you." He sounded it, but he seemed mostly

sad.

She shuffled in her seat. "About what you said yesterday …" How the hell was she supposed to say this?

"I said a lot of things yesterday." He was cautious.

Elle stood up, paced away. "You said you loved me," she said and it came out like an accusation.

He nodded. "I do love you. I love you and Toby. I want you to marry me."

Elle's jaw dropped.

He sat there, watching her, more serious than she'd ever known him. He couldn't say that. He couldn't possibly mean it. Not after all the things she'd said. Marriage was a whole other thing from love. Damn, she had to concentrate on one thing at a time. She closed her mouth and then said, "No one's ever said that to me before."

His mouth twitched in a smile. "Which bit?"

"Both."

Dean had never told her he loved her and he definitely hadn't wanted to marry her.

"I told you I didn't want a relationship. I wasn't ready. I had to sort out my life first." Twisting her hands together she walked toward him and then away.

"Sometimes you find things you're not looking for," George said, his gaze steady. "I can wait until you're ready."

Frustrated, scared and a little bit hopeful she asked, "What if I'm never ready?"

"I'll just love you anyway." He was calm and the expression on his face was so open, so sure and so loving Elle was caught up in it. She reached out a hand to him.

Dare she trust him?

Dare she trust herself?

George stood and took her hand, waiting. Always waiting patiently for her.

She entwined her fingers with his, looking down at their hands.

It felt right.

That's what being with George was like. A feeling of rightness, of being home, of being loved, and the giddy sensation of being wanted. He'd become the first person she wanted to call to talk about her day, to ask for help, just to talk to. Why hadn't she realized it? She loved being with him. Her eyes widened and she looked up at him.

She loved him.

George brought his hand up to her cheek. "Are you all right? You've gone a little pale."

"I love you." The words slipped out before she could think, before she could stop them.

He stared at her, hope, doubt and surprise warring in his eyes.

She laughed, the sound bubbling up inside her and bursting out. "I've been so slow to see it," she said. "I love you."

She kissed him and his hand came around her waist, holding her tightly as if he was never going to let go. He kissed her back and Elle thought her head was going to float away, it was so light.

"Say it again," he said as he drew back.

"I love you, George Jones." It felt so right to say it.

She laughed as he picked her up and spun her around. "Hallelujah!"

George put her on the ground as Toby ran up to them.

"What's going on?" Toby asked.

"Your mom told me she loved me." George beamed.

Toby frowned. "So do I."

George laughed and picked Toby up and swung him around as well. Toby's laughter-filled shrieks filled the air.

Elle wasn't sure she'd ever felt so happy. Here was this wonderful man who loved her, and loved her son, who she loved being with and couldn't imagine her life without.

The final piece clicked into place. She wanted to spend her life with George. Elle examined the idea from every angle. She loved him: he was kind, caring, funny and a wonderful person to be around. Toby loved him, had even asked if George could be his dad.

She smiled, her heart swelling. She could do this, she could take control of her life, give Toby a father and give herself what she wanted – a loving man, a best friend, a husband.

"There's just one thing," she said as he put Toby back on to the ground.

"Anything," he said.

Elle took hold of his hand. "Will you marry me?" Her heart lifted as she asked, soaring with hope. "Will you take Toby and me into your life?"

He looked at her, astonished, and then he grinned. "Absolutely. Just name the time and place." He kissed her again.

Elle couldn't stop smiling.

"Mom?" Toby tugged on her sleeve. His expression was a combination of hope and uncertainty.

Elle kneeled down to him. "George has agreed to marry me. That means we'll live with him and he'll be your stepdad."

Toby's eyes lit up like it was Christmas. He glanced between Elle and George. "George will be my dad?" he asked.

George crouched down, his eyes moist. "I'd love to be your dad, if you want me."

"Yes!" Toby dived into George's arms and hugged him tightly. "It's what I wished for."

Watching her two favorite males, Elle knew she'd made the best choice of her life.

# Epilogue

Elle locked the door to Eat, Drink, Read and turned the sign to *Closed*. She sighed with satisfaction. Her grand reopening had been an epic success with both music and poetry readings and people lining up for tables. It had been non-stop all day.

"I think we've earned a drink and a meal out," George said.

She grinned, turning to her fiancé. He'd been there all day, helping out when needed, chatting with and charming customers, and when Toby had returned from his day with Harry, he'd kept her little boy amused. "I'll say." It had taken them less than a week to reopen the café with George loaning her the money for equipment until the insurance paid up. "What do you feel like?"

"Chinese!" Toby voted. "Can we have Chinese *please*?"

Elle glanced at George to check that worked for him too, before saying, "Sure, Toby-boy. I'll just finish up here." She still needed to count the takings.

Her cell phone rang and getting it out of her bag she frowned.

"Who is it?" George asked.

"Martin." She hadn't spoken to Dean's father since they'd met in the park. Would he be angry about the arrest? The police had matched Dean's DNA to the cigarette butt found in the café and had charged him with burglary and criminal mischief. He was facing at least six months' jail, possibly more.

She answered the phone. "Hello, Martin."

"Elle. I'm so sorry." He paused. "Sorry about everything that has happened between you and Dean. When I heard about what he'd done to your café ..." He sighed. "I don't know where Lindsay and I went wrong."

He was clearly upset. "Martin, I don't blame you for Dean's actions. It's not your fault. I'm sorry it had to go as far as it did." She walked into the kitchen so Toby couldn't hear what she was saying.

"Me too." He paused. "Lindsay asked me to ask something of you. I don't expect you to agree, but I have to ask. He is my son."

Elle braced herself.

"Lindsay asked if you'd consider dropping the charges against Dean. She doesn't want him to go to jail."

"No." Elle didn't have to even think about it. "I'm sorry, Martin, but I have Toby and my welfare to consider. Dean is violent and unpredictable." She wasn't even certain she had the power to do it. The break-in was a police issue. And there was no way she was dropping the domestic assault charges against him.

"I know. I understand."

He sounded so tired. She wanted to offer him something. "Would you like to see Toby some time?"

"Yes. We'd love to. Would you consider bringing him out to the ranch?"

"Not with Dean there." There was no way she was letting him near her son if she could help it. "But if he goes to jail, Toby could visit you."

"All right. I'll talk with Lindsay and we'll arrange a trip to Houston. Thank you, Elle." He hung up.

She disconnected and stood leaning up against the bench. She hoped Dean would go to jail, hoped it would shake him up enough for him to turn his life around and not so much that he would blame her and seek revenge. She really didn't know what he would do.

"Everything OK?" George asked, coming in to the room.

"Yes. Martin wanted to apologize for Dean. Lindsay wants

me to drop the charges against Dean."

George scowled. "What did you say?"

"I told them no. Dean went too far."

"Good."

She smiled, walked over to him and wrapped her arms around him. "Martin and Lindsay are going to come to Houston to see Toby."

"Toby will like that. They're still his grandparents even if Dean agrees to give up his parental rights."

Elle was pleased he understood. When George had agreed to marry her, he'd asked whether he could adopt Toby. They'd consulted with Victoria and she'd put the necessary paperwork together. They were still waiting to hear whether Dean would agree to it.

"Come on. I'm hungry," she said walking back into the café area. "Let me count the till and we'll go and get some dinner. I need to grab some groceries for tomorrow as well." She was cooking dinner for her friends to thank them for everything they had done to help her.

"Cash register has been counted." George told her the numbers. "Toby and I did it while you were talking with Martin."

"Oh. Thanks." It was wonderful not to have to do everything, but it would take some getting used to.

Toby was sitting at one of the tables playing with his cowboy and astronaut.

"Ready to go, Pardner?" George asked.

"Ready!" Toby jumped to his feet, stuffed his toys into his bag and slung it on to his back. He grabbed George's hand and then Elle's. "Let's go, Pardners."

Elle grinned.

Toby was right.

They were partners.

# Thank you for reading!

I hope you enjoyed the book. It would be super awesome if you could leave a review wherever you bought it, because I love to hear what you thought of the story (yes, even if you didn't like it!)

If you've only just discovered the Texan Quartet, make sure you check out Libby, Piper and Imogen's stories too. The next story in the series is where Piper finds love in Into the Fire.

# Acknowledgements

A big thank you to the Houston Police Department public relations office for answering a myriad of questions regarding police procedure so I could ensure I had all the details correct.

And as always a huge thank you to the team at Momentum: Joel, Patrick, Ashley, Michelle, as well as Kate and Jon, for being so supportive and helping me make this book as good as it can be.

# Into the Fire

## The Texan Quartet # 4

*Piper Atkinson uses the truth as a weapon, but her latest interview candidate is more than just a headline.*

Piper wants to be the kind of journalist who makes people sit up and take notice of the issues, and in Houston, Texas, there are plenty to go around. In the city's high-end restaurant world, reclusive Native American chef Taima Woods is discussed in reverential whispers, so when the opportunity to interview him arrives, Piper jumps at it.

But getting to Tai is tougher than she expected. He has a deep mistrust of reporters, and a private life he'd prefer to keep hidden. There are two passions in Tai's life – his cooking and his tribe – and he means to keep it that way. But the closer Tai gets to Piper, the closer he comes to conceding a third.

Through Tai, Piper discovers a world she knew nothing about – a damaged and ostracized community in need of a voice. But the more Piper wants to help them, the more Tai understands that to love Piper is to turn his back on his people.

Will Tai reject the one woman who's ever understood him? Or can Piper show him that hardening his heart helps no one?

http://www.claireboston.com/books/the-texan-quartet/

# What Goes on Tour

## The Texan Quartet # 1

*What goes on tour, stays on tour … or does it?*

Few people know that socially awkward Adrian Hart is actually rock God, Kent Downer, and that's the way Adrian likes it. His privacy is essential, especially now that he has guardianship of his orphaned, ten-year-old niece, Kate. But when the nanny quits in the middle of his Australian tour Adrian finds himself in a bind.

Until Libby Myles walks into his life.

Libby has only ever wanted to become a full-time author and prove to her parents that she can make it on her own. On the surface, the temporary job as the nanny for Kent Downer's niece looks perfect—the pay is fabulous, the hours are short and Kate is a big fan—it's the rock star that's the issue.

Arrogant and way too attractive for anyone's good, Kent Downer has enough swagger to power a small city. But when he's out of costume he's different—shy and uncertain. For Libby it's a far harder combination to resist. She needs to find a balance between work, writing and ignoring her attraction to the rock star, because if she falls for him, it could mean the end of her dream.

But when a horrible scandal is unleashed—putting young Kate in danger—there's more heat between Libby and Adrian than just sexual attraction. Libby must figure out if Adrian ever cared for her, or if it was all just part of the show …

http://www.claireboston.com/books/the-texan-quartet/

# All that Sparkles

## The Texan Quartet # 2

*Imogen Fontaine is living every girl's dream.*

She is a fashion designer for her family's haute couture label, lives in a mansion, has a great circle of friends and is the apple of her father's eye. Everything is perfect.

Until the day that Christian, the boy at the center of her childhood heartbreak, walks back into her life.

From there her life starts to unravel, as long-kept secrets are revealed. Imogen learns that her past was built on lies and betrayal, shattering the illusion of her perfect existence. She must seek out the truth if she has any hope of forging a new path for herself and discovering true freedom.

But can she convince Christian that there is a place for him in her new life?

http://www.claireboston.com/books/the-texan-quartet/

www.ingramcontent.com/pod-product-compliance
Lightning Source LLC
Chambersburg PA
CBHW032119180726
48284CB00002B/619